"Yes—for you—you're so lovely, Margaret. May I see you? All of you—"

"Oh—yes—yes!"

Stepping away, her face flaming, but not with guilt this time—rather, the erotic excitation of an impulsive and generous desire—Margaret Elston swiftly removed the red satin peignoir and let it drop to the floor. Sonia caught her breath as the tall brunette stood before her, naked but for the narrow black satin-elastic garter belt, the panties which ardently clung to her sleek buttocks, and the diaphanous off-black nylon hose and open-toe sandals.

Also by PAUL LITTLE:

Slave Island
Captive Maidens
Chinese Justice and Other Stories
The Discipline of Odette
The Prisoner
Double Novel
All the Way
The Tears of the Inquisition

The Best of Paul Little

PAUL LITTLE

MASQUERADE BOOKS, INC.
801 SECOND AVENUE
NEW YORK, N.Y. 10017

The Best of Paul Little
Copyright © 1996 by Masquerade Books
All Rights Reserved

No part of this book may be reproduced, stored in a retrieval system, or transmitted in any form, by any means, including mechanical, electronic, photocopying, recording or otherwise, without prior written permission of the publishers.

First Masquerade Edition 1996

First Printing December 1996

ISBN 1-56333-469-0

Manufactured in the United States of America
Published by Masquerade Books, Inc.
801 Second Avenue
New York, N.Y. 10017

The Best of Paul Little

Chinese Justice 7

Lusty Lessons 38

Discipline of Odette 69

The Prisoner 129

Turkish Delights 169

CHINESE JUSTICE

"Oh master of sublime justice, genius of castigatory improvisation, what delicious spectacle comes next before this tribunal?" Guey Wong pantingly begged his august friend, the lordly Mandarin of Hanchow, when he returned to the dais after his much satisfying assfuck with the first of the accused!

"This time, old friend, we shall punish two wicked foreign sorceresses who, from the information I have received from a worthy officer of the Boxers who was employed in their household, were guilty of no treasonable crime against Her Celestial Majesty, but who have sinned in the most abominably depraved manner. Their turpitude is therefore a crime against the morality of our great, ancient, and honorable land, and it must be made known to those worthy spectators so that our ancient laws still stand unchallenged by such wicked evasions by these accursed white devils!" the fat mandarin sententiously declared.

Clapping his hands, he now ordered Soo Fa and Ma Loo to bring before him Nadia Kaplinski and her buxom aunt Katerina Ourosoff, as well as their accuser, Lieutenant Peng Chu, once that solemn and taciturn steward who had served the portly Russian Consul Piotor Vorshilof and who had spied upon their Lesbian love of lash and lust!

Katerina and Nadia, their wrists bound behind them, did not appear to be too greatly distraught. From time to time, Katerina glanced at her niece and gave her a tender smile, as if to tell her to have courage and that soon this insignificant moment would pass. But both of them had not reckoned on the fiendish cruelty of Li Woo, whose power to administer the justice of Tsu Hsi furnished him uninhibited opportunities to satisfy his own insatiable hunger for naked female flesh. The wheat-hued hair of Katerina Ourosoff was formed in an upswept pompadour, which made her buxom figure all the more imposing. She had been clad in a red satin evening gown, leaving her shoulders and arms bare in all their ivory pale splendor. The piquant contrast of her extremely light blonde hair with an almost brunette-like skin tint, together with her voluptuous curves of bosom and bottom and thighs, caused a murmur of lecherous admiration to rise from the avid spectators, as well as from the old peddler who again leaned forward to squint at them with glittering eyes.

Chinese Justice

Nadia, clad in a dainty pink muslin frock, her golden hair tumbling just below her shoulders, was equally appealing.

Li Woo studied the two women, and then made a sign. There rose the crash of a gong, and once again the little door to his right opened, the door whence had come these first three victims of Boxer cruelty. Dressed in the white robes of the Society of Clenched Fists, and with the yellow circle over his left breast, came the tall, grave-faced Peng Chu.

"A thousand thanks, good Lieutenant," Li Woo obsequiously greeted the former steward of the Vorshilof household, "for the valorous deeds you and your brave men have achieved on behalf of our beloved land! Twice blessed are you, not only for leading them on to victories that will drive all these white devils from our soil, but for giving up the glorious chance to wet your sword in their offending blood, that you may stand as the accuser of these two sorceresses now before us!"

Nadia and Katerina exchanged a frightened look. Peng Chu bowed low to the mandarin, then turned so that he could address the entire courtroom: "Sons of China, defenders of her honor and her glory, hear me! Before our immortal Empress deigned to have me summoned to serve her as a soldier, I was employed in the household of the Russian Consul, whose cousin that older sorceress is, and so had occasion to observe her and the yellow-haired girl who is her niece. Upon the graves of my ancestors, I accuse them both of filthy and unnatural lusts, lying together naked in their harlots' bed, imitating the sex of the man and corrupting it into an illicit and forbidden pandering among themselves!"

There was the sounds of gasps and of muttered oaths, "Punish them for their shamelessness!"

But Li Woo lifted his hand, then nodded to Peng Chu to continue, and the Boxer lieutenant resumed: "In all justice, I cannot condemn them for treason, for they did no harm to me, nor to the little housemaid whom I befriended, nor to any of the merchants or the people. They had no thought—indeed, their shallow minds are those of harlots, and incapable of scheming plots—of the tyrannies which their nation, like all those nations of the foreign devils who have come to our land to steal it from us, visited upon us. So I do not charge them with conspiracy against the Empire. I ask only, noble Mandarin of Hanchow," this as he turned back to Li Woo and moved his head, "that you deal with them severely for their depravities."

"It shall be as you desire, good Peng Chu," Li Woo decreed. While they had listened to Peng Chu's declaration, Nadia and Katerina had gasped aloud in shamed surprise, then constantly exchanged ever more fearful glances, their faces flaming. What most agonized them at this very moment was that Peng Chu had spied on them and actually seen them caress and girl-fuck. Overwrought, they both began to sob and to bow their heads, and Li Woo chuckled: "You see, good people of China? Already these wicked sorceresses know their guilt and are penitent. But they are ignoble bitches, whose bodies fear the male and so contrive to cheat him of their womanhood. It is therefore only just that they be furnished a surrogate husband, who will rudely and quickly acquaint them with what they tried so cunningly to escape. It is time they know the power of a good Chinese Kurdus!"

The last word was the Chinese equivalent of "prick," and jeering laughter applauded the mandarin's cruel jest. Dazed, not yet quite comprehending what was in store for them, Katerina and Nadia stared at each other again, each trying to take some pitiful courage from the other.

The mandarin clapped his hands, and two soldiers came forward, pushing a large square platform, upon which was a king-sized mattress. It was placed at the center of the court, offering an ample view to all.

At Li Woo's sign, both women were stripped naked except for their batiste drawers, fine clockwork stockings with flouncy garters, and pumps, and forced to lie down on the bed.

They faced each other, so that Katerina's more spacious, mature bottom was turned towards the spectators, while Li Woo feasted his eyes on Nadia Kaplinski's appetizingly rounded, deeply cleft bottomcheeks.

"Now," the mandarin instructed, "since the older sorceress undoubtedly corrupted her younger niece, her punishment shall begin first. And since her bottom is the more spacious and offers greater terrain for fustigation, let Soo Fa apply strokes with a cane, but strip them only to the waist."

"Why not on the naked flesh?" Guey Wong hoarsely whispered to his friend, again licking his lips in avid anticipation.

"I have a better idea, friend of my youth," the mandarin chuckled. "These sorceresses would have us believe that, because they avoid the honest lusts of men, they are chaste. Well, we shall let them keep the last veil of modesty, but their rumps shall feel the sting of the cane. We shall douse them with cold water and whack them just the same. The sting is quite intense this way." The air was filled with tension as they awaited their fate.

And in this position, they stared with fear at each other, and by stretching out her slim fingers, Nadia touched those of her beautiful buxom aunt. "Oh, I am so afraid, Auntie Katerina!" the golden-haired young beauty moaned.

"Have courage, have courage, galupchik. It will not be worse than I have given you. Just endure the sweet pain of the cane. Do not think about it. And they are letting us keep our drawers, so those heathen beasts will not see our private parts."

"But that dreadful man spoke of a 'surrogate husband,'" Nadia anxiously stammered.

"To frighten us and to mock us. Peng Chu knows that we are not wed, so they insult us. It is only their heathen way of talking, nothing else," Katerina Ourosoff carefully explained.

Then she shuddered and called out, "Oh, my God!" as she suddenly felt the douse of a pail of cold water dashed upon her bottom, tickling down her thighs, soaking the batiste drawers and making them cling immodestly to the jutting prominence of her opulent posterior. She heard the obscene catcalls and the derisive exhortations of the spectators. Then she saw Nadia's lovely eyes dilate, saw her soft red mouth gape as the other tortures laved Nadia's bottom with her pail of cold water.

Chinese Justice

Meanwhile, the third torturess, Kee Ming, who had flogged Lida so expertly with the eel skin, now approached with a bamboo rod two-and-a half feet long, with a sturdy handle. The end of it had been cut lengthwise so that only half the original thickness was left.

If Li Woo had commanded the punishment of the older woman to take place first, it was purposely to drive the dagger of atrocious suspense and dread into the sensitive soul of the exquisite golden-haired Nadia. By lifting her head, she could just manage to see the Chinese torturess take aim with the cane.

Her feet planted well apart, the stocky Chinese woman studied the water-soaked batiste sheath that outlined not only the hillocks, but also the cleft of Katerina's posterior. Then came the hiss of the cane, which made the Russian widow stiffen as the bamboo swept several times across her tautened bottomglobes.

The woman who stood behind poor Nadia, bamboo already in hand, counted aloud the strokes, and Nadia began to weep in compassion for her aunt. Her sobbing increased at each stroke, perhaps because Katerina Ourosoff had managed to suppress her cries. But her body twitched and contorted in such a way that you could see she was pained by the attack on her bottom.

"You repent your wickedness, sorceress?" the mandarin questioned, leaning forward. And once again, the gray-haired peddler, his face flushed, his lips wet and slavering, was fingering himself slyly under his silken robes.

"I repent, oh do have pity, it is too much!" Katerina Ourosoff cried.

Thus, Soo Fa laid down the cane on the tray and folded her arms, it was the turn of her compatriot Ma Lo, who took her station behind poor sobbing Nadia, the bamboo rod quivering in the air as if impatient to strike.

And with relish, the torturess lightly tapped the split ends of the rod against the very middle of poor Nadia's tightening bottomglobes. The old peddler licked his lips again, once more his hands sought his swollen organ. Then the bamboo hissed through the air and landed across the upper curves of both compact globes. Nadia cried out, seeking pardon: "Oh, no—aahrr—oh, have pity—oh! Aunt Katerina, it is worse, oh so much worse than when you thrashed me. I cannot stand it."

Nadia began to swear that she was innocent of any wrongdoing, to implore pardon from that fiery kiss which methodically thrashed her jutting bottom. It swerved, it bounded, it tried to flatten itself in any possible way, it squirmed in evasion under the painful kiss of bamboo as Ma Loo applied the switch with exquisite precision and never touched the same place twice.

When the final stroke had been administered, one could see the quivering of her warmed bottomglobes under the garment.

At the mandarin's sign, the two torturesses ripped off the wet drawers and revealed the two women, with Nadia crying out in shame, "Oh, Auntie Katerina, they've made me naked—oh, I want to die of shame—oh, what are they going to do to me now? Oh, no, no more, my bottom is sore, I can't stand it!"

At the same moment, a concerted gasp of mingled

astonishment and sexual excitement was heard from the audience as two soldiers entered from the same narrow doorway, and they were escorting their comrade Pen Chu, who had been bathed and robed for his performance and pleasure as the "surrogate husband" to the cunt-loving lesbians. Little did they know how many a night he was forced to take hold of his own swollen cock, intoxicated by the lustful sessions between the two women. For reporting their sins, he would be awarded with their hot, pink cunts.

The women looked at each other in horror as they saw the former house boy swathed in silken robes, with a humongous, erected cock sticking out from the opening, pointing menacingly their way.

"For your courage in reporting the sins of these lesbian sluts," said Li Woo, "you are to choose the best punishment before you have your way with them." He looked approvingly at Peng Chu, knowing that they had before this trial already decided that the two would be forced to display their lesbian love for the anxiously awaiting audience.

"I think the most fitting punishment for their deviant acts is to perform those acts, to show those among us here just how corrupted these two are in the ways of pussylove."

"An excellent idea," Li Woo said, looking over at his friend Guey Wong with a wink. Wong, his cock about to explode, had both hands wrapped around the rod of his pleasure, jerking himself off into oblivion, overcome with rut by the proceedings of the day.

The two torturesses, blazing lesbians, were told to

"assist" Katerina and Nadia in commencing with the activities. And thus, it was Nadia who was spread-eagled across the huge bed, her cunt lips held open by Ma Loo, while her legs were pinned down by Soo Fa. Katerina was ordered to gamahuche the luscious cunt in front of all who stood to observe. When she resisted, Lee Ming pushed her head down between the legs, toward the girl's open twat.

"Lick her cunt, now," Li Woo commanded, "or we will bruise that lovely fat behind of yours." And thus, Katerina went down into the fury slash of her younger lover, as she had on countless other occasions, and gingerly licked the loving cunt lips until Nadia began to moan in pleasure. She spread the pussy hole as far apart as she could and darted her elongated tongue into the sweet tasting hole and in those moments of revived lesbian lust, she forgot about her stinging behind, the audience, the humiliation. All she focused on was the pink, precious cunt petals which unfolded the treasure before her. And soon, she found her way to the engorged bud of love and began to slowly flick it this way and that, until the younger woman moaned and panted in exquisite joy.

The pussies of all three torturesses were on fire at the sight of this glorious gamahuche, and it was Soo Fa and Ma Loo who could barely control their lust at this sight and began to twiddle each other's pussies. Upon seeing this, Li Woo thought it would be fun to let the girls take possession of the lovely cunt that Katerina was so anxiously devouring, giving Nadia a chance to experience a wider spectrum of pussy love. And during that

Chinese Justice

time, Peng Chu could have his fun with the broad bottomed, big-breasted Katerina, whose face was totally buried into the creamy cunt of her intimate partner.

Winking at the two Chinese girls, Li Woo silently granted them permission to Nadia's body. And before either woman knew what was happening, the cunt-lapping Katerina's lips were pried from Nadia's pussy lips, as the Chinese women took over.

"Treat the young one as a man would," Li Woo ordered. And thus, Ma Loo strapped a dildo harness around her sister and guided the false penis to the wet pussy on the bed; Nadia flinched and whined as the head of the leather dildo neared her hole and gritted her teeth as it drove inward. Soo Fa kissed the lips of her new lover, and tongue kissed her deeply as she prodded the tight pussy hole with the dildo. The strap, and the inner part of the dildo, were rigged with soft rubber ticklers and thus the Chinese girls clit and cunthole were stimulated while she fucked Nadia like a man. And Ma Loo, to add to the intense enjoyment, came over and straddled Nadia's face, after her mouth was made good and wet by Soo Fa's kisses, and thus the girl was told to reach her tongue into the slim, thin-lipped slit and gamahuche the torturess as her own cunt was pumped with the male-like iron.

Nadia began to respond to the feel of the dildo, and to the essence of cunt which intoxicated her as Ma Loo's pussy slapped down on her lips and tongue, and she felt the gurgling familiarity of orgasm bubble through her loins, and soon, her creamy come emission splashed onto the leather dildo, which was then removed from her hole. She continued to gamahuche the woman sitting on her face, until again there came the juicy slish of girlcome, as Ma Loo spent on Nadia's lips. Then, Soo Fa brought the leather dildo to her mouth and urged her to lick off her own come. And for the final lesbian scene, Soo Fa turned herself around, now free of the dildo, and laid her own swollen cunt upon the slippery lips of Nadia as she dived down into Nadia's juicy, come-filled cunt hole, and the two women pussy-licked one another until the jism poured onto each others lips, and the aroma of sex juice filled the room.

Katerina, held back by the third Chinese girl, Kee Ming, was getting her bubbies rubbed and her nipples pinched slightly as her niece played pussy fucking with the other women. And her own cunt, at this point, was a massive ache of burning desire. This was exactly what Li Woo had wanted, because now the buxom Russian would beg for the hard cock of her former manservant.

Nadia was led to a bench across the way, where all three Chinese lesbians worked on her orifices and her tits, with Soo Fa licking her asshole, Ma Loo sucking her clit bud and Kee Ming kissing her titties and sucking her tongue, as the men on the dais watched with great lust.

Now, the soldiers led Katerina to the big bed, tossed her on her stomach with her head close to the edge, and held her down by the arms as Peng Chu, now disrobed, stood before her face and presented to her his cock, which now ached with the pent up longing for the white woman's wet pussy and mouth.

She resisted at first, until the soldiers, twisting her

arms, helped guide their comrades swollen prick to her mouth and warned she should suck it with the same care as she would take sweet cunt meat. And thus, the rock hard sword of a prick was brought to her fat pink lips and she took it in, sucking on cock, an alien notion to her for so long, and feeling her cunt swell with the excitement a man had not instilled in her for many years. She pulled free her hands so she could take hold of the instrument and fully pull the prick into her sensuous, suckling mouth.

The betrayer of Katerina's lesbian lifestyle was now the recipient of her artful sucking and he was ready to place the swollen sword into the depths of her, and swim inside her uncharted waters, so unused to male meat. He pulled his swollen prick from her hands and mouth, motioned for the soldiers to turn her over, and watched in joyful ecstasy as her charming cunt chink was opened by the soldiers, and made accessible for the charge of his raging prick. He bent over her, drove his tongue deep into her mouth, and then kissed the huge bubbies, taking one tit bud between his teeth and gnawing it, then the other, creating shooting spasms of lust inside the juicy cunthole and up and down her loins. Katerina felt herself fill with fire, an unfamiliar longing for cock, and in the moment of passion spread her legs as open as she possibly could to greet the rampant manhood that she prayed would in moments be filling her engorged, swollen cunt hole with it's own engorged, swollen stiffness.

Peng Chu now got on his knees between her legs, and taking hold of his aching weapon as he had so many a night while watching the two women rub pussies and eat cunt, he directed it this time into the receptacle of his longing and pressed with full force to achieve entry into the tightness of Katerina's cunt.

"It has been long since a man has thrust himself into this charming spot," he panted, pressing his prick deeper, "and your cunt is like that of a virgin. I honor you in a way you don't deserve with my manhood, and will honor you, white bitch, with Chinese seed."

And with that, he implanted himself firmly within the grasp of her tight cunt and moved in and out of her wet, juicy hole with vigor and lust, until he could feel the magnificently succulent orifice, with it's clenching cunt muscles, pulling from him the pent up seed of so many unrequited sex sessions, with his eye glued to the peephole, and his hand firmly glued to his manhood, making himself come.

And here, the opportunity to spill himself into the lesbian's wet cunt made him crazy with rut and he began to pump and drive himself into her, filling her to the hilt, until at last the wild expression of his lust poured into the lovely pussy and dripped gingerly over the soft folds, onto the tight asshole.

Peng Chu slumped onto the ample breast and lay there, and in that next moment you could hear the howl of Nadia who was coming in the wildest of ways at the hands and the mouth of the three Chinese seductresses.

Li Woo, Guey Wong, the men of the dais all watched in lustful agony, knowing that they themselves had to have the next cunt or they would die of pent up rut, their pricks bursting for a white woman's sex flesh!

The first day had ended. It was night, and Li Woo,

having first bathed and been anointed with exquisite oils and scents, waddled into his bedchamber where Lida still lay spread-eagled on her belly, lifted by the pillows under her belly. He was overcome by savage rut, having observed the wildly stimulating sessions of his court, and all he desired was to plunge himself into a sweet, warm receptacle and pummel a woman with his male meat.

Li Woo approached her, naked, his prick already swollen with desire, she began to stir, remembering how he'd buggered her that afternoon. She was like a little girl who yearned desperately for the protection of the parent but now it was too late. Gripping the sensitive cheeks of her bottom, the mandarin yawned them apart once again and pressed his cockhead against the shrinking cleft of her asshole. Lida's head rose, her shoulders tensed, as he began to bugger her in a madly maniacal way, pressing his huge organ deeply into the tight ass crevice. And all she could do was receive his thrusts, and his seed, for she was now the bondslave of the mandarin and would be until Tsu Hsi herself ordained the release of all the hostages.

In other bedchambers in this ornate palace, the Russian women commenced their servitude to their male captors. Tender golden-haired Nadia, shaken from her ordeal with the combination whipping, exposure of her lesbian lifestyle, and public pussy fucking with her aunt and with strangers, was taken to Fa Joe, the prosperous merchant from Wosan and there encouraged by two Chinese matrons, plying bamboo rods over her back and titties and thighs, to suck her pro tem master's cock and then to pillow her head on her arms at the foot of the bed and present her bottom for his rut. As he contemptuously explained, "I will not drive my worthy blade into an opening reserved for this bitch's proper mate. But I will fuck her in the posture which her mate would adopt to remind her of her vileness." So saying, he proceeded to bugger the golden-haired captive, cramming his prick back and forth inside her asshole while she simply pressed her lovely asshole to the merchants charging cock, having discovered on this day that she was powerless to deny him access to any hole he desired.

And in a nearby bedchamber, the beautiful widow, Katerina, was similarly ravaged by the Boxer colonel who, to show his own imaginative lovemaking abilities, had her watch him fuck two Chinese girls, and even watch the them rub pussies together, before he would plow her with his engorged weapon. In fact, he had one of the women don a pair of leather gloves, pinch Katerina's nipples playfully and rub her shuddering titties and belly and thighs while the virile officer, kneeling before her, pretended to aim for her cunt but actually delved his elongated, swollen cock into the sensitive trough of her bumhole. He fucked her asshole quite vigorously never even considering placing his cock into her swollen snatch. Thus, she was well-acquainted with the ways of anal lust that night.

The second morning of the trials of the captive females attracted an even larger and more vociferous audience, for those who had thronged into the huge courtroom the day before were loud in

Chinese Justice

their praises of Li Woo's ingenious and highly appropriate justice meted out to these white sorceresses.

Claudia was summoned first to appear before her vindictive and salacious judge. Her face was haggard, for she had spent a sleepless night. Not only had she been compelled to watch the eel skin flogging of her young stepdaughter, but she had learned of her husband's assassination by the Boxers. And she had had to brood upon Lida's wanton conduct with her own Chinese houseboy. Her efforts as a mother had failed, and now she had been brutally widowed. Perhaps for the first time, she could really give way to fear for herself, since there was nothing left of her little world except her own captive person, now in the hands of the ruthless and lustful Boxers!

Soo Fa and Ma Loo seized Claudia Garconniere by the shoulders and forced her down upon her knees before the sinister mandarin. Her eyes widened with revulsion as she saw his fat lips curl in a lecherous smile, his eyes glittering with lust. And then she started, for kneeling to her left was the homely little housemaid Ma Sue who had been summoned to testify against both Lida and her stepmother.

"You, sorceress," Li Woo began, "consort of that traitorous French dog who delivered our beloved country up to the depredations of France's mercenaries who look upon our wise and ancient people as no better than barbarians, I now accuse you tribunal of full knowledge of his wrongdoing. In addition, from the lips of your own housemaid, who is here by my express order, you are accused of complicity in the harlotry of your stepdaughter, whom we chastised yesterday. Admit your guilt, confess your sins, and throw yourself on the mercy of this court!"

"I was the wife of a man your accursed Boxers killed without reason, for his only crime was that he loved his country as much as you love yours!" Claudia Garconniere said in a trembling but courageous voice. "And that girl lies if she had told you that I had any part in poor Lida's shameful behavior. If she saw so much, surely she must have seen that I whipped my stepdaughter for her impertinence and her flirtatiousness, and that I was often scolding her because she did not behave as a proper young lady and a daughter of an important representative of France."

"Oh, yes," Li Woo blandly retorted, his smile deepening, "Ma Sue has told us how you whipped the girl. But come now, admit freely that you took sport from it and that it pleased you, more than the thought of righteous chastisement."

"What are you saying? That is an abominable lie!" Claudia Garconniere gasped, her face crimsoning.

Li Woo's face was mottled with rage at this insult. "You dare accuse me, chief magistral of Hanchow and under orders from Her Celestial Majesty, of being a liar? I should have you flayed alive for your temerity! But since you speak with so forked a tongue, you have suggested to me your punishment. Prepare her!"

The two torturesses seized the unfortunate young widow and proceeded to rip off all of her clothes except her corset, her lisle hose and shoes, heaving her splendidly high-perched, firm and delectably rounded titties bare before the tribunal. Since she had never had a

Chinese Justice

child, the areolae were large, with a dark coral tint, while her nipples, though ripe, were soft and exquisitely pink. Her skin was marvelously tawny, smooth and sleek. Claudia turned scarlet with shame at this enforced disrobing, struggling with her tormentresses, but to little avail because her hands had remained bound behind her back.

Then they dragged her to kneel before Li Woo, who had pulled his hardened cock from the confines of his silk robes, and before his old friend Guey Wong, whose own rut-filled manhood was thrust out from his loincloth. Claudia was commanded to suck the two cocks, making sure each received sufficient pleasure simultaneously, which meant that while one was in the grasp of her lovely lips, the other would be held firm in her hand.

Her corset was torn off, and from where she knelt, her fat bottom cheeks were yawned slightly apart and so many an audience member observed them with the secret thought of filling the tight, dark hole.

But this was the moment for the old chums to have their cocks pleasured together and, mortified, the ever-so-moral Claudia was forced to first go down on the huge weapon of the magistrate, while taking Guey Wong's prick in hand, and she sucked on the purple-headed spear, then shifted her mouth to the other elongated cock, with each man demanding her mouth come back to his organ. It wasn't long until she managed to make the two of them come at once—they were so hot from the idea of their two exposed cocks receiving the same lascivious treatment at the same moment—and she was told to lick the creamy dew from each organ, catch with her tongue any semen on their bellies and legs.

She relaxed her hand and jaw, but not for long, for Li Woo, showing off before his old friend, turned the woman over on her belly, and had the lesbian torturesses place pillows beneath her so that Guey Wong could gleefully take possession of her yawning butthole, stabbing the tight bung with his still hard-prick.

Mounting the woman like a dog in heat, and thrilled to be fucking the white woman beneath the stares of a jealous audience, he plunged his cock into her backhole with little fanfare burying it to the hilt in just a few thrusts, for she seemed so stretched, as if she'd taken the male meat in that hole before. He held fast to her shoulders and fucked her, finally bringing his prick to a full boil and spilling his seed into her arched asshole.

She was left there, her butt up in the air, for the pleasure of the spectators, who feasted their eyes on her magnificent bottom, the big, spacious ovals, broadly set apart so that the shadowy furrow them was, thanks to this exaggerated straddle of her legs, lewdly distended.

"Sorceress, hear me well," Li Woo intoned as he leaned forward. "Before I absolve you of your guilt, you must learn the lesson of humility. When you are ready for it you have but to nod your head three times and your punishment will halt.

Voiceless plaints and groans were wrested from the naked auburn-haired captive as she remained in the position in the most leisurely way, her shuddering thighs, wriggling this way and that as she tried to maintain her balance.

Chinese Justice

As a further humiliation, Soo Fa was directed to tongue fuck Claudia's exposed asshole, creating a public display of lesbian sex. This is where the brazen widow drew the line and decided to bow to her captives, as her bottom wiggled with discomfort at the Chinese girl's probing tongue. "Enough," Claudia cried out.

"Come crawl before me and lick my feet in token of your humility, sorceress," the mandarin ordered. And Claudia Garconniere, distraught from the anguish that consumed her magnificently beautiful body, cast aside all pride and shame and ignominiously prostrated herself before him and, holding each foot in turn with her cuddling hands, kissed the fat mandarin's feet.

She was taken to his bedchamber to await his dalliance with her that night, where he would plow his huge organ into the depths of her ass, following the path to anal lust blazed earlier that day by his friend Guey Wong.

Next it was the turn of Wilhelmina Preusser, the spinsterish secretary of the murdered German Consul who had been assassinated by the Boxer soldiers at the very moment when he and his secretary were about to make love.

When the two principal torturesses forced her down to her knees and Li Woo threatened her with serious punishment to reveal all she knew about the infamous treachery of the man she had served, Wilhelmina Preusser indignantly cried out, "How dare you judge so wonderful and kindly a man as Herr Reimath! You yellow beasts murdered him without cause! And I, a good German citizen, demand that you release me, or you will answer to the Kaiser himself!"

The audience gasped at this insulting defiance, and loud voices cried out for stringent punishment. But Li Woo chuckled and smiled, held up his hand, and then replied to the fuming mature brunette: "Sorceress, you too speak with a forked tongue. If you mourn your master, it was because he was about to make a woman of you. But since you call our noble and valiant Boxers yellow beasts, I will acquaint you with a true beast who will complete what your dead master could not finish!"

He clapped his hands, and then there was a cry of mingled horror and lustful anticipation from the spectators as, through that narrow door, a huge Chinese soldier entered the room. He was 6'4", fat, and apelike, with a cock the size of a small tree trunk.

Wilhelmina Preusser shrank back, her mouth gaping at the incredible sight. Then she shrieked and tried to rise, but Ma Loo and Soo Fa forced her to remain on her knees until the soldier came forward. He lifted the fräulein and carried her to the huge bed which still stood in the great courtroom. Its rectangular frame seemed barely large enough to accommodate the monster-sized man. Wilhelmina Preusser was stripped naked by Ma Loo and Soo Fa and spread-eagled on the bed while the huge Chinaman stripped naked himself, exposing to her startled eyes a cock she could have never imagined—12 inches long and almost two-and-a-half inches in diameter.

Soo Fa applied a special sex oil to the German woman's snatch and helped lower the long, fat cock to its mark as the soldier climbed atop her naked body with a grunt and pressed his weight upon her petite frame.

The fat cock head rested at the opening to her twat, and rubbed for a moment against the oily lubricant, but the soldier, filled with rut at this opportunity to fuck the virgin white woman, plunged himself into her twat without stopping for air, ripping the hymen immediately as the cockhead speared the virgin pathway and blazed toward the depths of her womb.

She moaned and groaned, overcome by the weight and force of the gorilla man, but the Chinese girls kept her legs far apart, so as to accommodate the huge weapon. Then Soo Fa whispered in her ear to try and wrap her legs around the man, to give him greater access and her less pain, and as she did, she felt the humongous cock pierce the final shreds of her virgin sheath, allowing him greater entrance to her snatch, and suddenly the virgin began to feel an elasticity in her cunt that propelled her to meet the animal thrusts of her first sex partner, who was now pummeling his rut with great intention into her newly gaping hole.

She felt him release his jism in a wild, pumping, pummeling spasm and he fell, spent, upon her breasts. Wilhelmina lay in shock contemplating this spectacular loss of her virginity.

When the tribunal resumed its third day of deliberation, Li Woo summoned Dorothy Trowbridge and brown-haired, widowed Katya van der Groot before him. The charming young coppery-haired daughter of the provincial minister, still mourning her father's assassination, was stripped naked by Ma Loo and Soo Fa, while the third torturess, Kee Ming, using her short bamboo stick liberally, compelled the weeping Dutch widow to strip completely naked.

"Here, good people of Hanchow, we have two sorceresses whose male warlocks have for long years cast their vile spells over our nation," Li Woo decreed. "The young sorceress, I have discovered from the most reliable sources in the village where she dwelt, is still a maiden, while the older white devil-bitch, though wed to a Christian minister, took little joy in the mating. Of her I say also that my spies have learned of her eagerly sought-for adultery, for she lusted for a young soldier of her own country and willingly cuckolded her righteous husband with this man. Her sin did not last because the Boxers entered her village and captured her before she could bring more dishonor upon the name of her rightful state."

Pausing to glance at the faces beyond and above him, he was able to note that he had held their attention and that there was not the slightest murmur against his autocratic judgements. Li Woo resumed, "Accordingly, we who believe in the ancient laws see here a sanguine opportunity to correct these wretched sinners and turn them back to the understanding of serenity and obedience. The switch shall warm them as they learn affection and comfort from each other.

At his sign, Soo Fa stationed herself behind Dorothy Trowbridge, her eyes devouring the voluptuous virginal nudity of the young redhead, while Ma Loo took her station behind and at the left of Katya van der Groot. Each torturess was armed with a springy, whippy switch

Chinese Justice

taken from the branch of a ginkgo tree. And at a signal, they began to lash at the writhing naked bottoms and thighs of their luscious victims, whacking them just until they felt a slight sting.

"You shall both be whipped until you seek to console each other, until you make love as women do!" Li Woo encouraged.

The two torturesses accelerated the tempo of the switching momentarily and Dorothy Trowbridge, rubbed repeatedly against her naked companion in attempts to get away from the switch. Expertly the two Chinese women plied their switches, until in desperation the young coppery-haired girl began to grind her cunt against Katya's. When this was observed, the woman flogging the Dutch widow terminated the punishment and watched as the two women began to girlfuck one another. Katya, panting now, lunged frantically against the triangle, rubbing her cunt against Dorothy's as if she were aggressively seeking to glean Sapphic pleasures.

Now the tempo was accelerated still more; the Chinese women prodded at the tight anal apertures of both women as they ground their cunts, forcing them to push their juicy folds even closer together as their behinds flinched. As the women began to revel in each other's naked, perspiring flesh, the daughter of the murdered minister cast aside all modesty and began wantonly to rub her pussy back and forth against Katya's. The latter, her bottom, burning from the kiss of Dorothy's pussy flesh, responded in kind until at last, both naked women began to feel the tides of passion seething in their cuntholes.

Both women spread open their legs, and hence, the inviting pink of their cuntholes, positioned their legs in such a deliriously delightful pose, that they were now pressed up against each others clit buds, furiously rubbing the tiny engorged organs against one another. They held tight to one another now, while rubbing the fully lubricated snatches, causing an exquisite friction that began the tingly sensation of orgasm in both their red hot love holes.

And just as the women's creamy love juice began to pour down, they were shocked to find Guey Wong and Li Woo's huge cocks shoved into their mouths. The two men, obviously heated by the furiously rubbing pussies, pressed their respective cocks into the depths of the cunt-rubber's mouths and releasing their semen almost simultaneous to the sweet ejaculations of the engorged pussies.

The women were then made to lie against each other and, still pressing their luscious cunts together, to tongue kiss one another deeply so as to taste the salty dew of sex resin left behind by each men as they kissed.

And when at last they swayed, half-fainting after the turbulent and coerced lovemaking, the fat mandarin had Dorothy Trowbridge and Katya carried off to his bedchamber where they would accept his sexual offerings this very night.

That same night, Dorothy and Katya were also to submit to the further lusts of Guey Wong, and all the other men of importance whose pricks they were to suck and accept into their orifices without question.

That very night also, by courier, the fat mandarin

received the dreadful news that Tsu Hsi had taken flight from her palace to her most loyal province in the north, and that much of the Forbidden City was in ruins. With this news had come word of the Lord Duke Lan that all the white hostages must be guarded with the greatest vigilance and that utmost care must be taken to preserve their lives so that China would have better bargaining power with the foreign usurpers when the inevitable peace terms were to be discussed.

And Li Woo, beating his breast and crying out upon the graves of his ancestors, knew the bitter truth—that the cause of the Boxers had failed and that the rebellion would not be a triumph as had been dreamed by those who ruled this mighty nation.

Yet no foreign troops had as yet approached Hanchow, and he could grant himself and his people a few more spectacles of Chinese justice. Hence, the next morning he commanded the German Vice-Consul Kurt Hullweg, his wife Ernestine and his stepdaughter Erika, be brought before him.

Flaxen-haired young Erika wept in terror when she was led in and saw her beloved mother and her handsome stepfather (to whom she was secretly drawn, although she had no way of knowing that he secretly lusted for her ripe young body). The mandarin had no charges to bring against this trio, particularly since this old amah Mei Fong testified that they had acted with courtesy and kindness to the merchants and the poor of Peking as well as to herself. Yet as she extolled their virtues, she unsuspectingly suggested to the sadistic magistrate a pretext by which he could furnish his enthusiastic audience with the lecherous spectacle they all desired. She had insisted that Kurt Hullweg was a devoted husband as well as father to this girl who was not of his own loins. And at this point, Li Woo mockingly interposed, "Why, then, to be a proper father he should indeed not hesitate to grant her the same love he would evince to his own spouse. Yes, you shall make a choice. Either you will make love to the young sorceress, who, though you claim her as your daughter, is not truly of your own seed, or the wife you profess to love so dearly will be taken by me before your very eyes!"

As much as Kurt lusted for his eighteen-year-old stepdaughter, and as much as he longed to bury his huge cock deep into the tender folds of her luscious cunt, he would not take on the act of deflowering her in public, nor would he hurt his wife with such an act. He stood strong and told the mandarin he would not commit such an act. He looked lovingly at his wife, and longingly at his stepdaughter, and silently said a prayer that neither of the women he loved would be harmed.

But the mandarin demanded a sexual spectacle and thus Ernestine Hullweg was to be it. And when her husband tried to fight on her behalf, he was pulled to a corner by two huge guards and chained to a heavy chair.

Meanwhile, the lascivious torturesses were directed to remove every strip of clothing on Ernestine, and to tie her open arms and legs to the posts of the bed. And, as he promised, Li Woo then fucked the wife of Kurt Hullweg as Hullweg himself was forced to look on, helplessly.

Li Woo, filled with rut still, but tired from the days and nights of jabbing these victimized white women in

Chinese Justice

every orifice imaginable with his cock, was slow to erect, and even slower to penetrate the woman. Finally, he managed the head of his prick through the tightened portal and, once inside, came alive to the touch of the cushy cunt flesh as it so naturally swallowed up his engorged organ.

He raised his hips and then dug them into the woman, who tried not to look at her handsome husband as she could do nothing less than accept the mandarin's humongous manhood, and he pressed himself into the hilt, wriggled his butt so he could get himself even farther inside, and shortly released his jism deep into Ernestine's womb, falling upon her breast with a sigh.

When he was done, he allowed the whole family back to their cell, and he called forth some new, nubile Chinese women to wash his prick and balls, and re-robe him, right before the captivated court audience.

But in the distance he could again hear the slight mumbling of those fellow countrymen who were jealous that Li Woo was so abundant with pussy and ass to fuck, and that he allowed his friends the same privilege, while the common men were forced to sit and watch in boiling rut as the parade of pussies and punishments commenced throughout the week.

The link to power was weakened now, for the fat mandarin and his old friend Guey Wong, the soldiers and all the others, had truly had their fill of fresh pussy meat and the common men would no longer put up with it.

This sentiment was, of course, strengthened by the fall of the Forbidden City, and that night, when Li Woo, his lesbian assistants and his horny friends were to partake in the lust orgy of pussy and ass-fucking, the magistrate found a surprise. During the course of the day, the natives had grown restless and, sneaking into the bed chambers and cells where the women were being held, plotted to stop the sexual greediness of Li Woo.

Thus, as he reconvened a special court that night, and brought in every "sorceress" who had been tried that week, he had the lesbians line them all around the huge bed, their butts and pussies wide open, accessible, their heads touching as they all met in the center. With that, he gave his comrades and friends, the special members of the dais, the thrill of playing musical cunts, stopping at anyone they would to fuck, a pussy or ass, and plow the waiting female meat with their male machines.

Dorothy, Katya, Ernestine, Erika, Claudia, Lida, Jane, Wilhelmina and all the captives were there, being offered to the iron-hard male swords, the pounds and pounds of male flesh, that wanted only to plunge deeply into the open clefts between their legs and leave behind their seed, in their cunts, their assholes, or splat across their bellies, their chins.

And as these grown men all stepped out of their silk robes and loin cloths with the help of Chinese girl servants who began to suck their cocks to hardness so they could fuck the waiting holes that yawned deliciously on the bed in front of them, a small army of commoners and countrymen stormed into the special night court. Without shedding a drop of blood or causing a battle, they were able to capture Li Woo and his gang, for they were all so tired from so much sex in four days that they were easily overcome.

Chinese Justice

Cuffed together like a Mongolian arban of captured warriors, they were carted off to the jail. And although the small army of rebel soldiers was tempted to claim the gaping cunt and assholes that abounded for their own pleasure, they knew that the war was over, and the hostages were to be freed. And the women who endured the lusts, and who accepted their sexual fates, were to later develop great strength of character for surviving what they endured, and also the knowledge that the men who pillaged their towns and took them sexual hostage, who killed their men and took their daughters, were not the fair representatives of the whole race. They were simply people of perversity who at one time in the history of China had power and wielded it wickedly.

The Dowager Empress understood that she was no longer invincible, no longer feared by all those nations who had paid homage to her in the past. The Imperial Palace had been looted, and on its walls were obscene pictures and vilifications of her reign. Old as she was, her spirit was now broken and she began to feel the burden of the long years of her reign. Thus it was that she decreed that the hostages Li Woo took should be surrendered to the emissaries of the Red Cross. They would then be taken to Peking to be repatriated, and they would be given gold to compensate them for their suffering and their imprisonment.

Li Woo, it was decided, would serve hard time in jail with his other perverted friends because he made the mistake of trying to conquer women in lieu of truly fighting for his country.

LUSTY LESSONS

It was Sonia Magaloff's custom to check every cabin as soon as the guests had departed, not only to ascertain whether anything had been stolen—towels, sheets, the Gideon Bible, lamps, the TV set—but also to see whether they had forgotten anything of their own.

Before driving to Chicago, she entered the cabin which had housed Jane and Dave Elston on their wedding night. Everything seemed to be in order. She opened the closet door, glanced in, and saw the little cosmetic bag on the top shelf.

Retrieving and opening it, she discovered the plane and boat tickets and the check, as well as a little envelope which contained a note of good wishes from Margaret Elston to Jane. On the envelope, Margaret's address label was a fortunate clue for the worried motel owner.

"What a shame—they'll need this on their honeymoon," she exclaimed out loud. "And they didn't tell me where they were going. Well, there's only one thing to do—take this to this Margaret Elston—she must be his sister."

As she left the cabin, she shook her head and frowned. "Such bad luck," she mused. "A very bad start for a marriage. They were not happy here last night, and when they find they lost the money and tickets—"

She stopped, perplexed. Perhaps they might drive back in search of the missing cosmetic bag. But more than an hour had already passed since Dave had driven off with his lovely young bride. And if she left the bag with one of the waitresses or the motel maids and they shouldn't come back…No, decidedly, the best thing to do would be to take it back to the sister of that fine young man. She surely would know where they were going.

Dave and Jane arrived at the Dells about 12:30, and Dave chose one of the less advertised resorts which boasted a tennis court and swimming pool. He hadn't asked Jane about her check—it had been certified to facilitate cashing out of town—because he'd taken along more than enough money of his own. Besides, money wasn't his prime concern. What happened this week would establish the level of harmony on which their marriage would be predicated. He was still fretting about last night's fiasco. Jane was such a sweet, shy, wholesome, lovely girl, he didn't want to do anything that would be in bad taste and change her opinion of him. He knew she loved him, just as he loved her. Of course

Lusty Lessons

he oughtn't to be so gloomy; lots of young couples had trouble adjusting the first few weeks of marriage, and after all, everything else was fine between them. Jane liked the same books and sports, she shared his fondness for classical and semi-classical music and for historical-thriller movies. Just the same, he wished it had been perfect for her last night...

Margaret Elston looked flushed and happy. She was wearing her provocative red peignoir under which she had only a pair of black panties, offblack nylon hose hooked to a tiny garter-belt, and open-toe sandals. Ken Davidson had called her long distance from New York last night and told her he was flying to Chicago the next afternoon. He was going to confer with his agent, who had a commission for a new travel book with photographic illustrations from a new Chicago publishing firm that wanted to head its autumn list with a sure-to-be best-seller by a nationally acclaimed author. It would mean he'd stay through September, and nothing could have made Margaret any happier. Now that her son was off on his honeymoon, however short, she could look forward to at least a week of uninterrupted amorous bliss with Ken. If only Dave and Jane could experience the ecstasy born out of candor and honesty and unabashed desire that she and Ken shared. And it wasn't all sex between them, either; Ken was a wonderful conversationalist who stimulated her to be at her own mental peak, which helped to keep her young. She would hate to think of ever becoming as stodgy and narrow minded as Frances Corley.

The doorbell rang. She frowned and rose from the

living room couch. That surely couldn't be Ken; he wouldn't be at the airport till three this afternoon.

Wonderingly, she opened the door.

"I'm sorry to disturb you. Are you Margaret Elston?"

"Why, yes, I am."

"Oh, good! I was afraid you might be out. My name's Sonia Magaloff. I run the Danson Motel out on the highway to Milwaukee, and your brother and his wife stayed at one of my cabins last night—"

Margaret Elston couldn't suppress a giggle. "My brother? You must be referring to my son, Dave."

"Your son? But that doesn't seem possible!" Sonia incredulously exclaimed.

"What a compliment! Thank you so much—but I'm afraid the truth is I am Dave's mother. But—is anything wrong?"

"Oh, no. I mean, they're fine. But after they'd left, I found this in the closet." Sonia handed Margaret the cosmetic bag. "You see, I found your note with your address in the bag, so I thought I'd bring it right to you. I left a good hour or so after they'd driven off and they hadn't come back, and I didn't know where they were headed."

"It was awfully kind of you to do this. Well, actually—do come in; I'm forgetting my manners keeping you standing here at the door. May I get you a cup of coffee? I'm sure there's a piece of wedding cake—I took some home yesterday."

"I'd like that very much, yes, thank you," Sonia beamed.

Appraisingly, her eyes fixed on Margaret's trim figure

Lusty Lessons

which the peignoir delectably molded as Margaret left the room. His mother! But how youthful she was, and what a lovely complexion—and such a firm, fine figure—she must be in her mid- or late forties, at least. And she seemed so pleasant and modern. Surely a woman like this must have inculcated in her son the understanding of how to please a woman.

She seated herself on the elegant but comfortable Chippendale couch, glancing about the tastefully furnished living room. What a lovely house! She and Sergei had never had much more than a hotel suite when things were breaking for them, and sometimes a tiny, cramped, dismal room with a bath down the hall that had to be shared with a dozen other tenants. Even her motel cabin, which she had decorated herself and of which she was pardonably proud, couldn't compare with this beautifully appointed place. It would be nice to have one's own place, to have roots. She envied Margaret Elston.

Dave's mother returned with a tray on which two coffee cups and a plate of cake were arranged, put it down on the glass-topped table in front of the couch, then seated herself beside Sonia. Deftly she cut a slice of the rich torte-like wedding cake and handed Sonia one of the smaller serving plates and one of the cups, then took coffee and cake for herself, leaning back and contemplating her unexpected visitor. What a striking woman, and what a very becoming outfit...she must remember to look for one like it for herself. The sheath-skirt and jacket fit beautifully, and the ensemble did wonders for a good figure. Margaret Elston was not vain, but she was nonetheless grateful that the years had dealt kindly with her feminine charms. So long as they still had the power to ignite Ken Davidson's exciting passion and inspire his satisfyingly artistic lovemaking technique, she would have no cause for complaint.

"Now then, Sonia—I like first names, and you've earned that and more by coming to see me at such inconvenience—" she began.

Sonia shook her head with a smile. "But there wasn't the least bit of inconvenience, Mrs. Elston. I was coming to Chicago anyway, and all I did was take one freeway instead of another."

"Just the same, it was good-hearted of you, and I appreciate it, just as Dave and Jane will. Now tell me something about yourself."

"But there really isn't much to tell, Mrs. Elston," Sonia smiled. She felt very much at ease; this handsome woman had the adroit gift of knowing how to make her, a stranger, feel perfectly natural and welcome. "I just own the motel where your son and his wife stopped last night. Nothing very glamorous, really."

"But you yourself look exactly that way—are you sure you weren't ever a model?"

Sonia threw back her head and laughed delightedly. "You're doing wonders for my morale, Mrs. Elston. Thank you for that nice compliment. No, I'm afraid I was just a very ordinary girl who eventually got married, and then—" she shrugged, extending her open palms to either side in a typically Slavic gesture, it doesn't really matter.

"And then what?" Margaret pursued, with a sympathetic smile.

"Oh, then my husband decided it was time for him to find a younger girl. He was always restless, I suppose. But we had fun and laughs for twelve years, and I can't really say he—what is the American phrase you have—oh, da—he didn't leave me 'in the lurch'. As a matter of fact, he was very generous in the settlement."

"But what a shame to be left alone with the worry of running a business. It must be very tiring for you."

"Oh, not so much. At first, maybe, till I began to find good, steady help. Then I opened my little restaurant—I love to cook, you see. And now I have fine people whom I can trust, so that I can drive into Chicago whenever I want and feel sure that things will be run right when I'm gone. No, it's not too much work at all."

"I still admire you, Sonia."

"You're so nice, Mrs. Elston—"

"Margaret, please!"

"Margaret, then, spassibo. But you, what do you do besides being the very nice mother of that so pleasant young man?"

"I'm in real estate, Sonia. And there's a lot of similarity between us. You see, my husband left me, too, for another woman. But he was a competitor of mine; he was in the same business and I think he resented my being a success. Maybe it was a mistake to show him I could be independent—men aren't fond of it, that's for sure."

Sonia's large, dark-green eyes darkened with compassion. "Da, I know what you mean, Margaret. But with me, it wasn't the same. Sergei was a mining engineer—when he wasn't gambling. I think he always wished he had been born to the aristocracy in the days of the

Czars, so he could have used the family estate for his stakes. Not that he wasn't very lucky at times. And we did have twelve wonderful years." Her eyes softened, her full red mouth curving in a reminiscent smile. "I always thought of him more as a lover than as a husband, if you know what I mean."

"I do indeed. So you really have happy memories—and that's very good for you now."

"Da," Sonia laughed softly, "but at night it is not so very good. I would far rather have Sergei in my bed than all the memories."

"More coffee, Sonia dear?"

"Well, if I am not a pig to say so, yes, and another slice of that delicious wedding cake."

"Of course. I'm sorry I can't take credit for it—the caterers baked it. But like you, I enjoy cooking too." Quickly, she rose and went to the kitchen, returning with the silver coffee pot. "I'll join you—but not in having the cake; I have to watch my waistline."

"You?" Sonia exclaimed in wide-eyed surprise. "But you have an adorable figure, Margaret. So slim and girlish—surely you don't have to be afraid of calories. I am the one who should be—but Sergei always said to me that if I grew too slim, he would leave me, and that a man, especially on a cold winter's night, enjoys the substantiality of flesh."

Now it was Margaret Elston's turn to laugh wholeheartedly at this quip, and Sonia joined her. When they fell silent, it was to eye each other with a new comprehension; a bond of camaraderie had been established between them.

"That was delightfully put. I wish I could have met your Sergei."

"He's in Buenos Aires by now with his new wife, preparing to go down the Amazon in search of treasure. Doesn't it sound like the kind of story right out of the magazines?"

"A little bit, yes. I don't have anything nearly so lurid to relate about my marriage. John just wanted to be the one who brought in the money and he didn't like my working, especially when I got good at it. But we're still friends. He even had me meet Elsie—that's his second wife—to see if I approved of her. I did—she was the opposite of me, happy simply to be a housewife and mother."

"And now you live alone without love?" Sonia boldly posed.

Margaret's olive skin flushed deliciously at this intimate and unexpected query. Then, meeting Sonia's frank gaze and seeing only candor and not a trace of insolent prying in it, she replied as frankly, "I live alone, yes. But I don't deny myself love."

"Da, that is good, that is the way it should be, Margaret. You are a wise woman if you know this. In Europe, women understand these things. Here, many women are—how do you say it—repressed. Or is it suppressed?"

"Sometimes I think it's both, Sonia," Margaret laughed.

"It is true, and it is nothing to laugh about, I think. Because if parents are secretive and guilty about love, then their children inherit this attitude and it makes for difficulties when it is their time for marriage, is that not so?"

"Yes, I'm afraid so, Sonia." Margaret frowned and pursed her lips. Then, eyeing her guest very intently, she slowly asked, "Will you tell me something in confidence?"

"But of course. Already I feel a warmth toward you, Margaret, as if we are old friends. What do you wish to know?"

"You saw my son last night—and his wife?"

Sonia emphatically nodded. "Yes. And I thought to myself, what a lovely couple they made. Only—"

"Only what?"

"Only I think your son worries too much and is not relaxed, as a man should be when he goes to his bride. He came out of his cabin to take a walk, and I met him, and we said some words, and I felt he was nervous and feared how it would be with his Jane."

Margaret Elston sighed deeply. "I can be frank with you, Sonia, too. I also had fears about the wedding night. You see, my son's inexperienced—he and his wife have been sweethearts since high school. She's never had any kind of love affair, and her parents are very old-fashioned, so I'm sure they gave her no education about such things."

"Still, she is not a child, and these days girls grow up quickly and have inquisitive minds, Margaret. Often the woman is wiser than the man about love, and she will guide him. Of course, if she is really wise, she will not let him find out that she is doing the guiding."

"That's very true, except that Jane's inclined to be shy and not at all self-assertive. I wish Dave had had his father with him these past few years. I did try to tell him, just before the wedding, that he ought to—well, have an experience so he'd have more confidence."

"In Europe, it is not unusual that a boy in his teens has this experience arranged for him by his parents."

"I know. But that's still a bit too advanced for us puritans, I'm afraid," Margaret laughed. Just then the phone rang in the hallway. "Excuse me, Sonia."

"But of course." Her eyes thoughtfully studied Margaret Elston's sinuous, balanced movements in the clinging peignoir as she sipped her coffee.

"Hello—oh, Ken—are you at the airport? Oh, what a shame. How dreadful for you. Do get well, darling—I miss you. You're sure it's not serious? That's good. Now you take care of yourself, do you hear? All right, dearest —let me know, and I'll drive out to O'Hare to meet you. All my love, my dear one. Yes, you don't know how sorry I am you won't be here today. Good-bye, Ken dearest."

Margaret's slim hand replaced the phone, her brows knitted in disappointment. He'd come down with a virus attack and the doctor had forbade his leaving his hotel room till at least the middle of next week. She'd looked forward so much to this reunion...it helped, to keep her from remembering that the years were catching up. And in Ken's arms, it was so thrillingly easy to forget.

"Is something wrong, Margaret?"

Sonia put down her coffee cup and rose, her exotic face solicitously taut as she saw her hostess return slowly, eyes downcast and frowning.

"Oh—no, not really. Forgive me, Sonia. It's a— friend. I'd expected him today, and he's taken ill. Nothing really serious, except I was looking forward to meeting him."

"Oh, what a shame, Margaret. I'm sorry to intrude."

"Don't be silly, Sonia dear. You had no way of knowing. Besides—" she brightened, "I haven't been able to sit down and talk in ages. Not, at least, with somebody I like."

"Well, thank you, Margaret. It's mutual. I like you too, very much."

The svelte olive-skinned matron crossed over to the couch and seated herself beside her guest, with a cordial little smile and a nod of thanks. "I guess I was feeling sad because Dave got married and left the nest. Typically maternal, Sonia—you don't have children, do you?"

"No," Sonia's beautiful face was shadowed a moment. "Perhaps if Sergei and I had had them, he would have lost his restlessness. Though I don't think so—and so it's just as well. It's a tragedy for the children if their parents break up."

Then, quickly, catching her blunder, she contritely added, "Oh, that sounds awful—and I didn't mean it for you, Margaret. Please forgive me."

"I know it wasn't personal, Sonia dear, and it's forgotten. But you're right, of course. Sometimes it's economics that breaks families up, and then the children suffer. But when it's a divorce or a rift between the mother and father, the children can't help teeing involved and drawn into the fight. That's the worst of all for them. Fortunately for me, Dave wasn't traumatically upset when John decided he wanted to go his own way and find a less independent female to share his life and

Lusty Lessons

his bed. Just the same," she paused, pensive, "I do wish he'd had the advantages of a father to talk to him about things."

"You mean about how to satisfy a woman," Sonia bluntly interposed.

Margaret Elston nodded.

Sonia put her hand on Margaret's knee, her eyes warm and understanding. "I can read your mind, Margaret. You are thinking that you know the delights between a man and a woman and that you wish you yourself had explained as much to that handsome son of yours, so that he would not have been so distressed last night."

"You're telepathic, my dear Sonia. That's exactly what I was thinking."

"And," Sonia shrewdly went on, her luminous gray-green eyes studying Margaret's exquisite features, "you are also thinking that it is a shame your…dear friend… did not come and that, instead, you have to put up with a talkative woman, isn't that so?" Margaret's cheeks turned a fiery red at this and she lowered her eyes. "Oh, good heavens, no. Really, no, Sonia. It—well, it is true the—the man who called is my—my—"

"Your lover, dear?" Sonia breathed, edging closer to the peignoir-sheathed, voluptuous brunette matron.

"Um hm…Sonia, you're an amazing creature."

"Not at all. Very ordinary, Margaret. I told you I had no glamour to my background, only experience—and, as I've told you, it wasn't quite enough to hold my man."

"He was a fool, then," Margaret firmly declared.

"Spassibo, darling!" Her hand, still on Margaret's

knee, pressed down more intimately as she turned towards her hostess. Then, born out of an irresistible impulse, their eyes met and held, locked in the interchange of affection and understanding in a communal awareness of their own loneliness. Slowly Sonia's other arm curved around Margaret's supple, slim shoulders, and drew her closer, very gently, very lingeringly, as their lips softly brushed in an evanescent salutation.

Margaret stiffened at the warm, humid touch of Sonia's amorous mouth. Then her eyes widened; a wondering, half-reproving, half-delighted look dawned in their blue depths, and her mouth opened like an eager flower to accept and bestow the most intimate and gracious of kisses.

Sonia raptly sighed, arching herself towards Margaret Elston; her hand slid along the svelte column of a firm thigh, and now Margaret's arms enfolded her with a passionate readiness as their mouths fused with a total awareness of their emotional needs. It was not so much of the flesh, this unison, but rather a communal desire, a quest after the urgency of being loved. Sonia, even as her mouth wooed Margaret's, even as her fingers stroked the quivering sleek stretch of satin-draped thigh, was remembering Sergei's imaginative romancing. This current expression of yearning was the joyous recollection of love that had been supremely shared, unforgettably bestowed. In her turn, Margaret Elston, disappointed at being denied consolation by Ken Davidson, attuned for love not only by his expert tutelage but also by the nostalgic sadness of her son's marriage which recalled to her her own youth and sexual rapture, experi-

Lusty Lessons

enced a wakening of all these past ecstasies in Sonia's gently compassionate embrace.

The kiss ended. Nervously, Margaret drew away and rose, stammering, "I'd better draw the shades—somebody might see and get the wrong idea—"

Sonia lazily laid her head back against the couch, stretching her superb body with a breathtaking felinity. Her voice was husky-soft as she murmured, "But there could be nothing wrong in a kiss of friendship, Margaret dear."

"N-no, of—of course not, Sonia. I-I'm a little flustered, that's all. My mind was—"

"On your lover, I know. And that was why I kissed you, to make up for him, to express the fact that you are loved, very much loved—for you are a woman who deserves and demands it, Margaret dear."

"Win—what must you think of me—" Margaret covered her face with her hands and stood, trembling violently.

Sinuously, Sonia rose and moved beside her hostess. Then gently she took Margaret's hands and put them against her ripe, full breasts, her eyes tender and beseeching as they sought Margaret's startled, gaze. "I think," she whispered, "that we are both lonely and in the mood for love, and that it cannot be wrong if we give each other consolation for what we have lost."

"Ohh—Sonia—you do sense what I feel, then—"

"Yes, because I feel it myself, darling. Come—"

She drew the unresisting brunette by the hand down the hall till she saw the open door of Margaret's bedroom.

She whispered, capriciously, teasingly, "But you see,

you have already drawn the shades here. It was a preparation for love with your man. So it will not be wasted, after all."

"Sonia—oh, dearest—" Margaret's voice was choked and vibrant with her exacerbated desires as she hugged her new friend to her, and again their mouths met. But this time, Sonia delicately prodded her soft pink tongue between Margaret's tremulous lips. Margaret's slim fingers dug into the hollow of Sonia's back as she responded with her own lingual intercession toward a yearned-for bliss. Sonia's hands soothingly stroked the slim shoulders, descending down the patricianly chiseled back to the lithe, compact, youthful hips, and Margaret softly moaned and pressed herself against the Slavic beauty, her tongue probing more boldly, more eagerly now as her nostrils flared with rising excitement.

"Oh—my dear—my dearest—so sweet—"

"Yes—for you—you're so lovely, Margaret. May I see you? All of you—"

"Oh—yes—yes!"

Stepping away, her face flaming, but not with guilt this time—rather, the erotic excitation of an impulsive and generous desire—Margaret Elston swiftly removed the red satin peignoir and let it drop to the floor. Sonia caught her breath as the tall brunette stood before her, naked but for the narrow black satin-elastic garter belt, the panties which ardently clung to her sleek buttocks, and the diaphanous off-black nylon hose and open-toe sandals.

The proud, small, pear-shaped globes of Margaret Elston's breasts surged with an erratic rhythm. Sonia's

Lusty Lessons

limpid eyes fixed on the wide, dusky-coral aureoles, on the stiffening love-buds in their amorous centers. Then she took a step toward the half-nude brunette, and putting her hands on Margaret's shivering sides, bent her head and daintily kissed each of the exquisitely flinty buds, then prodded each with the artful tip of her nimble tongue.

"Ohh—Sonia—oh—you—darling—ohh—" Margaret's voice was harsh with longing, as the sensual imagery of those magical hours spent in Ken's arms was rekindled, resharpened, revivified; eyes closing, lids fluttering, she was recalling them now under the delicate harmony of this omnisciently talented new friend with whom she shared the rueful souvenir of a lost marital union.

The slim brunette's hand locked against Sonia's cheeks to prolong that ethereally stimulating tribute, her own head falling back, the pulse in her slim olive-sheered throat beating with maddened intensity.

Sonia's fingers caressed the smooth-sheered sides of her amorous partner, while her lips and tongue alternated their delicious dalliance against the swollen tips of Margaret's surging tits. Tiny whimpering sobs and gasps escaped her now exultantly eager partner. Then she halted this prelude to love, straightening as her fingers deftly grasped the top of the black panties and pulled them rustlingly down Margaret's quivering hips and thighs, settling around her sandaled feet.

"Ohh—Sonia—dearest—Sonia—oh—now you," Margaret huskily pleaded.

"Yes—yes—I want you to, darling," was Sonia's ecstatic reply.

Tremblingly, Margaret's slim fingers unbuttoned the aqua jacket and drew it off. For a moment, she held it, admiring the exquisitely decorated mandarin collar, then carefully placed it over the back of a straight-backed chair. Sonia's lips curved in a voluptuous, acquiescent smile as she faced her hostess, her round breasts swelling against the lace trimmed white silk blouse which now drew Margaret's hesitant, then emboldened attention, till it, too, was draped over the back of the chair.

The dishabille of the Slavic divorcee was breathtakingly exciting now; the fulminating splendor of her breasts was held in tempting check by a strapless white satin bra; the bare shoulders, the smooth curve of the naked sides that were olivesheened, but a nuance darker than Margaret's own alluring epidermis.

"Oh—Sonia—you—you're beautiful!" Margaret breathed, entranced.

Now it was the turn of the sensual, candid motel owner to blush like a schoolgirl at this emotion-throbbing tribute. Her eyes feasted on the lithe loveliness of her hostess, on the suavely slim belly with its wide, shallow dimple an inviting oasis for oral and factual adoration, thence to the crisp dark triangle of womanhood which promised the ultimate seduction and the smoothly pink pussy lips that peeped invitingly below.

The brassiere fluttered to the floor, and Sonia, hiding her scarlet face in the crook of one uplifted, classically rounded arm, stood waiting, her round naked breasts in sumptuous offertory. Already the crinkly, ripe love-darts of that widely spaced surging bosom prickled with anticipatory tumescence, and the swell of the olive-satiny

Lusty Lessons

globes was enervatingly, shiveringly uneven, a tell-tale sign of their amorous owner's heady yearning for this carnal conclave.

"Oh—they're so beautiful—I have to touch them—I have to—" Margaret gasped. Her fingers softly sank into the smooth niches of Sonia's palpitating armpits, and her graceful head bowed as her lips and tongue returned, with passionate interest, the delicious tribute which Sonia had paid her own shuddering breasts a moment before.

"Oh—Margaret darling—I love you—" Sonia huskily moaned, her head turning from side to side, her eyes dilating and humid, the wings of her nostrils shrinking and expanding with convulsive rhythm as Margaret licked her tits.

Margaret Elston hesitated no longer. Now her fingers swiftly, knowingly, tugged the sheer panties past the nylon sheaths which revered the luscious curves of Sonia's calves and thighs, then husked them from those opulent loins.

"Yes," she sighed, "your skin is just a trifle darker than mine—but oh how soft and warm it is, my dearest Sonia—"

"Come—dearest—take me—hurry," Sonia groaned.

An arm round each other's waist, the two naked beauties moved toward Margaret's wide lush bed, sank down upon it, turning to each other, lips and hands exploring, learning, feasting, dallying in the passionate prelude to sublimity.

Then, locked together, mouth fusing with hungry, questing mouth, their bodies writhed and surged in the intolerable pilgrimage towards ecstasy, flesh fulfillment.

Their tongues entwined like serpents, darting and slithering one around the other. Their hands caressed quivering breasts and found engorged nipples that stiffened further under the special attention they received. Then Sonia inverted her body and buried her head between Margaret's thighs, while Margaret's lips found the secret grotto that in turn hovered before her. Those serpentine tongues again darted and flashed, only this time they each penetrated a fragrant cavern that offered solace and passion and refuge from loneliness. Fingers took the place of tongues, or shared that fine and private place, and came away dripping with the nectar of fulfilled womanhood.

"Darling…"

"Hmm?"

"It was so lovely, so very tender and sweet."

"Oh yes!"

"I feel so at peace with you. It's almost like being with a man—but it's bitter-sweet, and oh, ever so much more tender."

"And for me it was the same way, Margaret dearest. I wasn't sure at first."

"Nor I. And yet, maybe inwardly my body felt yours wanting to console me for his not being here—when I needed love."

"Yes—it was that way with me—when I first saw you walk in that red peignoir, Margaret. Your body is like a young girl's, but your mouth, your tongue, your hands have a woman's joy to give."

"As do yours, Sonia, my dear one. Cigarette?"

"Please, dear."

Lusty Lessons

Languidly, Margaret Elston reached a slim naked arm toward the silver humidor on the night table, her tapering, aristocratic fingers rummaging, finding, and then proffering the white tube to the moist red lips of the opulent nude woman beside her. Then she leaned over Sonia to flick on the cigarette lighter. In the darkness the red tip glowed and shimmered, then the aromatic wreath of fragrant tobacco smoke wafted over their palpitating naked bodies.

"Won't you have one too, Margaret?"

"Uh-uh. I'll share yours, dear."

"Yes. I love sharing—with you."

"And I with you, Sonia, my very sweet. To think your Sergei left you for a simpering young girl—what a fool he must have been!"

Sonia Magaloff lay in drowsy, satiated reverie, her right arm cradling her raven head; the curls were rumpled, the stylish coil unraveled by Margaret's ardent fingers in the lusts of love. Margaret reached over to retrieve a tiny bowl like brass ashtray and, with a slurred giggle, bent her head to place a kiss on the soft dimple of her lover's belly before laying the cool metal atop that delightful oasis. Sonia squealed and squirmed, and Margaret soothingly cupped one of her swelling round breasts and kissed her on the lips, chastely, like a benediction.

"A fool," she repeated, very softly and evocatively. "You've so much more love to give than any childish, empty-headed girl."

"I know," was Sonia's half-whispered reply, "but a man thinks he must have variety. Perhaps by now Sergei is tired of her—" she shrugged kiss-warmed, dimpled shoulders, "—but he must learn this for himself."

"A man can learn about women only from the source, dear," was Margaret's wistful answer. Then, suddenly, as if her casual words had kindled some secret spark, she sat up, frowning, cupping her chin, her eyes narrowed and staring into space.

"From the source," she repeated. "Yes, that's it, of course."

"What's it, darling?" Sonia tapped the end of her cigarette with a fingertip to drop the gray ashes into the little bowl atop her quivering belly.

"Sonia, you told me David seemed high-strung and overanxious, didn't you?"

"Yes, Margaret."

"I shouldn't wonder but that their first time together —Jane's and his—was a fiasco. The danger is, they may grow apart, just from the psychological frustration they both have."

"Oh, but they're young, Margaret. They'll experiment till they succeed."

"It's not so easy as that, Sonia. I didn't tell you Dave had a very stern governess, with a gloomy outlook about lovemaking. Otherwise, she was a perfect jewel, and I needed her desperately, because I was working, too. Now I think maybe it was a mistake." She sighed, shook her head slowly. "Dave's a fine wholesome person, with a lot of quiet reserve, and easily hurt, because he's sensitive. Jane's the same way, I'm sure, though she outwardly looks to be a happy, serene girl. But if they blunder and keep blundering, they may lose so very much."

"Especially your son, if he has to fight shadows of guilt."

Lusty Lessons

"Shadows of guilt—that's it exactly, Sonia dear. For there's nothing guilty or shameful in love that's honestly given and shared. But the moment you start to think of moral limitations and prudish conventions, you lose the spontaneity and beauty of joyous sex. The kind you have, dearest...the kind you and I just now shared."

"I know," Sonia murmured, her red lips softly evocative, curving in a beatific smile as Margaret bent her head to kiss them with a poignant tenderness. "If you could only teach my son and his wife that joyous abandon, that uncalculated pleasure which comes from letting a wholesome nature take its course," Margaret went on, a wistful nuance to her throaty voice.

"Margaret Elston, are you proposing I try to break up a brand-new marriage?" Sonia giggled, crushing out the cigarette and leaning over to put the little bowl-tray on the table, a maneuver which made her wide-spaced, round, full breasts jounce with a tantalizing resilience. Her nipples were still dusky and heavy-tipped from love.

"Well, yes, if you want to know the truth!"

"But that—no, you can't be serious—"

"But I was never more so, Sonia darling. Look, I told you that I was often tempted years ago, when Dave was in his teens, to send a discreet, capable woman to minister to his needs, to educate him in love, so that when he married Jane, he'd come to her with an understanding compassion and a self-control most men never gain no matter how many so-called affairs they have. You see, Dave's the intellectual type, the type that broods and frets about things and magnifies them out of all proportion. A less perceptive man would content himself with notching conquests and never care whether he satisfied his partner. That's the Don Juan complex men have—they think they have to try to prove something, and what they're really proving is that they're not good lovers at all."

"Oh, I do so agree with you, Margaret!"

"But let's suppose you could seduce my son and teach him how to give pleasure as well as receive it."

"Hmm," Sonia squirmed on the bed, her hands reaching behind her to smooth her tousled raven curls. "It would be interesting to try. He is very handsome, that one. And I think too, considerate. That is always good to start with."

"If you could rid him of that hidden streak of Puritanism he has, you'd guarantee the success of his marriage. I'm convinced of it, Sonia."

"You know, Margaret, this is really an amazing conversation."

"Yes, isn't it? Here we only met a few hours ago—and already we're lovers and I'm shamelessly asking you to go out and cold-bloodedly seduce my son who has been married exactly one whole day."

"Not...cold-bloodedly, though," Sonia giggled softly as her arms reached up towards Margaret's looming form.

"Oh no...not that...oh dearest—" Their lips met gently; then, as the secret flame of desire was rekindled, with an urgency of passion.

"Touch me...here...yes...ahh...ohh...it's so thrilling ...so good—"

"And you too—your lips here...and here...and again there...lick my cunt...oooh—ahh!"

"Dearest—"

"My lovely one—your kisses are so thrilling, your hands so knowing—"

"They delight in learning all of you, my sweet one—like this, maybe?"

"Yes, yes, oh, that especially—let me, to you, too—"

"Oh please—and don't stop—don't ever, ever stop—ohh, darling…Sonia again went down on Margaret, thrusting her tongue into her, drinking up her juices as Margaret cradled Sonia's head against her steaming cunt. After a few minutes she rolled off her and pulled a strap-on dildo from her bag, much to Margaret's shocked delight.

"One never knows when one is going to need something of this sort," purred Sonia. "It's always better to be prepared, don't you agree?"

Margaret nodded enthusiastically then closed her eyes when her visitor began rubbing the dildo against her clit.

"I'm going to fuck you until you come, my darling," whispered Sonia, and with that she inserted the dildo into Margaret's pussy.

True to her word, Sonia pumped her until her hostess exploded into a senses-shattering orgasm. Sonia then withdrew, straddled her face, and pushed the dripping dildo into Margaret's mouth, order her to suck her "cock." Margaret did so as if it were a real meatpole, tasting her own juices while she began to finger fuck her charming partner.

There were no demons in the darkened bedroom of the house on Sheridan Road. Even had they dared to venture in, the rapturous paean of delight which two entwined, quivering, ardent lovers expressed in sighs and gasps and stammered or whispered words, would have driven them forth.

But they pursued the young couple in Cabin D of the Miranda Lodge, two hundred feet away from the serene lake on which the twinkling stars and the full moon cast down myriad prisms of dancing lights.

The afternoon had been exhilarating. Dave and Jane had played three sets of singles, one of which he had gallantly though not overtly let her win. In shorts and blouse, even with a tight bra, the sight of her delectable young body darting about the tennis court was enough to tempt an aged ascetic into hedonistic longings. Then a pleasantly prolonged dinner in the resort restaurant with dance music in the background, of which the honeymooning couple took full advantage after a suitable period to allow for proper digestion.

Now all the elements of romance had been accounted for—a sharing of activity from sports to dining with enjoyable conversation, then the intimate nocturnal ritual of dancing which can be a potent aphrodisiac under normal conditions. Indeed, as Dave held Jane in his arms, his cheek against hers, inhaling her delicate perfume, to the measures of a dreamy song, he was already beginning to tell himself that tonight would be unforgettably different and that their honeymoon would really start from this night on, completely obliterating last night from their book of memories.

There was only one thing wrong with this prognostication. As they broke apart when the last dance ended,

Lusty Lessons

Jane murmured to him, her eyes dreamy-soft and her face glowing with pleasure, "Isn't this lots nicer than Nassau, Dave honey? And lots less expensive. You see, you married a practical girl who keeps your budget in mind."

"Uh-huh. I married an angel, if you want to know." Whispering into her hair, his left arm about her supple waist, Dave was beginning to feel that at last he was acting like a romantic to the manner born and that perhaps, at long last, he had banished the specter of Miss Mathis.

"Ohmigosh—oh Dave—ohh, my Lord—do you know what I went and did?" Jane suddenly uttered a cry and clapped her hand to her lovely forehead.

"Honey, what's the matter?"

"I just now remembered—I left my cosmetic bag in the closet of that motel we stayed in last night."

"Yes, but—I can get you another, honey, don't take on so—"

"You don't understand, Dave I put the check and our tickets in that bag—and now it's lost."

"Oh, it's not that bad. Look, I'll just phone there. I'm sure they'll have found it by now and kept it in the safe."

"Oh, what a forgetful idiot I was—three thousand dollars, Dave, and I forgot it."

"Now don't get panicky, sweetheart. Worst happens, you can phone your folks and tell them to stop payment on it."

"Oh—yes—I didn't think of that. But just the same, I'm worried. I never did anything like that before in my whole life!"

"No, and you never got married before, either. Now you just sit down on that couch over there and I'll phone the motel—lucky I remembered where it is and the name—the Danson Motel."

"All right, but I still feel so stupid for forgetting it," Jane said in a doleful voice.

He felt a warm surge of pride; now he could take efficient charge of things and convince his lovely young, new wife that she was married to a man who knew how to handle matters during a crisis.

Five minutes later, he returned, beaming with satisfaction. "Now don't you worry your pretty head about it any more, Janie," he assured her. "I talked to that cook, you know, Dolores, I guess her name is. She says Mrs. Magaloff—that's the owner's name—already found your bag and left word she was driving to Chicago anyway and would take it to my mother."

"Oh? But why would she do that and not take it to mine?"

"Maybe you had something in your bag with Mom's name and address on it."

Again Jane clapped her hand to her forehead, her face rueful. "There I go again, forgetting! Yes, I did—a lovely note from your mother wishing us well. It had her name and address label on it. Well, thank goodness, it's safe. That was so thoughtful of that woman, wasn't it?"

"Yes. We'll have to stop by and thank her when we drive back, Janie."

"Uh-huh."

"Let's take a walk in the woods before we go—er—before we turn in. Want to?"

Lusty Lessons

Jane's ivory cheeks colored at the implication. Demurely lowering her eyes, she nodded and rose, holding up her hands to Dave, who drew her to her feet and kissed her on the forehead.

"Everything fine now, honey?"

"Everything's just heavenly, darling," was her vibrantly whispered answer.

But it wasn't.

THE DISCIPLINE OF ODETTE

For the past three days, Odette Delage had lived in anguish. Through unbelievable clumsiness, she had overturned the inkwell on her writing table. Fortunately the rug had been spared, but her dress, a new dress from the Lanvin shop, was irremediably ruined. Her first impulse, after having tried to amend the damage with soap and water—and only meeting with disaster in the attempt—had been to confess the catastrophe to her mother.

But it was eleven o'clock at night, her parents had gone to bed, and so she had put off to the next day the confession, the sermon that would follow…and the inevitable and fatal punishment.

Undoubtedly a severe punishment, the birch or the martinet, perhaps applied by her father!

So, for the past three days she had held back that confession. Twenty times she'd been at the point of speaking, but the memory of past corrections made her a coward. For she well knew the frightful anguish of a whipping. A week scarcely went by without, for one reason or another, her being made to lower her panties and endure a few dozen smacks, vigorously applied.

A stained dress, coming home late from school, a gesture of impatience, a bad grade from school (for her father had insisted, despite her nineteen years, that she go on studying till her bachelor's degree)—that was all that was needed for her punishment. The birch or the martinet was reserved for the gravest faults. Now, just last week, she had behaved improperly at an afternoon dancing party, in her mother's view. Oh, nothing too serious—a somewhat prolonged chat with a young man. But on such matters her mother was not at all indulgent; when she left the party, she had been summarily informed that she would be whipped when she got back home. Her mother had found the young man's card in her purse; then her resistance and her cries when the whip began to fall had cost her a severe flogging with the birch. And when her father had heard the story, he had inflicted another whipping with the martinet. It had left her shrieking for pardon and marked her bottom with angry blisters and weals superimposed on the stripes left by the birch.

The next day at school, when she had had to sit all day on the hard wooden bench, had been sheer torture; even now her bottom was excruciatingly sensitive in certain spots.

The Discipline of Odette

So she put off that confessional, telling herself that in delaying the inevitable chastisement she would make it less painful, but deep down inside she trembled with fear at the threat of the augmented punishment her silence would cost her if her mother should discover the disaster before she herself avowed it.

By Sunday at the very latest she must explain why she wasn't wearing her new dress. And Odette, in her bed this evening, ruminated over this hardly enjoyable prospect: "Here it is Friday, and by Sunday morning at the latest I'll be whipped!"

Lifting her chemise, she nervously glided her hand over her bottom, pausing to press a finger here and there over the still visible marks, wincing at the sensitivity of those areas, her anguish growing at the fatal certainty of what awaited her.

Getting out of bed and in front of the mirror, twisting about so as to see better, Odette examined her tender bottom. It was wide, firm and rounded, jutting out sumptuously from her slim waist, a true womanly bottom, on which the visible marks of the lash evoked in disturbing fashion the memory of her many spankings since childhood.

Back to bed and now flat on her belly, her face in her pillow, she imagined herself awaiting the first strokes, demeaning herself to utter the most piteous prayers to delay the whipping. At last she fell asleep, and she had nightmares of seeing her father, birch rod in hand, advance to her, his face stern and menacing.

When she woke she was still more cowardly, resorting to the pretext that in the afternoon she wasn't going to school and that if she confessed her fault after her father had left the house, perhaps only her mother would whip her.

But when she returned at noon, she was haunted by the fear that in her absence her mother might have opened her closet and made an inspection, as she sometimes did, and discovered the ruined dress hidden back in the darkest corner. The threat of a flogging manifested itself into a chilling fantasy: she imagined her mother's glacial welcome, her embarrassed, faltering explanations, the announcement and sentence of punishment, her tearful undressing. The more she thought about it, the better she saw the scene: As she stood on the porch of the house waiting for the door to be opened to her, she felt tugged down, waiting for the whistling kiss of the fist lash. Agony made a tightening knot in her belly...

Her first act, before going to kiss her mother, was to run to her closet. A false alarm! The dress was still there, and her mother kissed her as usual. But this time, she made up her mind. After lunch, when her father had gone, she would confess.

Alas, during lunch, her mother remarked. "Ah, by the way, Odette, I had a phone call from Madame Lacaille. She's asked us over for tea today and since you don't have classes this afternoon, I accepted her invitation. That will give you a chance to wear your green dress."

Odette paled. So the punishment would take place at once, aggravated by the fact that her confession hadn't been more spontaneous. She stammered a few words to express her pleasure at this promised outing, was for a moment on the verge of admitting all. But the sight of

The Discipline of Odette

her father chilled her and a shudder seized her, accompanied by a bizarre twitching of her bottomcheeks as if the whipping were about to begin.

And she was silent.

After dessert and coffee, Odette's heart was pounding fearfully. At last, her father left, and her heart seemed to stop beating entirely.

"You'd better go dress, Odette, for first I want to take you to the Spring Shop to buy some things."

"Mama."

"What? What's the matter?"

"Mama…I…I have to tell you something."

"What, then? What foolishness have you done?" And she made a characteristic motion with her hand, the gesture of spanking.

"I…I don't dare, Mama."

"Now then, no more comedy, tell me everything at once, that's still the best way to lessen your punishment, Odette!"

"It—it's my dress."

"What, your dress?"

"My—my green dress you—you want me to put on now—well, I—er—I spilled ink on it the other day."

Her mother's gaze took on an icy expression of intense severity. "Get it at once!"

"Mama, it's not my fault, I—"

"Get it!"

That tone admitted no reply. Her legs weak, Odette left the room: her hands trembled as she returned to the salon, for by the light of day the disaster of the stained dress seemed more irreparable than ever.

Without a word, her mother took it from her hands and remarked impassively: "How long ago did you do that?"

"Last night, Mama."

"Don't lie. It's much longer than that, I can see you tried to remove it with water, and the material's dry now."

"Y-yes…it…was W-Wednesday, I—think."

"Why didn't you tell me then?"

"I—I don't know, Mama, I—I didn't dare…Oh, Mama, I beg of you, pardon me, I didn't do it on purpose!"

Two slaps rocked Odette's head to right, then left and wrenched plaintive sobs from the unhappy beauty.

"Enough! You know I don't care for these silly scenes of yours. You know what to expect, don't you? In your unpardonable clumsiness, you've ruined a dress worth fifteen hundred francs; you tried to conceal your fault from me; and you've just now lied. All that deserves an exceptional punishment!"

"Oh, Mama, Mama, don't whip me too hard, I implore you!"

"I shall begin by myself applying a sound whipping, and I advise you not to struggle or act up, if you don't want your father to give you a still more severe thrashing this evening."

"Oh, Mama, please don't tell Papa, I promise you I won't resist. Whip me as much as you want, but don't tell Papa, please, not Papa!"

"Be still! I'll do what I think best and all you say will only aggravate your punishment. I was saying, then, that I was going to give you the martinet at once, a whipping you'll tell me about as to its effectiveness, my girl. After which we'll go to Madame Lacaille where, if you haven't been perfectly docile, I shall tell everybody what you just got and what awaits you tonight. I hope that the shame you will feel will do you good. Now then, not another word; go fetch the martinet and also bring me back the old leather slipper with which I sometimes whip you!"

Sobbing desperately but without a word, Odette went into her mother's room to get, in the cupboard where they were placed in readiness, the instruments for her correction. Still weeping, she put them into her mother's hands.

"Now get down on your knees," her mother told her, "and ask pardon before preparing yourself for your whipping!"

Odette obeyed, in tears. Her voice interspersed with sobs, her hands clasped, her eyes imploring, she repeated the humiliating formula which her mother had long since taught her: "My dear Mama, I very humbly beg your pardon for my clumsiness, and I promise you—"

Brutally, a pair of stinging slaps interrupted her: "That's not the only fault for which you're to ask pardon. Begin all over again!"

Lifting her elbow, Odette had almost sought to ward off another such reproof, but the instinct of obedience —acquired through many a harsh spanking—had halted her gesture and, her cheeks burning, she docilely resumed: "I beg your pardon for my clumsiness and my l-lies...and...and I'm going to force myself to submit with gratitude and docility to the correction which— which I've deserved." But, that formula hardly uttered, she burst out into noisy sobs: "Oh, Mama, pity, don't be too severe…oh, not too hard…I…I still have marks from the last time."

"Have you finished with this ridiculous nonsense of yours? If you're whipped, you've only to blame yourself. Aren't you ashamed, at your age, to be such a crybaby? All right now, prepare yourself, and I promise you that your correction will be a proper one!"

"Oh, Mama—"

"That's quite enough now! Yes or no, are you going to prepare yourself? Once again, I don't advise you to prolong this silly farce of yours. I'm not going to struggle with you, but if you resist, you know how your father will treat you this evening. I don't think you've quite forgotten the ration you got last January?"

The threat must have been really serious and the memory of that referred-to whipping particularly burning, for Odette with an expression that mingled anguish and resignation, sobbed, "Yes, p-pardon, I—I shan't resist, but it hurts so much."

"Yes or no, are you going to lift up your dress, take down your panties and stretch out over my knees?"

Docilely, the lovely girl rose, stooped, seized the hem of her dress and began to lift it up in back. She wore no combination. Thus at once her thighs appeared, deliciously bare, above her stockings which were simply held up just above her knees by the garters over which they were rolled.

She wore a rather short and very ample pair of panties, with narrow crotch, and she attempted to uncover her buttocks just by lifting the two sides of the

The Discipline of Odette

panties, but a violent lash of the martinet clacked across the base of her thighs as her mother angrily exclaimed: "Do you imagine that you're to get a playful spanking? Will you pull down those panties of yours at once; and just to teach you not to play jokes on me, my girl, you'll receive a little supplement!"

Odette had let her dress fall back, uttering only an "Oh!" in which could be detected tones of suffering, humiliation and resignation, and now she began to bare herself once again. Her skirt again lifted and held up at her waist with one hand, she used the other to widen the elastic waistband which held up her panties, and shoved them down to her knees where, squeezing her legs together, she retained them.

"Come now, spread your knees…lift up your chemise, turn your behind toward the window and bend over. First, I'm going to examine you to see if that tender behind of yours is as damaged as you pretend!" her mother commanded.

Odette obeyed, her panties now clinging about her ankles, her bottom twitching in terrified anticipation of the first stroke of her whipping.

But her mother didn't begin the dreaded punishment at once. She examined the girl's naked flesh astutely; on the rondures of the full bottomcheeks there appeared only a few, almost faded red marks, a last vestige of the recent correction.

"And it was for this you made so much fuss, was it? Well, my little one, if you thought you could soften me, you were very much in error. Now, an end to this—stretch out over my knees!" was the terrible decree.

Odette didn't utter another word. But she sobbed softly and her hands, tightly gripping her uplifted garmeets, visibly trembled. Docilely she stretched out over her mother's lap.

"Come now, bend down more!" And a violent smack rang out as her mother's palm flattened over both quivering naked buttocks. "Pose both your hands on the floor. Lift up your behind more, now!"

With her right leg, she pinioned her daughter's calves; with her left, she raised the skirt and chemise higher still along that beautifully dimpled back. Odette waited. The shame of her juvenile posture was blotted out by the dread of the spanks about to be applied, and her naked bottomglobes tightened spasmodically to diminish the exposed surface, as much as out of instinctive modesty.

"You're going to get three corrections: fifty spanks with the slipper for having stained your dress; fifty lashes of the martinet for not having told me right away, and to finish up with, a good hand spanking for all these little comedies you've played with me!"

"Pardon…oh, pardon…p-pity," the poor girl could only sob.

"Attention, I begin!"

Odette's bottomcheeks convulsively tightened at these ominous words; brandishing the slipper, the correctress descended it with all her strength across the naked globes of Odette's delectably rounded behind, marking the flesh with a bright red splotch. A cry from the girl responded to that first spank, with a gesture of instinctive resistance, quickly suppressed by a second

The Discipline of Odette

spank. And the correction continued. A fearful suffering burned Odette's naked bottomcheeks, abolishing all her shame and outraged modesty.

This young beauty of nineteen, so completely ripened in her bodily charms, was now only a little girl wriggling and writhing under the domination of pain, arching up, then flattening her naked behind in convulsive starts, crying and piteously groaning: "Ohhh, no more! Ohh, it hurts me—ohh, enough—pardon, pardon, Mama, I'll never do it again...never again... ohh, have mercy... Ouuuuunuueeeeeee! Ouuuuueee! Arrrrh! Ohh!"

Pitilessly, her mother counted the spanks: "Twenty-eight...twenty-nine, thirty! Will you be quiet, you crybaby...thirty-five...and thirty-six...Will you take your hand away? You'll get three extras right now for that, my girl"—smack—thwack—crack! "And now I continue... thirty-seven...thirty-eight...thirty-nine... and forty! Ten left—ah, you'll be more careful next time, I hope!"

"Ohh, please, ohh, enough, enough, I can't stand it any more," the lovely weeping culprit tearfully implored.

Or, if she didn't cry out such pleas during the methodical whacking of the leather slipper on her quivering bare bottomcheeks, Odette, biting her hands to stifle her cries, uttered muffled groans of anguish.

Finally, the fiftieth spank fell, leaving the lovely naked bottom a brick red? swollen, quaking with enervated torment. Madame Delage now sought to regain her breath while Odette continued to groan and wriggle her flaming bare seat in every direction to ease the fiery heat of the spanking.

"So, you've finished your playacting, my girl? You

know your punishment is only just starting. Next it will be the turn of the martinet. Save your voice a little for it, I think you'll need it. I allow you two minutes to meditate. Tell yourself that if you'd admitted your stupidity to me at once, your punishment would now be over, while because of your lies the worst is yet to come."

And, to prolong the anguish of the lovely victim, she added: "Fifty lashes with the martinet, in the state in which your bottom's in now, I should say you'll be sure to feel each one!"

Then she was silent for a moment while, still stretched out, her blazing bottom in the air, poor Odette continued to weep and to plead for pardon.

At last Madame Delage lifted up the chemise and dress, which had fallen back down a little during this interlude, and seized the martinet. "Attention, I begin! "

The martinet, whistling, swept its thongs across the naked, huddling, inflamed buttocks. A cry was torn from Odette, and with a desperate twist of her body, the young girl slipped off her mother's knees.

"Ah, would you now," Madame Delage cried, beside herself with anger, "well, you'll see, my girl!"

Odette had raised herself on her knees, her hands parrying off possible slaps. Her mother bent over her and seized her by an earlobe; "Listen to me carefully, my little one. Since this is the way it is, I'm not going to hold you at all. You're going to kneel with your face against the divan. Besides, I'll have more strength in my arm whipping you that way. And you'll hold up your own skirts, and if before I'm finished you dare let them fall, I'll send for Marie the maid to hold you, I'll make you spread your

The Discipline of Odette

thighs and I'll whip you where you can guess. Apart from the shame you'll feel, to be seen and held by our maid, I think from the special viewpoint of your cowardice, it will be a session you'll not forget so soon!"

As she spoke, Madame Delage jerked at the girl's earlobe, and Odette, without trying to free herself, redoubled her sobs. As soon as she was released, she let herself be pushed without resistance toward the divan, and her face buried itself against one of its thick cushions. The divan was low, so that her head was bent lower than her bottom, which was thus marvelously offered up to the kisses of the martinet,

Once again, skirt and chemise were lofted at Madame Delage's imperious order. "Now put your hands in back of you and hold them up yourself. If you let them fall, you know what to expect!"

Her poor little hands trembled, a veritable terror contorted the flushed, tear-stained face of the unhappy culprit...and on that swollen bare posterior, another lash of the martinet now curled!

A shriek responded to it, as Odette's right hand dared a gesture of protection, half covering with her dress the right globe of her all-too-vulnerable and martyred naked behind.

But of her own accord, she bared it again, but that, in her mother's eyes, was not quite enough submission. Brutally, Madame Delage thrice lashed the guilty hand which, in an effort of desperate self-control, did not withdraw itself.

"Ohhhhh, Mama, pity, I can't bear it any longer—oh, I've hardly resisted any! Ahhh—ohhhh!"

But the correction resumed as before. But now, as if all will were annihilated in her by sheer terror, Odette's hands didn't budge, always holding her skirt and chemise well above her jutting naked seat; though the martinet swept its thongs across her bare behind, the thongs sometimes slipped toward more sensitive parts and drew wild shrieks of torment from the lovely young sufferer.

The ten first lashes had been applied with a sort of fury, almost all over the same place, and a few excoriations were inflicted to the creamy bare skin. Now, the correctress spaced out her lashes, applying them to the base of the naked behind and the upper thighs; but there too, toward the thirtieth lash, a few scratches could be seen amid the bluish weals that crossed the shuddering, squirming naked globes of Odette's beautiful condemned behind.

It was not the first time she had been whipped to the blood, though for more serious sins. Her fault this time did not merit such treatment, and Madame Delage took note of the fact that the punishment she had decreed was excessive. So she halted the flogging but, so as not to give any sign of weakness, she pronounced: "All right, you've been docile, and I acknowledge it. So we shall pass at once to the final spanking, and I shall see how you behave, before I decide to start you the last strokes of the martinet."

Odette, plaintively sobbing, did not reply to this sanctimonious declamation.

"Well, is that how you thank me?" Madame Delage at once demanded.

The Discipline of Odette

"Then get up and stretch yourself again over my knees," was her order.

She seated herself. Odette docilely stretched herself out, or rather, couched herself as a child might, for she had no strength or will left. The same punishment as with the slipper spanking was imposed upon her.

In the room, one heard only noisy, crisp smacks on the naked flesh of that poor swollen behind, for, breathless by this time, Odette could only groan.

It was energetic, but short, for the scratches and swellings inflicted by slipper and martinet, presently being exacerbated by Madame Delage's hard palm, grew more and more tumified, giving the unfortunate bottom a truly piteous aspect. Then, over the quivering, shuddering body stretched out across her lap, the mother pronounced her sentence; "As you've been very docile, I shall spare you the last twenty lashes of the martinet. But in return, I shall tell everyone at the tea, in front of your dancing partners too, that you've just been whipped almost to the blood, on your naked behind!"

"Oh, no, please, no, Mama, not that, I'd die of shame!"

"Choose—twenty lashes of the martinet or that, and hurry up, or you'll get both!"

A terrible alternative! Doubtless, Odette's friends were, all of them, whipped more or less the way she was. With Janine Lacaille, she often exchanged stories of their punishments, and Odette had even, one day, witnessed a whipping administered to her lovely friend. But, in front of an assemblage of amused mothers, laughing friends and ironically amused dancing partners, oh, she would surely die of shame hearing her humiliation detailed.

Still stretched out with skirts held up, her naked bottom burning and twitching uncontrollably, poor Odette sought to bargain: "Oh, Mama, just five, would you, and don't tell them?"

"So that's the way you show your gratitude for my indulgence! Well, you'll have your five, and maybe you'll choose more quickly afterwards!" And without waiting, Madame Delage seized the martinet within reach of her hand, and brought it down five times over the burning naked bottomcheeks, tearing from the unfortunate victim the most despairing cries: "Noooo. Ohhhh, Mama, no more—tell them anything you want. I can't stand any more—oh, it hurts too much—I can't bear it any more!"

And, her hands clapped to her bottomcheeks, she rolled to the floor and groaned: "Oh, I hum so, I hurt so, ohhh, my bottom, I can't bear any more, oh, no, oh!"

"Very well! It shall be as you wish!" Madame Delage remarked. Odette remained a few moments that way, wriggling shamelessly and groaning, till finally her mother's dry, cutting voice resumed: "Well, have you finished this indecent performance of yours? Will you get up at once! There."

The martinet brandished anew, she swept the thongs over Odette's lovely rounded thighs.

Odette then uttered a wail of pain and slowly rose, her skims held up in one trembling hand, fearing, as it seemed, the very touch of that thin fabric against her swollen, burning bare seat.

The Discipline of Odette

"Go to your room and dress. You'll wash your behind, put some antiseptic to stop the bleeding, and don't you dare stain you chemise!"

Skirts still trussed up, her head hanging, Odette was ready to leave the room.

"And your panties? Do you think I'm going to pick them up after you?"

Shamefully, Odette stopped down to retrieve them, hampered by her skirts, which she still held with one hand.

"For your shame, you'll put on instead your penitence panties, open panties—you still have some, don't you?"

"Y-yes, I…I think so…M-Mama…"

"Excellent. That way it'll be easier if I have to whip you at the Lacailles'."

Odette started convulsively: "Ohhh, Mama, you won't do that, I implore you? Oh please, not that!"

"That depends on your behavior. Little Darcy will probably be there. If you act like the last time you were with him, I promise you nothing!"

Crushed, vanquished, piteous, Odette went slowly away. She walked with tiny steps, her bottom burning her, and she felt its increased weight, it seemed to her, at the base of her back like a mass of lead; an immense shame came over her to have that sensation of an enormous behind in which all the life of her body seemed relegated. Besides, the pain given by the kisses of the thongs which had stung the hollow of her buttocks and at the top of her legs at every step.

Entering her bathroom, she doused her bottom with cold water, which somewhat appeased her suffering;

twisting about, she was terrified at the sight of her bottom, and that sight intensified her shame. Little by little, only that remained: shame. Shame, feeling herself more than ever a woman through the confused sensuality which whipping procured: shame at the memory of the lashes dealt out, the shame of kneeling, the smacks with hand and slipper as if she were a child; her supplications; shame at the thought of what humiliation she was soon to endure in public; shame at the sight of the blisters and scratches and swellings with which all her naked flesh was marked.

Obeying her mother's order, she chose a pair of open panties and, having stepped into them, couldn't prevent herself opening the edges of the slit to see how much was revealed thereby. Alas, it would be all too easy to uncover her bottom entirely!

Her mother's voice, from the next room, made her tremble: "Hurry up! We leave in five minutes, and if you're not ready, beware of the whip!"

The whip, always the whip! Her voice drowned with tears, she humbly replied, "Y-yes, M-Mama."

She put on a light-colored dress, happy at being obliged to wear a combination, which instinctively seemed to her to protect her more from the whip. She bathed her tear-swollen eyes, applied powder and rouge. Suddenly the door opened and her mother appeared, hat on her head and martinet in hand. "Are you finally ready, or must I resume your correction?" Oh, what terror just seeing the instrument of punishment caused. In a humble, supplicating voice, Odette stammered, "no, Mama, I—I'm coming, I'm ready."

The Discipline of Odette

"You put on open panties as I told you to?"

"Yes, Mama."

"Let me see; come now, truss yourself up!"

Oh, that trussing up, that shameful maneuver again! But how could she resist before the menacing martinet? She stooped, lifted her dress and combination, trembling, with tears in her eyes, still fearing the lash. Her mother parted the slit of the panties, lifted her chemise, ran her hand over Odette's bare skin. "Perfect! This way, at the least naughtiness, my girl—" And her hand smacked twice, noisily, on the huddling bare bottomcheeks. "Will you stand still? What kind of manners are these?"

Odette didn't budge, really; she uttered two sobbing little cries at those spanks; then her mother closed the panties, pulled down her skirt, and said, "All right, let's hurry, the limousine must be waiting."

They went out. Odette followed her mother with tiny steps, her eyes red, her walk somewhat awkward— every step made her feel the throbbing heat still lodged in her bottom. In the hallway, her gaze crossed that of the chambermaid, who had obviously guessed what had been going on from hearing Odette's cries, and she regarded the anguished beauty with a half-ironic curiosity that made poor Odette blush.

The impassive chauffeur did not move when they got into the limousine. Had he been in the kitchen at the moment of that burning correction? In any case, he would surely hear about Odette's punishment. Indeed, as she got into the car, she naturally sat down beside her mother in the back seat—but it was the first time she had put her bottom on a seat since the whipping. And she couldn't suppress a grimace and a little cry of pain which her mother, observing her, rebuked with: "Enough of these ridiculous little games of yours! Well, since that's the way it is, instead of sitting down here, you'll use one of the folding stools. It's harder, you'll feel the bumps of the ride better, and I can keep a better eye on you."

After a futile look of supplication, Odette pulled out the stool which was scarcely padded at all, and with painstaking effort caused by the jerky movement of the limousine in heavy traffic, finally posed her swollen bottom on it.

"Now you're really beginning to annoy me, and you've got to stop these indecent mannerisms of yours! You'll do me the favor of lifting your dress, opening the slip in your panties, and sitting down with your bare skin on the stool!"

"Oh, Mama! Oh, Mama, not that in the car here, someone will see me!"

"No one will see anything. Your dress is quite wide and naturally falls back down along the sides. Moreover, even if someone passing by should suspect what's going on, so much the better."

"My dress will be all wrinkled."

"I'll tell Madame Lacaille why."

"Ohh!"

"Now that's enough of this!" Smack—smack—a pair of slaps rang out.

Odette, mastered, submitted to the frightful humiliation. She rose, stooped over because of the low roof of the car, and swiftly lifted up dress and combination.

"Turn toward me, I myself will open your panties for you."

The Discipline of Odette

Ah, the shame of the whip was revived by that denuding, for Madame Delage, passing her hand under Odette's dress, verified that the open panties allowed contact of the girl's naked bottom on the stool. Madame Delage remarked, "I had Marie wrap your stained dress. We'll stop at the cleaning and dyeing shop to see if Madame Roumier can do something with it."

The limousine rolled on. Odette, terribly embarrassed, scarcely held back her tears and tried hard to forget the shame of her situation. In a few moments, they arrived at the shop, and Madame Delage said, "Take the package and let's get out."

Odette got out first, hastily lowering her skirt, but without having time to close the flaps of her panties which, with distressing anguish, she felt yawn open under her clothes. The woman shopkeeper greeted Madame Delage, a regular customer, examined the dress which had been the cause of so many tears, and then remarked, "Had you brought this to me right away, I might have been able to save it, but now...well. How long ago did this happen?"

"At least four days. Only, this little fool only told me about it today."

"Why?"

"No doubt out of fear of being punished," was Madame Delage's dry retort.

Odette blushed to her very ears as she stood behind her mother, her head bowed, as if trying to hide herself. A worker in the shop looked at her curiously, which heightened her distress. The dyer said complacently: "She probably was, just the same, then?"

"You may well think she was, and much more severely than if she'd told me right away. So, finally, there's nothing you can do with the dress, then?"

"I'm going to try something, Madame, but to be truthful I don't have much hope."

"Thank you, Madame, I'll stop by in a few days," said Madame Delage, then, turning to Odette, "All right, come along, and try to walk straight if you don't want some more this evening.

Once back in the limousine, the completely dominated Odette had again to place her bare bottom on the folding stool; apart from the physical suffering caused by the hard seat and the anguish of being humiliatingly nude on it, she felt herself singled out like a child stood in a corner, and closed her eyes for fear someone outside might recognize her.

There was another short stop at the Spring Shop during which, her mother having gone in alone, she had to remain alone on her seat of penitence. As they were about to arrive at the Lacailles' house, Odette was authorized to rise to adjust her panties. Then, once the panties' flaps were pulled together and her skirts lowered, the poor girl, her face red with shame and tears, seated herself on the stool and uttered a woeful sigh: "Ohh, Mama, I implore you, don't say anything!"

Even before she had time to finish her plaint, she was slapped twice, as Madame Delage hissed, "Keep still!"

Crushed, Odette did not cry out; only her hands flew to her burning cheeks and this time tears rolled down unchecked.

"Now then, dry your eyes, we're here and you're

The Discipline of Odette

lovely. I don't think I'll need many explanations to make people understand what's happened, eh?" her mother ironically remarked.

Sniffling and drying her eyes, Odette mechanically began to powder her face, but she could not remove from her eyes the trace of tears, nor from her cheeks the marks of the slaps, one of which had been so violent that the imprint of Madame Delage's fingers clearly stood out on the rounded soft cheek. They went in, Odette with her legs weak beneath her, heart thudding, ears buzzing. It was in improvised little reunion, people were dancing to music from a phonograph when they entered, and there was a general outcry of welcome: "Oh, how late you are...good day, dear Madame Delage! Good day, my little Odette! How nice to see you both...welcome, Madame and Mam'selle!"

But almost at once someone remarked on Odette's strange attitude, with her reddened cheeks, her uneasy walk, her humble air of a beaten dog! And without hesitating, Madame Delage smilingly explained: "I must apologize, dear Madame Lacaille, for coming so late, but it's my daughter's fault. Imagine that before leaving, I had to give her the whip very severely. She wept, carried on, till it hardly finished."

So everyone stared at Odette who, under all those curious and slyly mocking looks, blushed all the more and shivered in her humiliation. The young men regarded her with covert glances at her bottom which in their mind's eye they were stripping bare, as if yearning to see the marks of the now-famous whipping.

Madame Lacaille broke the silence: "Oh, and I

thought Odette was so docile. So what did that child do, then?"

"By an idiotic clumsiness, she turned an inkwell over onto a brand-new dress which she was to put on today. Then instead of at once telling me what she'd done, she tried to put water on it, which ruined it completely, and I only learned of all this at the moment I was sending her to dress to come here."

"Ah yes, these little ones are unbelievably stupid! So, to escape the moment of a whipping and hoping to put it off, they lie and earn a worse one—for you whipped her severely, I'm sure?"

"Sufficiently enough: fifty spanks with the leather slipper and thirty vigorous strokes with the martinet, without counting three or four dozen smacks with the hand."

"On the bare bottom, I presume?"

During this dialogue, Odette had regarded her mother with poignant eyes in which tears began to well. But her torment at last ended when her mother shrugged and remarked, "That's enough talk about that little idiot, for I don't want to stop all these nice young people from having a good time."

"Will you allow Odette to dance?"

"Why certainly—I even order her to do it. Besides, I think she'd prefer that to sitting down."

The smile on everyone's lips made poor Odette want to sink through the floor. But as the music began again, her friend Micheline led her away, affectionately taking her by the hand, and said to her in a low voice: "Do you hurt a lot dear?"

The Discipline of Odette

"Oh, yes—if you only knew—and—and all the shame—"

"Yes, I know. Jeannine and I are so often whipped by our governess."

"I was just whipped to the blood," Odette confessed.

"And I had the nettles this morning—but you don't know what they are, do you?"

"Oh, no."

"Ah, they burn atrociously, and it lasts so long after. But come now, let's think of pleasanter things. Jacques Darcy is burning to dance with you. Why, he's asked me at least three times if you were coming so I'll leave you two together."

"Oh, no, my little Niquette! Don't you know that last Sunday I was whipped because of him, for Mama thought we'd flirted together too much? Today, she's threatened me with the whip if I give him more than one dance."

"Poor little devil! But here he is now, you can't refuse him a dance, surely?"

"How wrong it was of you," Jacques murmured, "not to have written me as you promised you would."

Odette felt herself before him more a coward, more disarmed, more humiliated, that ever, feeble and abandoned. She murmured, hardly raising her eyes: "Oh, if you only knew!"

"Yes, I do know, your mother's very severe with you, isn't she?"

Odette blushed to the roots of her hair. "You heard Mama a little while ago, so why ask me?"

"Excuse me, I didn't want to make you feel bad. I

only wanted to talk to you nicely to console you. Come sit down beside me a moment."

"No, dear Jacques, I can't."

Recalling her mother's words, he excused himself like someone who has just committed an error of tactlessness. But his eyes, nonetheless, covertly stole a glance at that bottom, which he imagined as bruised and striped with lashes under her dress. Yet Odette, to her anguish, divined his thoughts; and in a low voice and with lowered eyes, she swiftly countered: "Yes, Mama forbade me to sit down with you. 'Just one dance with trim,' she told me, 'and no carryings-on like last time.' Oh, my mother is looking at me—I implore you, let's dance! If you have any friendship for me, spare me the shame of a new punishment!"

And so they went out onto the floor and began to dance. It was a slow tango, and their limbs brushed together. He, feeling against his knee the roll of her gartered stockings, thought to himself: "It's so she can be more easily made bare for a whipping that she doesn't wear a garter belt." Besides, his hand felt Odette's waist and detected the waistband of her panties, and he could conjure up her mother's gesture as she made the garment slither to Odette's heels before whipping her. And finally, against his cheek he felt her troubled face, felt the heat and saw the mark of her mother's slap.

She abandoned herself entirely; between her thighs she felt the thigh and knee of her male partner; against her belly, she sensed the pressure of his male emblem of desire, and she was aware of the indecency of their dancing posture and trembled, feeling her mother's gaze upon

The Discipline of Odette

her. But even in that very fear, she found an inexplicable joy; and, recalling the threat made to her, of a public spanking, she experienced confusedly a monstrous desire to be trussed up and whipped before him!

In the salon where the mothers had gathered, the arrival of Madame Delage turned the conversation to the whip.

"So," Madame Lacaille remarked, "you managed all by yourself to truss her up and to keep her in position while you whipped her?"

"Oh, I didn't arrive at that by force, believe me! But she knows that if she struggles, her father will whip her and she gains nothing by her efforts."

"As for myself," another matron claimed, "I don't care at all to have my husband whip my daughter. I save that for really serious occasions, and I may say that in the past six months my daughter has been whipped by her father only once, and twice by me in his presence."

"Yes, in the main you're right," Madame Delage answered. "I admit that I'm a bit wrong, when I'm quite angry, in threatening Odette with the worst treatment. For in essence, there's a limit to the severity of a correction. And I manage to punish her almost as severely for a slight fault as for a grave one. Thus, this evening, I admit to you that if I had to punish her again, I should be a little embarrassed. After twenty strokes of the martinet, her bottom would be completely cut and I'd have to stop."

"But why don't you use nettles?" Madame Lacaille asked.

"Nettles?"

"Why, yes, the governess of my daughters came up with that idea. Nettles prick and produce a cooking heat that lasts a long time, without causing any wound or cut."

"But where can you buy nettles? I wouldn't know where to look."

"Why, in all the shops that carry whipping articles, of course; where do you buy your birch rods and your martinets?"

"I rarely use the birch, but when I do, I go to a novelty shop, and I don't think I've ever seen nettles there."

"Haven't you ever gone to the Rod and Martine on the Rue Saint-Honore?"

"I confess my ignorance."

"Well, go there, then. Besides, it's quite a curious shop. They sell all kinds of material you'd find in a house of correction: whipping horses, special benches, paddles, birches, martinets...and nettles too. They're sold in carefully tissue-wrapped packages so the stems won't prick the fingers of the buyer. Only, I'll admit there's just one inconvenience: nettles must be fresh; after twenty-four hours, even if you keep them in water, the leaves fade and have no effect. But the shop has a very good delivery service. So I've sub scribed to it, which means that every other day they deliver four bouquets, enough for four punishments. With the two girls I have, I often need that much."

"Why, I was absolutely unaware of such a thing," Madame Delage delightedly exclaimed.

"Truly? But this shop also offers the service of private

The Discipline of Odette

disciplinarians who'll go to your home. Why yes indeed, I needed their service before I engaged my governess. One day when my husband had taken a week-long trip, my little ones took advantage by running wild. Jeannine in particular, when I wanted to whip her, struggled with me and refused to adjust her clothes. I didn't want to call my maid in, so I telephoned the shop. And a quarter of an hour later two correctresses were there, two strong women between thirty-five and forty years old! Oh, things moved swiftly then, I can tell you! Two minutes later, Jeannine found herself lying on her bed, trussed up and her panties down. The two women began by administering to her a superb hand spanking—and each of the two hands that took charge of her saucy bare backside was as wide as a paddle! Then, without leaving her time to catch her breath after some fifty strokes of the birch, they finished her off with the martinet. I assure you that the next day I had only to make a gesture to have her come stretch out over my knees. And while the two women were there, I profited by having them give Micheline the same dose."

"But this is most interesting," said Madame Delage. "My husband goes away a good deal too, like yours, and I avow I'm often helpless when Odette acts up."

"Nonetheless, there's nothing better than a good governess like the one I was lucky enough to meet. She has an extraordinary control over my girls, and oh what rest I enjoy now! You must really come spend a few days at Easter time at my place in Brittany, you'd be astonished how docile my girls have become.

"I'm very grateful to you, dear Madame. Doubtless it

would be a fine example for Odette, who has been giving me trouble for quite some little time now. There, just look at her now, dancing always with the same young man in spite of my having forbidden it! Ah, that's too much! There she goes to sit down with him now. Evidently she's telling herself she doesn't risk another whipping here!"

"If you feel it's necessary, don't concern yourself on my account, I beg of you!"

"No, I don't want to inflict on all these ladies the squeals of that little idiot…and certainly I don't propose to take her panties down in front of all these young men!"

"To be sure, but you could take her into Jeannine's or Micheline's room."

"If you wouldn't mind, dear Madame Lacaille, there's another solution which I'd prefer, because it's much more humiliating. Mightn't I chastise her behind that tall folding screen? I'd thus protect her modesty, while at the same time it would be vastly more shameful for her since everyone would hear the noise of the correction."

"Nothing would prevent you, equally, from whipping her in public through her clothes. If need be, Mademoiselle will aid you," Madame Lacaille, gestured toward the governess.

"I'm definitely grateful to you."

"But it's nothing at all. It's not easy to deal with these little incorrigibles."

The dance had just ended.

"Odette, come here," Madame Delage said in a curt tone.

Odette, pale and trembling, moved toward her

The Discipline of Odette

mother. Everyone had overheard, and all conversation stopped. When she faced her mother, Odette saw Madame Delage fix her with a severe glare: "You again feel like getting the whip?"

Odette stammered some incoherent words, turning scarlet.

"You don't remember what I told you before you came in?" And with a nod, she designated the young man who was watching the scene with passionate interest.

"But, Mama, it's still the same dance."

"Oh, no you don't, don't start Lying again, at least be courageous to admit what you've done. And what did I promise you in case of disobedience?"

"Oh, M-Mama," was all poor Odette could murmur as her eyes filled with sudden tears.

"Will you answer, or shall I slap you? What did I promise you as punishment?"

Her stern hand rose, ready to smite Odette's shame-empurpled cheek; the anguished beauty murmured, "The...w...whip."

"Yes, of course the whip, but how?"

"On—f-from behind..."

"No, not from behind, on your behind, your big behind of a grown girl of nineteen! But that still isn't what I want to make you say. Where were you to receive your correction, at home?

"N...no...h-here...Oh Mama, pardon!" And her hands joined in fervent supplication.

"Yes, here, in front of all your friends. But you doubtless said to yourself that I wouldn't dare, especially in front of these young men."

"Oh, no, Mama, I never thought of it, oh, pardon!"

Her voice was low, stifled, as if to keep her words from the ironic circle of listeners she guessed was forming behind her; but the silence was such that not a word was lost.

"No pardon before punishment. You are going to be whipped and publicly, since Madame Lacaille consents to it."

Odette fell on her knees, and in a voice still choked with sobs, she implored, "Oh, Mama, it's too much, it's too shameful! In the house…you may whip me to the blood and I won't say a word. But not here, Mama, please not here!"

"That's enough of that! You shall be whipped here as I promised you. Yet because I have a little more concern for your modesty than you had a little while ago while you were dancing, I shan't inflict the shame on you of trussing you up before your dancing partners. I shall whip you behind that screen, since Madame Lacaille is gracious enough to permit it. Afterwards, you'll receive the martinet in front of everybody—but over your skirts."

Odette had heard this implacable verdict without budging; but at her mother's last words, she flung her arms around Madame Delage's knees and lifted poignantly imploring tearful eyes to that stern, relentless face: "Oh, pardon, not that, not here! It's abominable!"

"Little fool, you know very well that your sniveling does no good. Now get up and let's finish this!"

She was about to seize Odette by the earlobe, but the latter had risen and in her agonized eyes there shone the

The Discipline of Odette

glow of a desperate revolt. Madame Delage did not wish to give her friends the spectacle of a struggle in which her dignity was bound to suffer; she made a sign to the governess to approach. "Will you help me, Mademoiselle? This scene has lasted much too long."

"Be at ease, Madame. I've mastered more rebellious ones than her."

Odette tensed herself, ready to give battle. But before she could make a move, the governess clamped an arm around the girl's waist and with uncommon strength lifted her up in classic position. Odette, stupefied, began to kick and wriggle wildly, but without breaking her jailer's grasp. The governess, without a word, walked toward the screen placed in a corner of the salon. It was close to the wall, but a woman standing nearby drew it out to give Madame Delage room to slip inside. Now Odette was humbly pleading for mercy, conscious of her weakness.

The parents and the young people followed this scene in absolute silence; no one dared manifest his or her impatient curiosity, or move about in order to better to see the culprit; but perhaps by design—for the governess was capable of having thought up this refinement herself—though the lower part of Odette's body was now hidden, her head appeared in the narrow space between the wall and the screen thus exhibiting to all her lovely face contracted with indescribable anguish and shame.

In a loud voice, the governess, still holding Odette under her powerful arm, spoke to Madame Delage, who stood behind her daughter and whose head was seen above the top of the fragile screen. This gave the spectators a titillating emotion in reconstructing in their imaginations the scene hidden from their eager eyes.

"Do you wish me to aid you in trussing up her clothes, Mademoiselle?" said the maternal voice.

"There's no need, thank you. Her dress is rather wide, but if you'll just help me tuck it under my arm—there, perfect. We remove her panties?"

"Yes, yes, on the bare, as we've agreed."

"Of course, but I see she has panties with a wide slit."

"That doesn't mean anything, I had her put them on to humiliate her, but I'm going to have them off all the same, you'll be able to whip her better...Odette, will you stop kicking and wriggling like that. Now, wait until I tuck her chemise under your arm—ah, good!"

There was a short silence; then the governess exclaimed: "I see you've already whipped her very well, her behind is delightfully patterned. Then we'll simply spank her?"

"Yes, but go to it and don't spare her!"

One can imagine the state of Odette's emotions now. She had at first, before all those eyes fixed on her face, tried to hide that scarlet, contorted visage in both hands, then the words being uttered behind her revived all her shame, so while she kept her eyes closed, she clapped her palms over her ears in a frantic attempt to blot out those cruel words and also the whispers of the spectators beyond that infernal screen. Yet the words filtered through to her just the same, and besides that rustling of her trussed-up and descended garments and at last the sensation of air caressing her naked behind left her no

The Discipline of Odette

illusion. Then, feeling herself ready for the thrashing, feeling the hand lifted and ready to fall on her still burning, swollen, naked bottomcheeks, all else was obliterated by the fear of those torturing smacks to come.

"Mama, Mama, pardon, oh have mercy, oh, not too hard!"

But suddenly the very first smack resounded; Odette's anguished, contracted face instantly twisted with shame and suffering, and from her rosy mouth a cry rose, a wordless plaint. Then came a second, a third, and now an uninterrupted fusillade of dry, harsh, methodically regular smacks which to the feverish imagination of the tense listeners conveyed the graphic scene of that naked bottom bounding and wriggling, turning an infamous red under that avalanche of shameful open-palmed spanks, such as one would administer to an unruly child.

At first, Odette had tried to stifle her cries, but her suffering became such that it blotted out all pride.

And so there, behind that screen which was circled by young girls and mothers, some of them seeing her for the first time, and by young men whom she had met before, some of them being so timid that they did not even dare speak to her, she, Odette, a beautiful young girl envied for her family fortune and her desirable beauty, now like a wretched child, amid her strangling and heartfelt sobs, murmured endless words to beseech the end of her juvenile chastisement...one which, we must recall, assuredly hurt far more atrociously than could any ordinary spanking, in view of what her naked bottom had already endured at home.

"Oh, Ohh! Ohhh! Ohh! Mama! Oh, no more, no

more, it hurts me too much. Oh, it's too much. Oh, it burns—oh, please have mercy! Pardon me! I promise you to be very good—Ohh, mercy, mercy—Oh enough. Oh, please—aahhh! I can't bear it any more!"

At last her martyrdom had ended—that is, her physical martyrdom, for scarcely did she have the time to rise and to be aware of herself and regain possession of her senses, than her restored modesty was put to torture again. Inside the screen behind which her tear-stained face had disappeared, her mother's words now rose to prolong her public ignominy: "Will you take away your hands! Will you let your behind alone? Let your dress fall. No, I forbid you to put your panties back on. All right, come along now!"

Odette, her anguish a little appeased, regained full awareness of her horrible shame. She tried to resist a little so she might stay longer behind the fragile shelter of that screen, but the governess thrust her back into the salon and giving her a contemptuous smack on her bottom.

Her face red, sobbing, her eyes disconsolately lowered, Odette indeed evoked for all who saw her the image of a whipped girl. And anyone who had not witnessed that scene we have just described must certainly have guessed, just by seeing her, what treatment she had endured.

She was nineteen, she was tall, her superb breasts beautifully formed, her haunches somewhat vigorous in their glorious rounding, everything in her suggested the ripeness of womanhood. And yet, on her naked bottom, the humiliating slaps of a corrective hand had fallen.

Her behind, her behind, a ridiculous and disgusting

The Discipline of Odette

word with which she was always and ceaselessly lashed. Her rounded behind, her behind, this morning so soft and ripe and desirable—her young girl's behind, her modest behind!

For here exactly was the terrible contrast: it was for a behavior not sufficiently reserved that she had just been chastised; it was for having pressed too intimately, during the dance, her thighs to those of her partner—that was why in his very presence the bottom had been bared, and under his eyes she had had to arch and wriggle and jut out her naked cheeks. It was through the taste of the whip on her naked behind that she was being taught modesty. No, Jacques had not actually seen her behind the screen, but she knew very well that his vivid imagination could picture exactly what had taken place...see every detail of her panties being dragged down, of the governess holding her arms in such a way that the cheeks of her cringing and huddling bare behind had to stick out so piteously for the rude, burning smacks of that chastising hand. And this was perhaps the most torturing punishment of all for the sensitive and maturing beauty.

But perhaps this contradiction was only apparent. What were the reactions of a whipped girl? Did the baring of her most intimate bodily parts waken within her a disturbing sensuality, or, as most mothers believe, force her to see in that part of her virginal body only the instrument which was to be punished, the flesh which was publicly shameful because one unveiled it only out of necessity for the most animal of functions and in penitence to be flogged like a dog!

The voice of Madame Lacaille was first to break the silence as she addressed Odette: "You see, my child, the whip always has the last word. What have you to say about Mademoiselle after the whipping?"

Odette lowered her head without replying. The slaps of her mother restored her to order: "Don't you answer when someone speaks to you? Do you want us to go behind the screen again?"

Odette stammered, "Mama, pardon. I don't know—what I must do?"

"Madame Lacaille has asked what you think of the chastisement you have just received?"

"It hurt a lot, Madame," Odette murmured.

"Even more than when I whip you?

"Oh, yes!"

"You see that you are still lucky that none of your friends would like to be in your place. But you are preventing everybody from having fun with your ridiculous little acting. Come get your dose of the martinet and let's end this!"

Had Odette forgotten the recent minutes, or had she truly forgotten that mercy had been accorded to her? Whatever it was, this order from her mother made her fall on her knees and clasp her hands together. "Oh, Mama, no more! Oh, no, isn't it over? Tell me, isn't it over?"

"Just one more word my girl, and you shall have the martinet naked in front of everyone. All right, get on your knees on that armchair. Hang your bosom against the back, and prepare yourself for a good dose. Would you hand me the martinet?" Madame Delage added as she turned to the governess.

The Discipline of Odette

"Janine, go get me yours," the governess said as she spoke to one of the pupils.

Janine was, naturally, the pet name for Odette's dear friend, Jeannine. If the governess used this familiar sobriquet now, it was to announce to this interested audience that she had full charge of that charming young lady, and the girl promptly blushed. But without a word, she left the room and returned a few moments later carrying the shameful instrument.

All this time Odette, feeling that all resistance was useless, mastered by the correction she had just received, had taken the position her mother had indicated: her bottom arched out against the dress which tightly clung to it. That magnificent posterior was turned toward the group of guests, who, without a word, remained there forming a semi-circle as spectators.

The governess took the martinet from Janine's hands. Then, addressing Madame Delage, "Do you want me to whip her?"

"No, thanks, I'll take charge of that myself. I'll ask you only to hold her, because I'm going to give it to her good. Besides, Odette," she added, "if you show the least bad will, this evening you'll have an explanation with your father. You understand?"

The poor child had neither strength nor revolt left in her; she murmured a vague supplication and did not stir.

Already Madame Delage, running her hand over her daughter's bottom, made certain that under the dress the girl's chemise did not contain any fold which might lessen the efficacy of the chastisement. Meanwhile the governess took the girl's hands in hers and drew them behind her back, while at the same time maintaining Odette's body pressed against the back of the armchair. And thus the condemned backside thrust out still more boldly because her loins were hollowed by the ignoble and enforced position.

"I think you may begin, Madame," the governess remarked.

And once again, Odette felt all her modesty flee before the anguish of what awaited her; even before the first lash could be applied, she uttered a plaint.

Placed at a good distance from the condemned backside, Madame Delage brandished the martinet with long thongs, which whistled and flattened over the bottom-cheeks of the unfortunate girl. There was a cry and a convulsive start from the victim. But, heedless of that, her mother applied the second lash. Then, slowly, in spite of the cries—more and more numerous—and supplications of the unhappy culprit, the lash fell slowly at least twice, and Odette endured the frightful agony of her burning bottom which had already experienced such prolonged torment all this never-to-be forgotten day.

When it was finished and while the panting young girl still continued to groan and to squirm on her knees, the mother put her hand under Odette's dress and stroked the swollen bottomcheeks. This simple gesture had a curiously sensual effect upon the spectators; for the moment they had the sensation that they were at last going to be permitted to behold that burning flesh, that naked and intimate flesh, that beautiful bare bottom of a young woman, which they saw in their mind's eye swollen, striped and welted.

The Discipline of Odette

Odette herself, fearing that her clothes would be trussed up, felt her shame get the upper hand of her suffering. She uttered an "Oh, no, not that!" so heartbreakingly that even Madame Delage herself had pity.

"All right, don't be afraid," she said gruffly. "This time it's finished. Your behind is very hot, but it doesn't seem to be scorched. We'll see tonight when we get home. Ask my pardon and go thank Mademoiselle who took the trouble to correct you."

At the point to which Odette had arrived in the training, which her mother and father had so astutely given her, this supplementary shame awakened no reaction. She put herself on her knees before her mother, clasped her hands and murmured once more the shameful formula of thanks customary after a whipping.

She went then to the governess in her haste to finish the hideous ordeal, put into that formula more shameful humility than ever her mother might have demanded: "Mademoiselle, I thank you infinitely for the trouble you took in trussing me up and spanking me as you did. I ask your pardon for the trouble that I gave you, and I hope the memory of this correction will be profitable to me."

Madame Delage then said, "Now, push up this taboret. You're going to sit on it and stay there till we leave. If you just budge, if you utter the least sigh and even if you continue to cry, I shall slap you and you will be whipped tonight by your father."

This time, Odette was truly mastered; although sitting must certainly have been atrociously painful, she placed her bottom on the seat without stirring, and her hands crossed over her knees, remaining straight and motionless under all the curious and mocking glances which the mothers fixed upon her.

The dancing had resumed. All the young girls had followed this scene and, out of their own personal memories, could imagine only too well what pain and shame Odette had suffered, and they remained enervated and quivering with the prospect that perhaps some day too, they themselves might be condemned to such public mortification.

The young men had eyes only for the whipped young girl, seated motionless in her attitude of piteous repentance.

The mothers, standing near Odette, were still talking of the whip, comparing the different instruments of correction, discussing the most comfortable position in order to maintain a young girl during punishment, and each of their words was a new shame for the lovely culprit.

Finally Madame Delage rose to depart: "Excuse me, dear Madame, for leaving so soon, but I'd like to stop at the shop that you mentioned, for perhaps I shall have the occasion either this evening or tomorrow to try these nettles on my little one's bottom. It's on the bare flesh, isn't it, that one must use them?"

"Of course, otherwise she wouldn't feel a thing. Besides, they'll be very happy to show you down there the best way to use them."

"Thanks again, dear Madame, and excuse me for the disturbance I caused."

"Oh, that's quite natural. Who knows, perhaps I

The Discipline of Odette

myself one day may be advised to apply to you for service to my girls."

Madame Delage turned to her daughter and said harshly. "Get up, and excuse yourself to Madame Lacaille for the disturbance that you caused."

Odette rose, trembling, and, as she kissed Madame Lacaille's hand, murmured, "I pray you to excuse me, Madame, for having deserved a whipping in your house."

As she raised her eyes, mechanically, her gaze crossed that of her boyfriend, which she found to be tender and shining, strangely tender and harsh at the same time; such a desire was evidenced in his gaze that a sensual titillation composed of brutal sensuality and infinite shame invaded her, so that a flood of tears choked her, her voice strangled, and she almost felt like fainting. Jacques had looked at her as if he wanted to truss her up himself and, not content with feeling her bottom to determine how well she had been whipped, put his hard manhood into the intimate little spot between her legs. She felt her thighs shuddering, soft and molten, with a strange and inexplicable desire at that emotion; it seemed to her somehow that her public whipping and shame had now been justified because they had caused him to pay more attention to her than ever, to desire her physically as a man wants a woman...in bed, thighs entwined, his manhood prodding against the tender secret nook of her virginity.

"Very well," the mother said, somewhat softened. "Now say good-bye to your friends."

Perhaps here was the most humiliating moment of all: with reddened eyes, with awkward steps, her bottom burning furiously under the dress, she had to go shake hands of six or seven friends standing nearby. A heavy silence weighed upon all the salon, and it accompanied Odette as she said her good-byes.

Without a word, she and her mother went down the stairway, and got into the limousine, but once there, Odette humbly and pitifully murmured, "How shall I sit down, Mama?"

Madame Delage, her voice tranquil, replied "You have been corrected enough, my poor little one. Come sit beside me, and, about the nettles, we will see another time. I hope you'll be good tomorrow."

When her daughter had carefully seated herself, she put her arm around her neck and drew her affectionately toward her, saying, "You see, my child, it does you no good to disobey."

Odette abandoned herself to her chagrin with heavy sobs: "Oh, Mama, Mama," she choked, "how ashamed I was. I'll never dare go back to the Lacailles."

"Yes, you will, my little one, and the memory of your shame will be very beneficial, I'm sure."

As the limousine turned and made the two passengers sway in their seats, poor Odette murmured, "And it hurts me so much, Mama, if you only knew!"

"We'll examine your behind when we get home. I think, indeed, it must be a bit scorched."

When they went into the house, Odette supplicated, "You won't say anything to Papa?"

"Yes, I shall tell him, but I promise that he won't whip you. So take off your hat and come into the bathroom so I can examine you."

Following instructions, Odette, her clothes again

The Discipline of Odette

trussed up, stretched out flat on her belly on the wooden chair, offering up her wide, round bottom for inspection. It was a low chair, so her hands and feet touched the floor and her bottom was upreared quite high.

Over the red and congested background, the swellings of the martinet were designed in wide streaks which now began to turn violet, and here and there were some raw spots.

Madame Delage contemplated for a moment that poor flogged bottom: "Well, you have been very well chastised. I think that for the next few days you won't be able to sit down without remembering what you've done. All right, I'm going to wash your bottom for you."

She took a heavy sponge and soaked it in warm water. Then gently, even with caution, she grazed it along the upreared bottom. The water gave Odette an immediate solace, but then, in order to pat a raw spot, Madame Delage had to rub harder, and Odette was scarcely able to hold back her plaints, instinctively tightening her bottomcheeks.

This ritual was about to end when suddenly there was a knock at the door of the bathroom. Terrified at the thought that someone was going to see her like this, Odette tried hastily to rise, but her mother pressed her down with the palm of her hand called out, "Enter!"

The chambermaid entered, her eyes at once fixed on the shamefully spread out naked bottom, but she said only, "Dinner is ready, Madame."

"Very good. Thank you. Has Monsieur returned yet?"

"He has just arrived, Madame, and he is in his office."

"Very good. You may serve."

She went out with a scathing glance at weeping Odette, saying, "We're going to dine, so hurry—you've five minutes, not a second more."

Odette rose; alone now, her bottom still burning, eyes drowned in tears, she hurried, dominated by the fear of the lash. And, face flushed, hair disheveled, walking warily, she entered the dining room; just seeing her father there revived her terrified shame; but she went to him and said, "Good evening, Papa."

Glacially, he looked her up and down, remarked "Your mother's told me how you behaved this afternoon. I myself shall examine your behind after dinner, and I warn you if I find it hasn't been whipped enough, I shall finish it off for you."

"Oh, Papa!"

"Be still! Sit down and keep quiet, it's your only chance of escaping a new thrashing!"

The dinner was a moral agony for the unfortunate young beauty, especially as most of her parents' conversation revolved around the events of the afternoon. Finally, entering the salon for coffee, Odette going there with trembling thighs, half-fainting with suspense, her father commanded, "All right now, show me your backside." She burst into nervous tears, but obeyed…it was her fifth trussing-up of the day. He glided clumsy hands 'round her hips, lowered her panties at last, and the humiliating coolness of the air again caressed her well-marked naked behind. A terrible anguish made her heart pound wildly. He prolonged this shameful examination, palpating the flesh, parting her thighs to see if the lashes had marked the insides. Finally he said, "Yes, for today I think you've

The Discipline of Odette

had a fair share." He then allowed her to rise and replace her clothing, adding, "Ask once again, and very humbly, your mother's pardon. Thank her for the trouble she's taken to chastise you and then go to bed at once."

Docilely, Odette went to the armchair, knelt before her mother, and with clasped hands she murmured in a humble voice: "My dear Mama, I beg your pardon for my conduct this afternoon. I thank you for having offered to give me the whip, and I ask your pardon for the trouble that I gave you in doing it. I hope that the memory of this correction will keep me from starting my naughtiness again in the future."

"That's very good, my dear, I pardon you, and I hope also that the souvenir of your correction will be wholesome and profitable." She kissed her affectionately, and Odette rose. Odette then offered her forehead to her father, and was preparing to go to her room when the phone rang. Madame Delage went to the phone.

"Hello, is that you, my dear friend?" said the voice of Madame Lacaille. "Are you going out tonight?"

"No. Why?"

"Because I should like to ask you, if you aren't too tired and if it wouldn't disturb you too much, to come back to my place right away."

"With pleasure, but why, then?"

"Because Janine had just earned a severe chastisement, and I am going to give her the whip and then the nettles. So, if it would interest you to see how I proceed—"

"Yes, certainly, dear Madame, but won't it disturb you at this late hour? Just give me time to prepare myself, and I don't think it will take me more than half an hour."

"Oh, that's no bother. I'm going to prepare Janine, and this waiting, with her behind in the air, will be an excellent aggravation of punishment for her."

"If you don't mind, perhaps I might bring along Odette, for whom it would be a good example."

"Certainly Then I'll be expecting you both soon."

Madame Delage told her husband and her daughter of the conversation she had just had, and gave Odette the order to prepare herself, then rang to have the chauffeur get the car ready.

Not more than fifteen minutes later, both of them arrived at the door of the Lacailles' and it was the governess who opened the door.

"Madame is in Miss Janine's room, and if you like, we can go there right away," she said pleasantly.

As they came in, Madame Lacaille came to meet them. They went into Janine's room, and the first thing which struck Odette's eyes was Janine's behind.

Kneeling on a chair, the girl bowed her poor head onto the table against which the back of the chair was pressed; thus her backside was raised higher than her head.

Her dress—a very pretty silk—and her chemise had been lifted above her waist. Her little pair of panties had been pulled down to her knees, and along her thighs there hung, on each side, the garter tabs from her rolled-down stockings. Thus she was naked from the waist to her knees.

At the sound of their entry, she had tried to lift herself up and pull down her skirt, but the governess had applied her hand on her shoulders and had scolded her, "Janine, you stay still."

The Discipline of Odette

Her thighs clenched together, Janine thus remained immobile, softly sobbing. Madame Lacaille then spoke.

"You see, dear Madame Delage, this position is, in my opinion, the most favorable for this kind of correction. The behind is at a suitable height, the buttocks sufficiently parted, and by making her open her knees, the leaves of the nettles can penetrate into the most sensitive region and thus punish efficaciously. Janine, will you open your knees? There, like that. You see, Mademoiselle Odette, that it isn't only you who is whipped. Janine is going to receive a punishment which in no way will be inferior to that which you have just endured." Odette blushed at this reference to her own shame, but a strange and troubling emotion now rose in her being as she watched the humiliation of her friend, which was evidently much worse than hers. Janine's position permitted her in no way to hide her most secret parts, and Odette's eyes could not move away from that jutting naked bottom nor the mysterious amber groove between those twitching bare bottomcheeks, nor still less from the dainty pink-lipped orifice just below, framed with silken thatch of golden hair, Janine's virgin slit.

During all of her mother's discourse, Janine had not budged, and her shame could be judged only by her sobs, which shook her shoulders. Her mother resumed:

"I counsel you, dear Madame, any time you want to administer the nettles to Odette, to begin by a good hand spanking, either with a flat hand or some kind of paddle or slipper. That considerably augments the sensitivity of a bare bottom. As I intend to punish Janine very severely this evening, Mademoiselle is going to spank her with this leather sole. You see," she added as she smilingly took hold of the object, "the contact of this with my girl's behind has given it an enviable polish. All right, Janine, the moment has come. Prepare yourself to be severely chastised."

"Oh, Mama, pardon, not too hard, pardon?" the poor girl piteously groaned.

"I shall pardon you later. Now, enough of these jeremiads, you know very well they are of no use."

"But what has she done to deserve this correction?" Madame Delage inquired.

"Mademoiselle found in her room a book that she bought without permission."

"A book that wasn't for her?"

"Not precisely. If she had asked. I should probably have allowed her to buy it. But out of principle, I feel that she ought to receive the whip."

This dialogue had caused Odette an infinite distress, because it revealed an education that was even more rigid and severe than the one under which she dwelt.

But Madame Lacaille did not wish to waste any more time, and turned to the governess and said, "Mademoiselle, if you care to begin?"

The governess approached the table, clamped her left arm around Janine's waist, seized with her right hand the instrument of correction, shoved the girl's clothing up her back so it would be out of harm's way, and on the stretched and tightened skin of the plump bare behind, applied with the full strength of her arm a sonorous thwack! Janine uttered a cry, but tried in no way to escape the next smack, which fell with the same force, marking the other bottomcheek. The first blow had

The Discipline of Odette

been applied upon the summit of the nether globe; the second stroke equalized matters as regards the furious bright imprint of the whipping instrument.

So the correction proceeded, pursued amid the silence of the spectators, and the humble and supplicating cries of the culprit.

"Stop crying so loud," her mother said to her after a few spanks. "It's late, you'll wake the entire household. You want us to give you a gag, you little wretch?"

Biting her lips after this invective, Janine managed to utter only stifled groans. The spanking stopped at the end of some forty whacks with the leather sole, and Janine's behind was uniformly crimson, with several darker streaks (marks of an earlier correction, doubtless with the martinet) appearing at the base of her bare seat.

"Get up, thank her, and go bring the nettle as usual," her mother dryly commanded.

Janine rose, letting her skirts fall over her blazing bottom, and trying to remove the lowered panties from her legs, at last went to the cupboard where, in a case, a magnificent bouquet of nettles was displayed.

A formidable pair of slaps from her mother's hand stopped her immediately: "Well, what sort of manners are these? Is this the way you are accustomed to act?"

"Oh, Mama, not now—not here!" Janine implored, glancing fearfully toward Madame Delage.

"Yes! That will humiliate you all the more, since there are witnesses to your shame. So much the worse for you, my little one. It was your fault that you find yourself in this state. Mademoiselle, before you apply the nettles, to teach her to obey, correct her a little more."

"Oh, Mama, pardon, I'll obey. Don't have me whipped again before the nettles. I implore you, it hurts so much already!"

"Another word and you'll receive the birch!"

The young girl fell silent. The governess approached her, bent her over her arm m the classical position, without Janine's attempting a single gesture of defense. In a moment, her clothes were trussed up again, the unfortunate behind again revealed, in all its bare, jutting beauty.

Without any delay, and with the full force of her arm, some vigorous strokes of the sole rapidly inflicted were applied on the two naked bottomcheeks. Amid Janine's desperate cries, those luscious, furiously crimson gloves wriggled and writhed and clenched uncontrollable, yet Janine attempted in no way to escape either the grip of her governess or the smacks from the leather sole.

Once she had been released, she began to groan and to caress her bottom with trembling hands.

"Will you finish that indecent comedy?" her mother's voice dryly ordered. "On your knees, and truss yourself up high!"

Janine obeyed, holding up with both hands her lifted skirts, sinking down on her knees and turning toward the governess, then she murmured "Mademoiselle, I thank you for the trouble that you have taken in whipping me."

Then she rose in the middle of a severe silence of her mother, a curious one on the part of Odette's mother —and an anguished one, to say the least, so far as Odette was concerned. Still holding her skirts uplifted, she walked to the cupboard. From the vase she broke off —in spite of the stings and pricks it must have given her —one of those bouquets of nettles, whose stems, as has been said, were carefully wrapped with tissue at the end. She knelt again before the governess. Then, amid sobs which stifled her voice, she murmured, "Mademoiselle, will you please be good enough…to whip…my b-behind…with these n-nettles and punish me as severely as you think best."

"Have no fear, my child, I shan't spare you," the governess remarked, though no one could discern the least irony in her voice. "Place yourself as before," she added.

Janine obediently trussed herself up again. Her stockings, during the few steps she had taken, had slid all the way down her legs, and she leaned over the table, offering herself naked from the waist to ankles now.

"Pardon, pardon," she sobbed softly now, resigned before the nettles.

"And above all, keep your hands still, otherwise, the cravache!" the governess threatened her as she approached.

She applied her left hand on the loins of the culprit, both to hold up the girl's skirts and to force down her bottom the more. Then the correction began. Against the middle of Janine's naked behind, she at first gently rubbed the bouquet of nettles, and Janine trembled, uttering a plaint. Then, with little light taps, as if one were dusting off a cushion, she whipped.

Janine's naked behind, from top to bottom, quaked and wriggled while her plaints became more and more like moans. Through the redness of the earlier correction, one could now see a multitude of tiny white blisters rising, each one a torturing sting which added to the ferocious cooking left by the sole.

This quaking and wriggling became more and more disorderly; Janine's thighs instinctively tightened. The leaves detached themselves from the stems, falling on the floor.

"Janine, what sort of behavior is that? Will you spread your thighs? More than that—more!"

"Oh, Mademoiselle, oh, it burns me—if you only knew! Oh, no—I'm too ashamed!" Janine sobbed.

"One more word and it's the cravache! Come now, I shall put this book between your knees. If you place one of your knees upon it, tomorrow you'll wear your panties full of nettles."

Madame Delage questioningly looked at her friend. Madame Lacaille nodded and said, "Yes, Mademoiselle had the idea once to make Janine a kind of very thick jersey panties with nettles inside. One afternoon she had to go outside, walk and sit down with them in her panties. You can imagine what a state she was in that evening. Now, this is her fan and she is just gently cooling Janine's bottom. Isn't that so, Janine?"

Before that sarcastic voice, poor Janine sobbed, "Oh, Mama, it's too much. I can't stand any more—oh, pardon, have mercy!"

"Do you reply, you insolent one?" he mother said, as she got up and walked over to the girl. Then she herself applied two stinging smacks of her gloved hand on Janine's naked backside.

"Yes, oh yes, Mama, oh, owww!"

The Discipline of Odette

"Go on, quite deeply, you know where," she said to her governess. "That will teach her politeness."

The whipping resumed. Now the parted bottom-cheeks allowed the display of all the secret femininity of the lovely young girl. The governess made the tip of her bouquet penetrate between the open thighs, and turning the point 'round and 'round, irritated not only the tender cleft of Janine's virgin bunghole, but also the entrance to her maiden love-temple!

Then there were stifled cries, loud groans, desperate appeals, but those motionless knees did not try to clench together, so complete was Janine's domination by the governess and by her mother.

Little by little, the bouquet became shredded. A few more caresses on the thighs, then, so that nothing would be lost with a possibility of punishing, the governess collected the remnants of the bouquet into a mess and then rubbed all over the naked cheeks, and then finally with a sigh of fatigue, opened her gloved hands and let the stems and blossoms fall to the floor.

Janine continued to groan and to wriggle her bottom madly, her hands twisting together as if fighting against the mad desire to rush to her bottom and rub out the furious heat.

"Enough," her mother said. "Prepare yourself for the last part of your correction."

Swaying, Janine rose and holding her skirts up from the rear, she knelt before he governess.

"Mademoiselle," she murmured, her head bowed, amid her sobs. "Will—will you b-b-be good enough—to—to give me on my b-behind some—some more good smacks which—which will prolong the—effect of the—the correction that—that I've just received?"

"That's good," said Madame Lacaille. "She has been docile enough. Smack her only with your hand."

The governess seated herself. "Stretch out over my knees," she ordered Janine.

The young girl obeyed, was trussed up again, and upon the bare posterior, the sonorous smacks began to fall, amid the sobbing and stifled supplications.

"There," the governess said tranquilly, after the last spank. And while Janine, with all pride and modesty vanquished, continued to groan piteously and she wriggled and twisted and jerked her fiery backside.

"All right. Stand up," she added, as she applied a final slap. Then, putting both hands to Janine's thighs, she pushed her and made the poor girl fall on her knees before her.

Promptly Janine rose, and at once, with an instinctive gesture, brushed her hands to her bottom, which, with no thought of modesty, she began to rub and even to scratch.

"Is this the way you act in front of company? Take your hands away immediately, or I'll begin all over again!" was the fearful threat.

Janine obeyed. "All right. Put your panties back on, lower your dress, and go to beg your mother's pardon."

The little panties, slipped down to the ankles during the last part of the correction, were Lying rumpled at the foot of the table. Janine docilely went to pick them up, and was about to put them back on when her mother stopped her.

"No, come here first, so that we may see the state of

your behind. All right, hold your skirts up and put yourself back on the chair in the position for the whip."

"Oh, Mama, no!"

"Don't be an imbecile, it's not to whip you again."

"I'm ashamed—I'm so ashamed, Mama!"

"It's high time, a little while ago, during the whipping, you were wriggling so indecently. All right, hurry," she said, as she pushed Janine toward the chair. And once again that magnificent bare behind was exposed.

Madame Lacaille turned to her friend. "Would you like to come see, dear Madame Delage? Mademoiselle, bring the night lamp closer, if you will, please. Good. You see, there isn't a single raw spot or scratch, yet I guarantee you that she has been punished as severely as if she had fifty lashes of the martinet. The excellent thing about this kind of punishment is that the effect is prolonged for several hours afterward. So we can send Janine to bed right away. And I am certain that she won't be able to go to sleep till well after midnight, besides which she is forbidden to put cold water on or to rub or scratch!"

"How can you prevent her from scratching, once she is in bed?"

"We are going to tie her hands for the night."

"You tie her hands?" Madame Delage asked, wonderingly. "Oh, very lightly, with a simple silk cord, so that she can get free very easily, and thus the temptation of putting her hands to her bottom will be very strong. But she knows that if, tomorrow morning, that silk cord should be broken, she will be pitilessly whipped!"

During this time Janine had risen and put her clothes back in order.

"Say good evening," her mother ordered, "and go to bed. Mademoiselle, will you go with her? The hands as agreed."

The poor young girl, her face contorted with shame, chagrin and suffering, had left. Madame Delage remarked, "I see that your girls are brought up much more severely than mine."

"Well, I don't let them get away with anything!"

"You must whip then almost every day?"

"Oh, of course, but it really isn't so terrible. So for instance, today Janine only received the correction that you have just witnessed. As for Micheline, she got only a whipping with nettles this morning during her piano lesson…Oh, no, I was forgetting…she also got a dozen lashes of the martinet before dinner because she had torn one of her stockings."

"Listen to that, Odette, and reflect upon it," Odette's mother said, shaking her finger at her blushing daughter.

"You think I am very severe?" Madame Lacaille asked. "Why, that's nothing. In Paris we do not treat them as severely as we might like. You see, there are shops, there are parks, and you can not always watch over them. But in the country, it is another thing. Happily, in my estate in Brittany, we can take them in hand from time to time. We are going to spend two weeks around Easter-time, and I swear to you the birch and the martinet will not grow dusty there!" "That's what my daughter needs," Odette's mother remarked.

"You know, I should like to offer you my invitation. If you can't get away, why not turn Odette over to me, and she shall be in my care for a period. Besides, my

The Discipline of Odette

governess has already made acquaintance today with her behind," Janine's mother added with an ironic smile.

"Well, dear Madame, in principle I accept. But it will depend only on Odette's conduct from here on in."

One can well imagine in what state this incredible scene had left poor Odette, the more so since all the way back home, her mother kept insisting on how over-indulgent she was in comparison with Madame Lacaille. She also warned Odette that henceforth it might well be necessary to bring her up as severely as her friends brought up their daughters, too.

At last, back home, Madame Delage told her husband what she had witnessed, and he in his turn threatened Odette with real severity if she did not mend her ways!

THE PRISONER

The Japanese valet had prepared Edith Garvin for her ordeal. He had entered the room in which she had been incarcerated and secured a pair of silver handcuffs to her wrists. He had acted so swiftly that Edith barely had time to be surprised, let alone put up a defense. Moreover, resistance would have been useless, though she didn't know it, for Yoshio was skilled in both judo and karate. He had blindfolded her, and then, fixing a leather dog collar around her neck, had taken hold of the leash and peremptorily commanded her, "You will come quietly now, or I'll give you a good whipping!"

Appalled at what had happened to her, the blindfolded young woman had begun to stammer an agonized question, demanding to know why this was being done to her, why she had been abducted from New York, where she was now, what was to be done to her. But the Japanese valet had given her no reply whatsoever. Dragging on the leash, he had led her stumbling out of the room and guided her down the stairs. His left hand was at the scruff of her neck, and his right gripped her fettered wrists and guided her to the basement chamber where she was at last to be reunited with Judge Austin W. Black.

This chamber was extremely wide, with a low ceiling. Placed advantageously around its walls were several love seats, and a few tabourets and ottomans. In one corner there was an elaborate sideboard on which were placed decanters of liquor and wine. There was even a movie projection screen at one end of the spacious chamber, used at times by the Judge to stir his sexual appetite. He watched films which had been taken at Welfare Island or shot in this very house by his cooperative manservant. The movies were complete with soundtrack, and in a special room on the first floor just off his study library, there were metal cabinets containing hundreds of canisters of movie film, each meticulously labeled as to date and victim, and with a brief outline of what action could be enjoyed by watching the film. Many of these had been duplicated and given to members of the Syndicate, either for their own amusement or as documentation on some helpless female victim who was about to make her commercial debut.

In the center of this wide room was a pillory, solidly set into a rectangular platform about a foot high. But it was much shorter than the kind illustrated in history

The Prisoner

books dealing with the early colonies in New England, when it was the custom to flog errant citizens and then set them in the pillory or the stocks, to be mocked and taunted by the avid spectators. It was scarcely four feet high, which meant that victims whose neck and wrists were clamped in the yoke holes would have to bend over until their back was on an almost completely horizontal plane—and this, needless to say, would project their buttocks out for either the exploration of the executioner's fingers or for the lash!

Yoshio had fixed the beautiful woman in this pillory, removing the dog collar and the handcuffs, but leaving the blindfold in place. His eyes had glistened with lust as he had stepped back to contemplate the mouth-wateringly desirable victim. The round, firm globes of her behind excited his passions, even though she was still fully clothed.

Edith Garvin heard his receding footsteps and then the clang of the metal door which announced that she was alone in her suspense and terror. She began to sob helplessly, ineffectually trying to ease the constricting pressure of the yoke about her wrists and neck. Her back had already begun to ache because of the exaggerated stress of this bent-over pose.

She had been waiting there for nearly an hour when Judge Austin W. Black entered the chamber, clad only in a pale orchid-colored silk bathrobe and dainty leather sandals. He was accompanied by a golden-haired girl in an inadequate black tunic.

Edith Garvin uttered a stifled cry at the sound of their entrance. "Oh God, who is it? Oh please, please let me go! Why have you brought me here? Why have I been kept a prisoner all this time? In the name of mercy, will someone tell me?"

The clapped-out old lecher made a gesture to Martha Krankheit. She swiftly approached the panting, terrified captive and deftly grasped the hems of her modest brown cotton skirt and the chastely cut white nylon slip beneath it. She rucked the garments up over the victim's curvaceous hips. Making a snug roll of them, she then unfastened the two safety pins she had pinned to the bodice of her tunic, and secured Edith Garvin's garments so that they would not fall back down.

"Oh my God, what are you going to do to me? Who is it? In the name of mercy, I beg you! Who are you? Where am I? Why have I been brought here?" Edith Garvin wailed. She twisted her hips about, for the stress of her imprisonment was already beginning to prove an ordeal.

Judge Black's eyes were narrowed and burning with lust as he contemplated this scene. Edith Garvin was wearing white satin panties. Presented as she was, this final veil which hid her sexual charms from him was so stretched that it seemed to have become part of her very skin. It molded the full, fleshy hemispheres of her behind, and accentuated the ripe curves of her shuddering thighs by its contrast. The muscles of those luscious columns, and those of her delightfully curved calves, rippled and flexed under the gauzy nylon hose she wore.

Martha Krankheit watched her master anxiously for his slightest sign, for even though at this moment she was not the one incurring his disciplinary wrath, she

The Prisoner

knew very well that a single misadventure or mistake in executing his orders would condemn her to the same fate as this beautiful brown-haired captive in the pillory.

His prick was savagely swollen, thrusting out adamantly against the silk folds of the bathrobe. The sensation of being naked under the delicate, thin silk appealed to his hedonistic senses, sharpening his erotic imagination as well as his carnal lust. A patron of the arts, as he fancied himself, and a frequent (if somnolent) visitor to the local symphony, the Judge had once read that the composer Richard Wagner never wore anything but silk next to his body. He had quickly adopted that affectation as his own. It was indescribably exciting at this moment to feel his bare skin delicately caressed by the soft silk, to feel it brush against his straining cock, to feel himself virile and powerful, an artist, a veritable god-emperor. Edith would learn to understand this about him!

The silence in the strange room was broken only by the victim's sobs and gasps and by the Judge's quickened and heavy breathing. Martha Krankheit knelt beside him, her eyes fixed on Edith Garvin's jutting bottom. She was very pale and wide-eyed, but already, she had been thoroughly initiated into carnal servitude that at this moment she could only feel secretly grateful that the unknown female locked in the pillory before her was going to suffer, and not she herself. And at that moment, she was ready to do anything to add to the torment of the unfortunate Edith Garvin, if that meant that her own tender flesh would be spared.

The Judge glanced down at Martha Krankheit and he

read all this on her pale, frightened face. He grinned, gloating. The power this double life had given him made him feel reborn, like a young man. Seated on the bench in his courtroom, seeing lovely girls and women brought before him on one charge or another, pompously chiding them for their transgressions and then, with a kind of mournful solicitude, sentencing them to Welfare Island "for their own good," provided him with the most exquisite secret delight. For he well knew that, in a few weeks, he would preside over them in another capacity, that of executioner, torturer, ravager. A true devotee of sadistic joys, he savored the pleasures of anticipation; when he stared down with a benign smile upon some helpless woman who stood before him in his courtroom, it seemed to him that he could envision her stripped of the dress she was wearing, kneeling naked at his feet, her hands clasped in prayer, her eyes brimming with tears, and her naked breasts heaving with sobs as she begged him for mercy. It delighted him to conjecture about the exact quality of her charms when she was finally naked and enslaved, to imagine how she would behave under the lash or when her thighs were forced apart and a male prick was gouging the tight channel of her cunt. He was, he thought, a real sophisticate.

From the pocket of his robe he took another Havana Panatela, lit it, and suavely took a long drag, savoring its rich aroma. Then he blew a cloud of smoke toward the pillory and waited. Edith Garvin was still brokenly begging to know the identity of her captor and what he intended to do to her. As the fumes of the strong cigar reached her nostrils, she gasped and coughed. "Ohh—oh my God—who is there? Oh, speak to me! This is unbearable—have pity on me! I've done nothing. I demand to know why I am here! Please—it hurts me like this—my back is hurting so! Oh my God, if you have any mercy in you, tell me who you are!"

For answer, he sent another cloud of smoke in her direction. His face was a mask of lustful anticipation, and his cock was aching with the savage joy he had promised it.

Again she began to cough and gasp as the strong fumes wafted to her flaring nostrils. "Ohh—ahh—please—pl-please—who is it? Who's there?"

He chuckled softly, a soft sound that made Edith Garvin freeze in terror. Her body stiffened, and he could see the muscles surging out along her thighs and calves through the sheer brown fabric of her stockings. He approached now, transferring the cigar to his left hand as he extended his pudgy right forefinger toward her jutting bottom. Holding his breath, he approached the crevice shaped out by the tightly-stretched panties and mimicked his actions of five years past.

"Ahhhhhh! Ohhhhh! My God, please *don't*!" Her voice was frantic and agonized as she tried to swerve her hips away from his fat, stubby finger.

"You disappoint me, my dear," he purred. "I thought your memory would be much better than this."

"That—that—that voice—ohhh my God—no, no, it can't be—" she gasped, trying to reject the sudden dread that descended over her mind.

"But it is, my dear. Now that's better. I'm glad you're

beginning to remember. After our happy association in the past, it would grieve me to find that you didn't recognize me by now," Judge Black obsequiously declared.

"Mr. Black—oh my God—no, no, I can't believe it—where am I—oh my God, why have you done this?"

"It's *Judge* Black, now, my dear. And you disappoint me. When you were in my employ, weren't you aware of my legal abilities? Didn't you realize that I would go higher than the mere post of state's attorney, my dear?" he banteringly replied.

"But I don't understand—I came to Chicago and, oh …then it was all *your* doing—" she gasped.

"All of it, yes, my dear. That should flatter you, my charming Edith. To think that I remembered your charms so well after these five long years that I could not do without them."

"But this is insane! You—you kid-kidnapped me—that's what you did! Oh my God, let me go. Please let me go!"

"Come now, Edith, can it be that you are still as foolish as you were when you worked for me? But I've had reports that you're actually engaged to be married. Now surely, in these past five years—let me see, that would make you about thirty years old, wouldn't it?—you must have learned *something* about a man's desires for a luscious body like yours. As a matter of fact, seeing you like this in such an immodest pose and so scantily clad, I feel even more strongly about your charms than I did when you were my secretary. Yes, it seems to me, truly, my dear Edith, that your bottom and your thighs have taken on an even more enticing plumpness. Surely you can't have gone these last five years without some romantic experience, not with tempting charms like these."

With this, he passed his right hand over the surging cheeks of Edith Garvin's jutting bottom, and the young woman uttered a piercing cry and violently twisted herself away from that ignoble touch. "Gracious!" he laughed. "You seem to be even more sensitive than you were before."

"You—you filthy old beast! You know perfectly well why I quit my job! You know that I wouldn't work for a man who had no more respect for a woman than that —to do what you did!"

"You mean this?" the Judge guilefully asked as again his right forefinger prodded the narrow crevice of Edith Garvin's rectal fissure, pressing the soft material of her panties into her tender crack.

"Ohhh! Stop that, you disgusting pig. How dare you! Oh my God, if you're a judge, then the people who voted for you cannot know how vile and contemptible you are. You'll go to jail for this, for kidnapping me and treating me this way! Do you hear me? I demand that you let me go at once!" Edith shrieked, as she jerked from side to side.

Judge Black cleared his throat with an oratorical flourish. "Let me set forth your present situation, my dear Miss Garvin. You were brought here to claim an inheritance, and the people who helped transport you here to my house are all in my employ. You will receive that inheritance, with ample interest, I assure you. As

Judge of the Municipal Court, I have in my power to find you a vagrant and to sentence you to a correctional institution. No one can trace you here, and once you are imprisoned at Welfare Island, you will simply disappear from view. Even your fiancé, this Rosen fellow—and I shall have a good deal more to ask you about him in a few moments, my dear—won't be able to track you down. So my advice to you, my dear Miss Garvin, is to resign yourself to reality and to try to be less hostile to my displays of affection for your charming person."

The flowery rhetoric so dear to Judge Black's heart was, he fancied, the mark of an artistic and imaginative sadist. But Edith, unlike the almost naked girl who knelt beside the fat, greasy old lecher, was hardly aware of this. Again trying frantically to swerve her hips and wrench her wrists and neck out of the yoke holes of the pillory, Edith cried out, "I haven't the least interest in your *affection* for me, you repulsive idiot! It was criminal of you to have me kidnapped and brought here, and you know that perfectly well! And you can't legally hold me here. You know that, too!"

"I can, my dear, and I certainly *will*. But this is no way for two old friends to behave after five long years." His voice became soft and unctuous. "There's so much I want to know about you, my dear Miss Garvin. Particularly, how much you have learned about men in the last five years. Now then, my investigators tell me that you are 'engaged to be married.' Has this fiancé of yours seen you naked yet, or cuddled with you and put his hand under your skirt and felt your sweet little snatch?" The sudden transition from the gently solicitous words

The Prisoner

to crude obscenity struck Edith like the lash of a whip, and the Judge chuckled as he heard her horrified gasp. Then he resumed, "You must have learned something, my dear, or you wouldn't be shocked by that vulgar term for the dainty spot between those sweet thighs of yours. Martha, suppose we have a look at Miss Garvin's charms without the hindrance of those overly tight panties she's wearing. Be so kind as to drag them down as far as you can."

"Don't you *dare!* I forbid you to do that! You wicked, horrible old man! You have absolutely no right to treat me this way. I shall go to the police and complain, and then there'll be a real scandal! Oh, to think that a man who calls himself a judge should treat a decent woman like this!" Edith Garvin cried.

But Martha Krankheit, seeing the glitter in her master's eyes, had hastened to obey. She quickly fastened her fingers on the top of Edith Garvin's panties. The victim shrieked, twisted, and jerked herself in every way imaginable to try to avert the catastrophe, but the lovely golden-haired young woman tugged the waistband and shucked it down. Edith Garvin uttered shriek upon shriek and desperately tried to escape this outrage to her virginal modesty...for indeed, even though there had been a lapse of five years and she was now thirty, she still retained her maidenhead.

"Quickly, Martha, unless you're eager to have your own naked bottom soundly flogged," the Judge drawled. His bushy white eyebrows arched, and Martha Krankheit's heart sank at that sign which she recognized only too well. With a gasp, and with all her strength, she dragged down the panties to the middle of Edith Garvin's stocking-sheathed thighs and then drew back, trembling and pale with her own terror.

The beautiful brown-haired captive uttered a prolonged cry as she felt herself denuded before the eyes of her former employer. To him she made the most piquant and lasciviously exciting of spectacles, bent over with her neck and wrists captured in the yoke holes of the low pillory, her fleshy, olive-sheened buttocks jutting out, and the white satin sheath of her underwear twisted about her lower thighs and acting as a fetter of restraint.

The cheeks of Edith Garvin's naked bottom were magnificently sensual. They were round and solid upstanding hemispheres, whose warm olive skin was flawlessly soft and satiny. Even though she tried frantically to clench her thighs and to diminish her nakedness as much as possible, Edith could not help exposing the amber-shadowy groove that separated those glories. Nor could she hide the dark brown thicket of pussycurls that hid the edibly-pink lips of her virgin cunt and flourished along the inhibited and sensitive furrow that led from her mount of Venus to the dainty rosette of her equally virgin asshole.

His prick was now gigantic with longing, but as a man in love with the idea of sexual coercion and subjugation, Judge Black controlled his impulse to possess her then and there. Stepping to her left and placing his left palm on the small of her naked back, he glided his right hand over the cringing, tightening globes of her naked bottom. He delectated over the smooth, warm skin, tactilely appraising the elasticity of the jouncy hillocks

The Prisoner

and tracing their contours from the lasciviously jutting curves of their summits to the provocative swell of the base of her bottom just as it left the harmonious juncture of her full womanly thighs. Adding to his enjoyment was the convulsive interplay of the muscles of her bottom and legs, while she dug her nails into her palms and again tried desperately to wrench herself free from the pillory.

"What a magnificent ass you've got, Edith, my dear," he said pleasantly. "I wonder if your fiancé has ever felt you up. Tell me, my dear, have you and he been to bed yet?"

"Ohhh! My God, my God, take your filthy hand away from me! You disgusting, cowardly beast, I forbid you to touch me like that! I'm a decent girl, I'm going to be married, and he treats me with respect, I'll have you know! Oh stop it, stop it! You have *no right* to do this to me!" Edith Garvin was beside herself, and her voice was high-pitched and shrill with desperation as she twisted her bottom in a vain attempt to escape the sullying and lecherous caress of his pudgy hand.

"Can it be, from all these protestations, that you wish me to believe that you're still a virgin, my dear Miss Garvin?" he chuckled thickly. "I had thought that the excellent example I gave you five years ago might have turned you away from the ascetic life. You won't answer? Then I shall have to find out for myself, shan't I? Martha, stand there and hold Miss Garvin by the hips so that she won't twist around too much. And take care you hold her tightly, or I'll have you in one of those contraptions with *your* bare bottom stuck out for a good thrashing!"

Martha Krankheit did not need a second invitation; she hurried to the pillory, dug her slim, soft little fingers into the edges of Edith Garvin's olive-satin hips, and tensed herself. Judge Black chuckled again, and then slyly lowered his right forefinger and advanced it toward the thick cluster of dark pussycurls that shielded the succulent fig of Edith Garvin's exposed cunt.

The victim's body stiffened, and then a frenzied, hoarse shout burst from her: "Ahhhhh! Don't do that to me, you filthy brute—you dirty, horrible coward! Take your finger out of me right now and stick it up your *own* backside! No problem there—you can't have hemorrhoids, you're a perfect asshole!

For Judge Black's fingertip had pried through the thicket of silky pussydown, between the pink lips of that delicious cunt, and had penetrated up against the tight and resisting barrier of Edith Garvin's cherry! He had pressed in very hard, causing a twinge of pain; and in the midst of her shrieking protestations, the victim's voice had risen a full octave in pitch.

"I wouldn't have believed it, my dear," he said in a tone of feigned surprise, as he withdrew his finger and shook it at her waggishly. "Imagine that! At thirty still a virgin. This fiancé of yours must really be very backward. You'll have to send him to me, my dear Miss Garvin, so that I can give him a good lecture on what to do to you in bed once you're married. But that will be quite a while off, you know. Well, well, well! I congratulate you, my dear, for preserving your chastity at all costs for all this time. Why, you're practically a spinster at thirty, Miss Garvin. Don't tell me that you have the old-

The Prisoner

fashioned and quaint notion of saving your maidenhead for your wedding night? Yes, I guess that must be it. But I have first claim on it, you know."

"Ohhhh noooo! Oh dear God, help me, help me! Save me!" Edith Garvin shrieked to the impassive walls; but God's reply, if indeed there were one, was not evident to her.

"I think, Martha my dear," Judge Austin W. Black drawled, "we'll have those panties all the way off. And at the same time, you may as well roll Edith's stockings down to her ankles. I want to see as much of that lovely, warm, olive skin of hers as I can."

"Oh, please don't! How can you be so cruel, so inhumane, Judge Black?" the beautiful brown-haired woman cried, as she twisted herself and contracted all the muscles in her ass to diminish as much as she could the exposure of her naked behind—a tempting oasis of sexual pleasure as yet untried!

Martha had no time for compassion for poor Edith; she was concerned for her own safety, and she knew that the slightest hesitation in carrying out any of her master's orders meant that she would take Edith's place, either in the pillory, or in another of the cruel devices placed in this room for his sadistic amusement.

She therefore tugged at the satiny garment and dragged it off Edith's legs, whereupon the victim began to kick out and twist herself as she tried to prevent this last ignominious ceremony. Next Martha grabbed the top of Edith Garvin's left stocking and dragged it quickly down, making a neat roll of it at the captive's chiselled, olive-sheened ankle. Then, evading the victim's frantic kicks, she did the same with the other stocking, until Edith Garvin found herself naked from waist to ankles, bent salaciously over the wooden pillory, and unable to see what was to be done to her.

"What a magnificent ass, my dear! And you mean to tell me that your fiancé hasn't yet pinched or squeezed or goosed it—like this?" Suiting action to word, Judge Black once again inserted his right forefinger into the shadowy crevice separating Edith Garvin's ripe, resilient buttocks, and pried open the dark ring of her dainty asshole, lodging his finger up to the knuckle and then wiggling it about.

"*Oh dear God in Heaven stop that, stop that, in the name of human decency! You filthy, horrible, cowardly brute, to treat a helpless woman like this! Oh God, you're hurting m-me, please take it out, oh please take it out!*" Edith shrieked, and the pillory creaked as she jerked and twisted about, heedless of the bruises which the yoke holes administered to her neck and wrists. But all these violent movements only served to further inflame the Judge's lusts, for he could see the ample, olive-sheened cheeks of her behind jiggle and flex and contract in the most convulsive spasms imaginable, all of which set into relief the sensual glory of her voluptuous, mature, and still virginal body.

"But what I really can't get over, my dear Miss Garvin," he continued, with a smirk lighting up his fat face, "is that your fiancé has respected your cherry. I wonder, would he be so noble if he were here right now. On the other hand, perhaps he is the fastidious sort who would much rather have the work done for him in

The Prisoner

advance. That way he won't have the messy job of perforating your hymen, which at your advanced age of thirty must surely be very thick and resistant."

Edith Garvin was mortified at hearing her most intimate person discussed so callously, especially before an unknown female who was apparently aiding her cruel and vengeful ex-employer.

"Oh God, why are you doing this to me? I don't deserve such shame, such cruel treatment just because I did what any decent, self-respecting woman would have done in response to your reprehensible behavior five years ago!" she cried in despair.

"Let's say I'm a sentimental old fool, my dear," he smugly answered. Having withdrawn his finger from her asshole, he now began to caress the magnificently plump, firm, and velvety smooth cheeks of her squirming bottom, while the unfortunate young woman groaned and sobbed as she twisted hopelessly about, unable to evade his maddening touches.

"The fact is, ever since you stuck that luscious ass of yours in my face that memorable day, Miss Garvin, I've dreamed of nothing else but seeing it naked just like this and being able at long last to testify to my very earnest admiration for its tempting qualities. Martha, my dear, I think a good spanking on Miss Garvin's deliciously gravid bottom will make her more docile. You will apply it, my dear, and I trust you will give it to her quite smartly. I should say that about thirty good swats will be ample preparation for what I have in mind. By then her bottom should be well heated so that I can heat her front."

"Oh no! For God's sake, how can you do this to me?

How can you make that unfortunate girl help you torture and shame a helpless woman brought here against her will?" Edith cried.

But Martha Krankheit had already approached the half-naked captive in the pillory, braced her left palm against the small of Edith Garvin's naked, olive-sheened back, and, raising her right hand high over the condemned posterior, brought it down smartly with a noisy *SMACK!*

"Excellent, Martha! Excellent!" the Judge purred, his eyes devouring the bright pink outline of the young girl's palm, which was immediately imprinted on Edith Garvin's right buttock. "Give her twenty-nine more exactly like it, Martha, and you will have done me a service. And you may tell yourself, my dear Miss Garvin, while Martha spanks you, that if you had given me a little piece of tail five years ago, you would not now have your naked ass sticking out at me, nor would you be suffering so at the hand of a young woman whom I have rendered far more cooperative than you are. But perhaps with some training and a good session at the Island under the careful supervision of Marjorie Sayers, and the occasional physical examinations given by the prison's personal physician, Dr. Archibald Fenwick, you may yet turn out to make this fiancé of yours an enjoyable bedwarmer. You may proceed, Martha."

Stepping back and opening up his bathrobe so that it yawned to expose his hairy, paunchy, naked body and the gigantic thrust of this swollen prick, Judge Austin W. Black gazed with rapture on the scene before him. The young golden-haired servant, her eyes narrowed, her

The Prisoner

lips tight, assumed a severity worthy of a born executioner—an attitude evoked, needless to say, by her own dread of the man who was directing this insidious degradation of the other captive. Her hand rose and fell quickly but vigorously, for she did not need to be reminded that if her master found this spanking too benign, her own punishment would be nothing less than a sound whipping...one administered by a far more painful instrument than a human hand!

Edith Garvin ground her teeth and closed her eyes, striving with all her might to remain impervious to this humiliating and juvenile correction. The knowledge that she was being spanked on her naked bottom by her former employer via a young lady was absolutely annihilating to her pride, exactly as the Judge had foreseen it would be. But never having endured the slightest corporal chastisement throughout her life, she began to soon feel the stinging discomfort of those repeated smacks, as they alternated on the jutting cheeks of her bottom and soon covered the entire area with the flaming outlines of Martha Krankheit's palm.

By the twentieth spank she had begun to groan and twist herself about, for the cumulative heat generated in her sensitive bottom had become acutely irksome. By the twenty-fifth she sobbed, "Oh my God, oh stop it! It's vile to make her do this to me—ohh, it hurts—ohh, stop it!" And when the last blow fell with all of Martha's panting might against the base of Edith's right buttock, the half-naked captive tried to lunge forward while swerving her inflamed buttocks as she emitted a raucous and wordless cry of pain and spiritual despair.

"Very ably done, my dear," Judge Black murmured as he fondled his stiffening tool. "The next time I have occasion to punish you, Martha, remind me how well you performed just now and I promise to remit five lashes from whatever count I sentence you to."

"Yes, Master, thank you Master," Martha replied, blushing with shame, as her own insecure status was once more brought home to her.

"Well now, my dear Miss Garvin," the Judge continued in his mocking drawl, "that should make you feel more welcome here, I should think. You have no idea how exciting you look with your naked ass stuck out this way, and nicely red, like a tomato. Now that I consider it carefully, I see a few patches of skin that Martha apparently neglected. That will have to remedied, I think. But since this is a memorable occasion, our reunion together after five desolate years during which I have missed your company, Miss Garvin, I am going to let you have the pleasure of choosing the next order of business in our little program. Now then, pay close attention. Which is it to be? A sound spanking with a leather sole, which will make your bottom quite red and, I fear, quite hot, or are you ready at this point to ask me to undertake the difficult task of making a woman out of you? In a word, in the event that your vocabulary has not been enriched over the past years, my dear, would you rather be spanked on your bare ass until you can't stand it any more, or will you beg me to fuck you and break that tight cherry of yours, which has kept you so modest all this time? You have two minutes in which to make your decision, my dear Miss Garvin. Meanwhile, in order to

The Prisoner

stimulate your mental processes in so important a choice, I myself am going to aid you a little."

With this, he opened the velvet-covered case in which he kept the egret's plume and the thin, flexible little switch with which he had accomplished the subjugation of his enchanting golden-haired assistant.

Taking the egret feather and moving to the front of the pillory, he squatted down, his eyes blazing at the sight of the thick, dark brown bush of pussycurls that covered Edith's virgin cunthole. Slowly, holding his breath, he lifted up the feather and began to tickle her inner thighs, while she gasped and jerked convulsively, taken by surprise at this exquisitely titillating sensation instead of the stinging fire of the lash as she had expected. He continued this for a moment or two, then put the plume against the thickest mass of lovecurls at the apex of her muscular, olive-sheened thighs and began to tickle her cunthole.

"Well, my dear, you've got a minute left, I'd say," he cajoled.

"Oooooh, it's—it's vile—oh my God, stop it—oh you beast, you dirty, filthy, despicable beast, to do this to a woman—oh God, help me—oh Ben—Ben, save me from this horrible old man!" Edith Garvin wailed as she backed away and twisted herself in a desperate attempt to evade the caresses of the egret's plume.

"So," he rose in high dudgeon, "you think I'm an old man, do you, Miss Garvin? And you'd rather have your fiancé save you than have me teach you what it's like to be a woman, would you? Well, I shall make your decision for you, then. Martha, get me the leather sole. I am going to give your big ass a sound thrashing, Miss Garvin, and I am going to keep it up until you beg me of your own accord to fuck you—yes, my girl, fuck you and take your cherry. It's too bad that Ben couldn't have that privilege, but perhaps he'll be grateful to me in the long run for sparing him such a messy job. Now, if Dr. Archibald Fenwick were only here, he could do it for me. But you'll just have to put up with my implement, I'm afraid." He turned as his assistant brought him the slipper. "Thank you, Martha. Now, just to test the efficacy of this good leather sole, be good enough to bend over and hold your ankles and count five. Then you'll remind me the next time you're to be punished that I own you a remission of ten good spanks, you understand?"

Martha Krankheit had brought him a slipper with a black leather sole, murderously pliable and a good quarter of an inch thick. Grasping it by the heel, he waited until she had reluctantly—but obediently, all the same—bent over and grasped her slim ankles. This maneuver hoisted up the sheer black nylon tunic she wore well over her parabolically-curved bottomcheeks, and so he had the added stimulus of her unveiled and nubile loveliness to whet his carnal appetites, already grown ferocious through the exciting prelude with his major and most coveted victim, Edith Garvin.

"Don't move out of position, if you please, Martha. And count the spanks aloud," he instructed.

"Y-yes, M-master," the girl quavered. She closed her eyes and ground her teeth, relaxing her muscles and breathing deeply as she readied herself.

The Prisoner

With cruel deliberation, Judge Black rested his left palm on the small of her back. He then moved from side to side until he was assured of the proper angle. At last he raised the sole over the magnificent young behind. He hovered it in the air while poor Martha waited in dire suspense, and then it flashed down like a bolt of lightning, to flatten with a wicked *CRACK!* over the top of the girl's left hip.

"Ohh—*one*, Master," Martha groaned, unable to suppress a convulsive twisting of her hips and bottomcheeks.

"You monster, you heartless fiend, to brutalize that helpless girl and to treat me this way too," Edith Garvin sobbed as, once more, she tried to wrest her neck and wrists out of the implacable hold of the pillory. The second blow of the slipper attacked Martha Krankheit's upper right buttock, and the third—after a pause of nearly a full minute that made the unfortunate young girl moan and squirm restlessly—was applied full across the fleshiest curves of both bottomglobes, compressing the shadowy crack between the huddling, quivering hemispheres.

The final two were applied respectively to the base of the right, and then the left cheek, and each was tremulously counted out by the tearful captive, who did not forget to thank her lecherous master for this privilege of "testing" the implement on her.

"I trust you heard all that, Miss Garvin," the judge declaimed, as he placed himself at Edith's left and brandished the sole, "because that is the way it is going to sound, only louder, on your own naked ass. You needn't count either. I'm going to spank your big, juicy, naked ass, Edith Garvin, until you beg me to fuck you. So, now you know what is expected of you. Let us see if your sensitive bottom will overcome your scruples about retaining your virginity. Of course," he continued thoughtfully, "your resistance really doesn't matter. If this doesn't break you, something else will.

"In other words, you cheat, you flabby old short-stroke," Edith said bitterly. "This has nothing to do with whether or not I resist, or what you call my 'prudishness'." She spat the word at him. "You're just listening to your own voice run on and on, as usual, and you're going to do exactly what you please. And if it weren't for the fact that it'll hurt me, you know what your proposed plan would be?" Edith Garvin stared at the Judge intently for a moment. *"Boring,"* she said decisively. "It would be stupid and boring!"

At this direct blow to the most sensitive part of his person—that is, his vanity—the Judge's face turned an alarming shade, and he roared, *"Boring?!* I'll show *you* boring, young lady!" So saying, he began to apply the sole in wickedly horizontal blows over the misused, squirming, already uncomfortably inflamed hemispheres of Edith Garvin's naked posterior. Beginning with the tops of her hips and working down to the , he methodically and thoroughly regaled each cheek in turn, with about fifteen seconds between each loud and crisply sonorous *thwack!*.

Edith's eyes opened, drowned by tears that broke in rivulets down her contorted cheeks. Her nails dug into her sweating palms; her body jerked fitfully at every

The Prisoner

noisy crack of the leather sole against her swollen, steadily darkening bottom.

But the thought of humiliating herself by her extorted complicity, assenting to her torturer's rape of her maidenhead in exchange for relief from this atrocious and humiliating thrashing, proved at first too tremendous a barrier to be overcome. She believed that she could hold out, and perhaps win by her courage his grudging respect for her chastity. It was a pitiably ingenuous notion, for the longer she resisted, the more her groans and sobs and uncontrollably spasmodic twistings, wrigglings, kickings, and dancings roused his mounting lust.

Finally, at the twenty-fifth stroke, which bridged both hemispheres and seemed to pinch the pouting edges of those luscious bottomglobes together, Edith Garvin could bear the torture no longer.

"*Arrrgh!!* Oh my God in heaven, you're killing me, you're killing me, I can't bear such pain! Have mercy on me, have mercy! Surely you've had revenge enough by now, whatever I've done!"

"Why, not at all, Miss Garvin. Are you ready yet to ask me to be fucked?" he countered.

"Oh no! I'd rather die—*EEEOWWWOUUU!*" At her words, he had viciously brought down the sole, and with a downward sweeping movement the pliable leather implement bit against the upper, outer edge of her right bottomglobe. The pain had been excruciating, like a white-hot knife searing her oversensitized flesh. Her wild shriek and prolonged wild cry attested to the dreadful torture she was undergoing, one which had been so ingenuously supplemented by her having first heard the punishment of his young and lovely assistant.

"I will give you another chance before I continue," he said hoarsely, as he briefly lowered the sole. "Ask me to fuck you, to ram my cock into your virgin cunt, to take your cherry, and I'll stop thrashing your bottom. Otherwise, I may have to see whether a good cane or a leather martinet will persuade you more quickly."

"Kill me! I'd rather die than give myself to you, do you understand? I won't, I—*arrrhhhh!!* Oh dear God, let me die instead of suffering like this! *Oowwouuu! Aiiii! Eeeyarrhh!* Oh stop—no more, oh God, I can't bear it! Yes, yes, anything, only stop!"

Pitilessly, his teeth grinding with sadistic rage and lust, the white-haired judge had dug the fingers of his left hand into her tender belly. Then, standing up close, he applied a barrage of ten or twelve short, vicious, downward-biting cracks of the leather sole, all against the tender crease of those jutting hemispheres. It was too much. The unfortunate young woman shrieked out frenziedly as her body lunged and twisted, but she could not escape the ferocious thrashing.

"You ask me to stop? Very well, you know the alternative. Do you submit then?"

"Oh God, oh help me, oh Ben, where are you?" Edith Garvin babbled.

Thwack—thwack—thwack! Thrice the leather sole crashed against her naked bottom. Moving slightly backward, Judge Black had lowered the flexible leather implement and swept it up with all his might against the base of her bottom and into the shadowy groove itself.

The Prisoner

The pain was severe, and Edith Garvin relented at last, lunging and twisting, jerking her neck and wrists and rolling her eyes for effect, as she finally cried out: "Oh, bloody hell, all *right* then! No more!" When the Judge nevertheless went on with the beating, she added, in exasperation, "Yes, yes, oh, *do* it to me! Fuck me, fuck me! Anything except this dreadful whipping! Oh my God, I'm begging you to fuck me. In fact, I'll die if you don't fuck me right now. *Right now*, dammit—aren't you *listening*? Fuck me—oh dear *God*—oh Ben, forgive me, I can't *help* it any more—ooh baby, ooh baby, fuck me, Judge Black, fuck me now!"

The Judge dropped the leather slipper to the floor with a hoarse wheeze of greedy anticipation. At last, the moment had come for his supreme revenge!

Judge Austin W. Black rubbed his hands gleefully as he heard Edith Garvin's despairing supplications to be spared further abuse with the leather sole. "Now you're being really intelligent, Edith dear," he chuckled, as he proceeded to unlock the wooden pillory and take the petite, half-naked young woman in his arms while she sobbingly collapsed against him. "Let me slip off your blindfold because I want you to see what's going to happen to you, Edie baby." He chuckled. "So those virginal lips of yours have finally pronounced the word 'fuck.' You've made a great step forward in five years, but now I'm going to show you what the word really means. Let's see now, where shall we have your nuptial bed, hm?"

There was a low couch against the wall, to his left and the Judge said to Martha Krankheit, "Martha, help Edie slip off the rest of her clothes. I want her stark naked. And as fast as possible, or else!

"Yes, M-Master," the golden-haired slave expertly quavered. Gently, for now she could afford to show compassion for her fellow captive, the girl opened the safety pins that held Edith Garvin's skirt and slip up about her waist, and drew the garments over her head. Edith allowed this, overcome by a vexatious fit of tears in her supreme humiliation. She still wore spectacles, which gave her near-nudity a most exciting flavor in the Judge's eyes. Martha now removed Edith's brassiere, and then knelt down and slipped off the stockings she had rolled down earlier until Edith Garvin stood divinely naked.

The corrupt old lecher caught his breath in undisguised admiration at the sight of her beautiful breasts, her nipples broad as the whale-shouldering sea. They were firm and resilient, looking marvelously utilitarian in spite of Edith's as-yet-childless status.

"Marvelous, really marvelous, Edie," he breathed.

"Edith," she snapped back at him.

He thoughtfully put a finger on his lips, and then continued on serenely: "Martha, suppose you undo that tacky chignon of Edie's and let her hair down. It was passable if uninspired with the skirt and blouse ensemble, but it's entirely the wrong coiffure for her current look."

Martha swiftly obeyed. Edith tried to put a hand back to prevent this, but even that simple movement made a new wave of hot torment seethe through her bottom. She at once rushed both hands back to those succulent hemispheres and began to rub them energetically, heedless of the nakedness and vulnerability of her loins before this man whom she had every reason in the world to fear and loathe.

The Judge now let his bathrobe slip to the floor and was naked in his sandals. His prick was enormously stiff and throbbing, and it was all he could do to contain himself.

"What a shame," he said with mock solicitude. "Your ass hurts you a little, doesn't it, Edie? Never mind, you'll find it will make a new woman of you once you feel yourself getting fucked. That's true, isn't it, Martha? When a girl's ass has been thoroughly thrashed, she's so hot and squirmy that she wriggles when she feels a man's cock inside her cunt. Martha, tell Edie right now how true that is, from you own experience," he cackled.

A violent blush suffused Martha's pale cheeks, and she could not help clenching her fists. She shot Edith a significant look, then demurely said, "Oh yes, what the master says is true. Whenever he—he—whips me—I always feel *much* more passionate."

"Charmingly put, Martha. Don't you think so, Edie? Go ahead, Martha, help her to the couch and put a cushion under her ass. It'll ease the pain, and then I'll take over and make her forget it entirely!" He chuckled, in rare good humor now that his plan had come to complete fruition.

Martha, in the short diaphanous tunic, helped the still-sobbing captive over to the couch, pulled one of the cushions out to the middle and patted it. "There you are," she said with a wan smile, doing her best to keep this unfortunate woman from feeling rancor toward her. She longed to tell Edith Garvin that she hadn't wanted to give her that shameful spanking, that had been forced to because otherwise she herself would have been in terrible danger. Of course, she would have been exposing herself to the same danger if she had dared express her thoughts, and so she wisely kept silent.

Very reluctantly, wincing and groaning, Edith slowly seated herself on the cushion, and then closed her eyes as a violent shudder passed through her naked body. Her chaste shyness suddenly came back to her, and she put an arm around her heaving titties and pressed her other hand over the furry thicket of her virgin cunthole. Then she bowed her head and burst into hysterical sobs.

"Now don't start that again, Edie," the Judge said thickly as he approached the couch, his prick bobbing with every step. "Just in case you have ideas about going back on your bargain, I've brought along the leather sole, and Martha here will hold you down while I really give it to your tender ass if you don't get ready now for your fucking."

"Yes," his voice grew hoarse with gloating delight, "for five years I've wanted to see you like this, Edith Garvin naked, on the couch, with your legs spread and your cunt ready to be fucked. Do you understand me, my girl? And now the moment is here. *Will* you stop that crying?" He tightened his lips and lifted up the leather sole, delivering a cruel blow across the top of her left thigh. Edith screamed and grabbed for the wounded spot, lifting her

The Prisoner

head and staring at him with agonized eyes behind her thick spectacles. "Now will you be a good girl and get ready for your fucking, or do you want some more?"

"Oh no, no, please no!" Edith groaned. "Oh, p-p-please tell me what to do—I can't stand any more pain, I just can't!"

"Now that's being sensible, my dear. I'll tell you what to do. Lie back now…that's it! Now lift up your legs in the air. Martha, kneel behind Edie and help her as I tell you to. Good. Now then, Edie, grab hold of the backs of your knees and pull them tight against your tits. That's the girl! Martha, reach out and hold her calves so she doesn't lose that delightfully inviting pose of hers!"

It was true: never had Edith Garvin been more clinically exposed than at this moment when, stark naked, her buttocks upturned, her knees drawn back against her breasts, she displayed to the eyes of her ravisher the furry nest of her virgin cunt. The presumably pink lips could not quite be seen in the exaggerated and lascivious straddle of her beautifully rounded bare legs, but the tableau was made even more exciting because the golden-haired helper, kneeling behind Edith's head, was leaning forward to grasp the young woman's calves tightly and expose that virgin slit. On Martha's own exquisitely lovely face there was the shadow of her fear of and anger at this white-haired man whose power reached even beyond the state line.

"Now then, Edie, I'm going to make a woman of you. I'm going to put my prick into that sweet little slit of yours, and I warn you, it may hurt at first till I break that stubborn cherry of yours. That's why Martha's going to hold you in position, so you won't wiggle too much and make me slip out of you before the job's done. And you'd better not try anything, my girl, or back you'll go into that pillory, and this time I'll use the leather sole on those big titties of yours, and on the insides of your bare legs where it'll hurt the most, believe me! Or I might even give you a switch instead of a cock right up this dear little cherry spot of yours. You mean to tell me that Ben has never even *seen* this sweet little cunny? He poked playfully at her pussy with his forefinger.

Edith burst into heartrending sobs as she moaned, "Oh Judge, I can't stand this. Do it and finish it for the love of heaven! What more do you want of me? I can't stand any more torture. Do it to me, but at least end it and be merciful!"

"Who would have thought that chaste Miss Edith Garvin, glasses and all, would be lying stark naked with her knees pulled up against her titties and her cunt spread open, and her dainty little brownhole too, begging to be fucked by the man whose face she had slapped just because he goosed her five years ago?" the Judge gloated as he licked his lips. Crouching now and putting his hands on the wide couch to either side of Edith's shuddering body, he edged himself forward until the stiff head of his prong made contact with the furry fronds covering her exquisite pink cleft. "Pull those knees of hers back just a bit more, Martha," he instructed. Edith uttered a sobbing groan as she felt her titties mashed by her own knees, and at the same time felt the presentation of her loins and buttocks to the rampant cock of her former employer.

The Prisoner

Then she uttered a horrified gasp, her eyes bulging behind the thick spectacles. His prickhead had edged between the outer lips of her cunt, and she squirmed uneasily as he pushed forward. Suddenly her body stiffened. His spearpoint was up against the tough hymenal seal of the maidenhead which still denied his access to her hitherto unprofaned vagina.

"It's going to take a little work to plow through this defense of yours, Edie," he gloatingly informed the weeping young woman. "Martha, wriggle yourself over Edie's face until your pussy is right over her mouth. Now then, Edie, to take your mind off what's happening, you're going to suck and kiss and tongue Martha's sweet little pussy."

"Oh no! In mercy's name, don't make me do a thing like that! Oh please don't! I—I'm ready—I'm ready for my—I'm ready—but don't make me help you humiliate this poor innocent girl!" Edith protested, weeping.

"Innocent!" the Judge sneered. "This little bitch could earn her keep in a whorehouse after all she's learned under my expert tutelage. Isn't that so, Martha?" His narrowed eyes told the golden-haired girl that complete acquiescence to his will was her only safe course. She understood this, and quickly said, "Oh yes, that's true, I do my best to please my master! The best thing for a girl to do is to make Judge Black happy with her, Miss Garvin!"

"There, you see, Edie?" he purred sadistically. "Now then," his voice grew harsh and inflexible, "start licking Martha's cunt if you know what's good for you!"

Out of a sudden anguished compassion, indiscreet

and dangerous, but certainly pardonable, the young slave-girl hastily whispered to the victim over whose tear-stained face she crouched, "You have to do it, Miss Garvin, please! I—I want you to! He—he'll really whip you awfully bad unless you do everything he wants. I know!"

Judge Black pretended not to hear this, but he made a mental note to "reward" Martha for it later, though in fact he was not altogether displeased. "Get ready, Edie," he said. "I'm going to break through this cherry of yours if it takes all night!"

Martha at once tightened her hold on Edith's muscular calves, lowering herself till her own blond pussycurls rubbed against the woman's shrinking mouth. Edith couldn't believe what was happening to her as Martha's pussy hovered over her face. She could see the thick outer lips covered with curly blond hairs separate as the girl parted her legs and straddled her head. The deeper red interior of the girl's cunt seemed to shine with moisture from the deep canal. A sharp, musky odor assaulted Edith's nostrils as Martha used her own slim fingers to pull apart the outer lips, exposing even more of the tantalizing inner flesh.

"Hurry up," grunted the Judge, not wanting Edith to have time to acclimate herself to the task she was being forced to perform—a task so foreign to her reserved personality.

With a start, Martha squatted suddenly, covering Edith's mouth before the stunned woman had a chance to protest.

"Ah, that's better," the Judge chuckled, "but I don't

think Edith's quite got the knack yet. Am I going to have to teach you everything, my dear? Stick out your tongue now, Edie, and move it around on dear little Martha's cunt. That ought to get you started."

Her sobs muffled by the girlflesh covering her mouth, Edith tentatively extended her tongue, quickly recoiling at the odd sensation of slick flesh on her tonguetip. She could feel the Judge's fingers digging into her thighs, and she opened her mouth again before he could realize that she wasn't doing as he had ordered. This time, a little more accustomed to the taste and the odd sensation, Edith extended her tongue and ran it all over what she could reach of the pussy poised above her. Martha, deciding she might as well get as much enjoyment out of the situation as she could, moved her torso up and down, sliding her cunt over Edith's rigid tongue.

Edith, warming to the task and eager to take her mind off her ex-employer who, she knew, was staring at her own exposed pussy, sucked and licked at Martha's cunt as it moved above her. She quickly realized that Martha was, with greater frequency, grinding the small nub of flesh at the top of her slit against her tongue, encouraging her to explore that rigid flesh in the midst of all the soft tissue around it.

Obligingly, Edith opened her lips and sucked Martha's clitoris into her mouth. Martha's groan of pleasure told Edith that her efforts were appreciated, and she attacked the tiny organ with more intensity. Suspecting that such concentrated effort might be too much for the girl above her, Edith let go of the little sentinel and plunged her tongue deep into the cunthole. She lapped at the hole and then caught one of the labia majora between her own slippery lips and sucked on it. The squeals of delight she could hear despite the firm thighs covering her ears pleased her. Realizing that her hands were free, she brought them up to cup the younger girl's buttocks, kneading the firm hemispheres in her hands even as the Judge passed his gnarled hands over her own bottomglobes. Feeling that this way at least *someone* was having pleasure, Edith moved her hands hesitantly toward the girl's cunt, feeling her own cunt being attacked by those other, male hands. As she slid her fingers over the slick flesh, seeking out the tiny nub that had seemed to be the center of pleasure for Martha, the Judge's fingers sought out her own clitoris, causing Edith to gasp. She still didn't know the name of that fleshy nubbin, but she was beginning to understand the pleasure it could bring her.

As the Judge continued to explore her exposed cunt, Edith once again sucked the miniature girl-erection into her mouth. She sucked deeply, at the same time flicking the tip inside her mouth with her tongue. Feeling that some crisis was about to happen, she plunged three fingers of one hand deep into the girl's cunt. Martha's reaction was immediate; grinding herself furiously against Edith's mouth and grasping the delving fingers with her cunt muscles, Martha screamed her pleasure and rocked mindlessly on the prostrate virgin's face.

Violently excited by the tableaux being played out before him, and feeling the first slick moisture of Edith's excitement, Judge Black grabbed his turgid prick and positioned it at Edith's soon-to-be opened cunt.

The Prisoner

Then, with a grunt, Judge Black thrust himself violently against the resistant barrier to his rutting bliss, and Edith Garvin uttered a strangled scream that was muffled as Martha desperately ground her cunt against the young woman's mouth, while at the same time pulling Edith's calves toward her so as to keep her open for the sacrificial spear of destiny that would at once transform her and rob her of her cherished virginity.

Setting his teeth, the Judge drew back a little, and then lunged forward with all his strength. There was a piercing shriek and Edith Garvin's body jerked and twisted on the pillow; her face moved from side to side, her mouth rubbing against Martha's cunt. It was a wordless cry which expressed an eon of torment and despair, and the hopeless realization of the supreme disaster that could befall a chaste virgin. For the savage brunt of his thrust had broken through Edith's hymen, and Judge Austin W. Black was lodged to his balls inside her tight and quaking cunthole!

Edith barely had time to get over the pain of the brutal entry and the shocking feeling of fullness before the Judge began to thrust slowly in and out of her aching cunt. With so much going on, Edith hardly noticed the climactic convulsions of Martha, still poised over her gaping mouth. She didn't notice when Martha let go of her calves, a restraint no longer needed since the Judge was now holding her bent knees as he plowed himself deeper into her with every forward thrust. Concentrating on the never-before-experienced sensation of a male organ entrenched within her newly opened pussy, Edith barely noticed when Martha left her come-drenched face. The satiated girl stood next to the couch, confused as to what her role was to be now.

Her view unobstructed, Edith was forced to see what was being done to her. She gasped as she watched the ivory shaft of the Judge's cock pistoning in and out of the opening it had seemingly created.

Noticing Edith's interest in her own ravishment, the Judge pulled his rampant prick all the way out of his former secretary's cunt and let her look at it.

Edith's gaze took in the flared head of Judge Black's cock, streaked with her own blood; she looked at the thick column of hard flesh that had so recently been inside her, dropped her eyes to his hair-covered sac swinging pendulously between his legs—and her own. While she watched, the Judge grasped his weapon and rubbed the tip of his cock against her rigid clitoris. Edith gasped, realizing that this was her own version of the protrusion that had brought so much pleasure to the Judge's beautiful assistant. Pleased with Edith's intense reaction despite her newly initiated status, the Judge made a great show of aiming his staff once again towards his captive's cunthole and slowly, inexorably penetrating her once again. Edith could hardly believe her eyes as she watched the length of the Judge's tool disappear within her. He pushed down on her bent knees, lifting her cunt up and applying even more pressure against his straining cock. He groaned, thrusting faster and faster, ramming himself into the woman who had so stupidly denied him all those years ago.

Martha looked down on the fucking couple, and her heart went out to the poor woman who was experiencing

The Prisoner

sex for the first time right before her eyes—experiencing it much the same way as she had that memorable first time—at the hands and cock of her cruel taskmaster. Glancing quickly over at the sadistic Judge and noticing that his eyes were closed, Martha reached out and began to fondle Edith's breasts, which were jiggling in rhythm with the Judge's thrusts. Noticing the perky nipples stiffening in appreciation of this soft touch, Martha brought her other hand into play, running it over the woman's stomach and tickling the curly hairs at the apex of her cunt. Edith's eyes locked onto the adoring gaze of her new friend, and she smiled, silently thanking the girl for her ministrations.

Martha smiled in return. She was taking an enormous risk, but Edith had shown her more pleasure than she had experienced since being taken and held prisoner in this house. She only hoped that she could bring this woman to climax before the Judge spurted into her and realized what was going on under his own sweating body. Martha's slim fingers worked past the curly hairs and twirled around Edith's lovebutton. She quickly flicked the upstanding flesh back and forth, trying to communicate to Edith with her eyes and her caressing hands that she should try to get some pleasure out of the ordeal.

Edith didn't need much encouragement. After years of self-denial and pure thoughts, she felt the crisis overtaking her almost immediately. She gave herself up to the combined stimulation of the Judge's viciously thrusting cock and Martha's gentle caresses, and almost shouted with joy as her body was racked with great shuddering tremors. Her cunt muscles contracted, squeezing the Judge's cock and coaxing the sperm out of his prickhead and into the undefended depths of her own trembling body.

TURKISH DELIGHTS

Major Hakim Istefan scowled at the sheaf of papers on his desk, lit a long Turkish cigarette, and shuffled through them. He was forty-nine, lean, and weather-beaten, his head was bald and a supercilious black moustache adorned his thin upper lip. His ears were almost those of a faun —close to his skull, and his eyes were dark and hollow, his nose hawk-like. His slanting cheekbones gave him an Oriental mien, and indeed his grandfather had married a savage and passionate Tartar girl from Irkutsk while on vacation in that desolate terrain.

He was one of the most dreaded men in Constantinople, and not without reason. For Major Hakim Istefan was secret Chief of Intelligence, somewhat more than a glorified police chief of the city, and with far more martial powers. As a boy of fourteen, he had been a smuggler in the Balkans, joined the Turkish Army at twenty, suffered the ignominy of being whipped through the barracks while holding on to a gun butt and drawn along the double row of jeering soldiers by two corporals, while sticks, batons, switches, and leather belts slashed at his back and wiry shoulders.

Yet, just three years later, he had been appointed lieutenant of a small Turkish garrison in Munimez, about hundred miles to the north-west of Constantinople. There, against a secret attack by the Greek federalist troops, he had distinguished himself with such valor, as well as butchery, that he had been promoted to the rank of major. And although he still held the same military title more than twenty years later, the mere mention of his name was enough to send a shiver of terror through the bodies of those on whom he preyed.

The two Balkan wars had helped him distinguish himself as an active counteragent against Greek, Armenian, and Serbian spies who infiltrated into Constantinople to learn the strength of the Turks. The squat gray building on Rasouli Street housed his well-trained staff, and, in the cellar, isolation cells and torture chambers. One must remember that, except for the area south of Bulgaria and east of Greece on the European continent, Turkey lies in Asia, occupying the peninsula of Asia Minor, across the Black Sea from Russia and across the Mediterranean from Egypt. Its locale thus partakes of many Oriental influences and for centuries the people of the Orient have been noted for their methods of coercional persuasion, to use a euphemistic term.

Turkish Delights

But Major Hakim Istefan, apart from his own cruel Tartar blood, had still another reason for his sadistic persecution of all luckless victims who were brought into his luxuriously furnished private office at the back of the first floor of this building. He was impotent, and he had been rendered so by a woman.

At the age of twenty-nine, having already cut a swath among the maidenheads of many a beautiful girl in the villages where he was stationed, the tall, cadaverous-looking Turkish Intelligence head had fallen in love for the first time. It had been with a lovely Greek girl of nineteen from Delphi.

In that mystic and ancient city where once the fabulous oracle was consulted by the great and the near-great to learn the will of destiny, there was perhaps an ironic paraphrase of the legend when Irenee Vespegalos consented to wed the tall young officer.

Her face was a cameo-like oval, slim as a reed, with white skin like marble. Her voice was soft and gentle, her eyes deep blue like the Mediterranean, and she seemed permeated by the most docile and naive nature.

But what Hakim Istefan did not remember was that, three years before, while engaged in a mountain skirmish with marauding guerrillas he had stabbed a slim blond young man in mountaineer's costume who had crept into his camp and tried to assassinate him. And that young man had been the brother of Irenee Vespegalos.

Major Hakim Istefan did not learn this until his wedding night, and it had very nearly cost him his life. He had taken the virginity of his beautiful young bride, consoled her tears and fallen asleep with a smile on his face, triumphantly glorying in the proof of his manhood that appeared on the blood-stained sheets that had been hung outside his bridal tent to proclaim that the union had been consummated.

He woke with a sudden pain lacerating him. Blinking his eyes, he saw his gentle bride kneeling before him, the bloody knife in her hand. She had stabbed him in the side as he lay naked and defenseless.

"Filthy Turkish pig! Butcher! Rapist and defiler of honest women!" she spat at him. "You do not remember the man you killed in the mountains, the one who came into your camp to rid the world of your loathsome presence. But he was my brother. And tonight I avenge him!"

With this, she made another lunge at his heart, but Major Hakim Istefan rolled over onto his side and escaped the blow. He seized Irenee's wrist and tried to wring the knife from her, but in a last hysterical gesture of unbounded hatred for him, she wrenched her wrist free and slashed at his cock. The sweeping blow cut off his testicles and very nearly damaged his scrotum. His shrieks of agony brought his orderly into the tent. The latter, seeing what had happened, struck Irenee on the head with the butt of his revolver, then disarmed her. But from that night forth, Major Hakim Istefan could never again bury his hitherto invincible weapon in the tight, warm sheath of a passionate cunt; and he hated all women with the helpless fury of a man who was once their lord and master and had become an object of derision.

Turkish Delights

No one had ever dared to laugh or mock his powerlessness. He had other ways of gratifying his brooding, inimical hatred and lust. When he saw an aristocratic young woman strung up by the thumbs with her bare toes a scant inch from the wooden planks of the floor, heard her babbling hysterically for mercy and saw her twist her contorted face over her shoulder to watch Sergeant Bekir's arm raise the leather whip, when he saw her body jerk under the lash and saw the welts spreading on her tender flesh, then his depraved and thwarted instincts of passion were more than satisfied.

Few women ever left his office after having once gone in there, for usually they left via the back door into a van that transported them to a house of ill fame. This if they were lucky, to be sure. There were many women who prayed for death and were not given that boon of mercy in the cellar torture chambers of the ominous-looking building on Rasouli Street.

And of all the women who came before him for this or that reason, suspect as spies, as prostitutes who had not bothered to consult with the police to take out a license, as thieves or smugglers, he hated Greek women most of all. The ancient feud between those two countries lived in Major Istefan. And there were times when, directing the torture or himself applying it in one of the special cells in that damp cellar, he would imagine that the naked girl or woman wriggling and twisting and shrieking before him was the reincarnation of his faithless, traitorous Irenee.

To be sure, Constantinople, with its mixture of Oriental and European culture, such as the superlative Adbulla

Effendi Restaurant on the main street, the ancient Byzantine hippodrome, Constantinople's oldest church known as St. Irene, and the fabulous Yerebatan Cisterns, had long attracted cosmopolitan tourists from all over the world. Even in those days before the Austrian archduke was murdered at Sarejevo, his own work had been complex enough, ferreting out smugglers, international jewel thieves, brigands of all species, and conniving females who sought to gain entrance into the inner circles of the army and the diplomatic corps so that their price might set high on their bodies and they might turn another quiet profit when they blackmailed their casual lovers.

But now his work was intensified, for every beautiful woman was a potential spy, to his mind, just as she was a faithless, shameless whore when the necessity arose for it. He would not indeed, have credited the fat, complacent, fifty-year-old favorite wife of the Sultan with honesty or honor just because she was a female because she could, if it so suited her, deceive and betray her own Exalted Lord.

Unlike the Sultan, Major Hakim Istefan believed in nothing so merciful as the bowstring, or the sack into which a faithless wife could be sewn and hurled into the Bosphorus. He infinitely preferred the subtle and devious apparatus that he had had installed as soon as he had been given his new assignment and rank. It meant that in this entire teeming city, he alone might have an aristocratic woman undress before him in her shame, and defying her protests.

He might have her ravaged before his eyes or

Turkish Delights

buggered by the lowliest of his soldiers. And he could draw from her the most abject, pitiful babblings of mercy, offering to do anything in the world to stop the kiss of the *bastinado*, the piercing of her tender flesh in the most intimate regions by sharp, heated bamboo splints, or the nipping of her vulva and nipples with a pair of silver sugar tongs—a bridal gift from Irenee herself.

That treacherous bitch had had a jeweler engrave her initials on those tongs, and whenever he used them, he stared at the tiny amethysts that spelled the initials of her maiden name, and remembered. And when the victim before him would writhe and shriek an inhuman, prolonged cry, his lips twisted and his eyes grew bleak with remembered hate.

Irenee had paid him back for his loss of manhood by the degradation of her own womanhood. He had her staked out naked, between four heavy wooden stakes in front of his tent, her legs straddled widely and a sharp pointed wooden post planted under her belly to compel her to arch her loins and bottom to avoid impalement.

Indeed, the ancient sultans of Turkey had favored impalement as capital punishment for traitors. But theirs was perhaps more spectacular: lifting a man or woman up and then down so the spiked post entered the rectum. Then the hands and legs would be bound with yielding cords, ingeniously contrived so that gradually they would impale themselves upon the fatal stake. But death would be long and unspeakably terrible in coming.

At his order, Irenee had been buggered by twenty of

his strongest soldiers, all privates. Then she had been given the *bastinado* on her heels and tender soles. After that she had been smeared with honey so that the heat of the day brought flies. She had turned her face towards his tent and implored death, but that would have been too easy. His subaltern had been ordered to drive the flies away and to wipe off the honey with a wet cloth. Then she was whipped on her buttocks and between the legs until she fainted. And after that, she was ravished by a dozen men who thrust their stiff cocks into her bloodied, whip-lacerated vulva until the agony and her own weakness slowly forced her down upon the pointed stake. She did not die until dawn of the next day, and he lay on his couch gloating over her cries and incoherent, maddened entreaties.

The Sultan himself had given Major Hakim Istefan an ivory-handled riding crop made of supple, polished white leather as a mark of favor, for the first month of the war, as a reward for having brought to justice a dangerous Greek spy and his mistress. The woman had been so exceptionally beautiful that, before she had been executed, she had been blindfolded and stripped naked, and the Sultan himself entered her cell and fucked and buggered her.

But there was a nest of spies operating out of Constantinople and he felt they were mainly Greeks who sought to learn by their perfidious ways what the Turkish army intended doing about the Dardanelles. Distrusting Greece as he did as the result of his fatal marriage, the Turkish Intelligence head firmly believed that the Greeks might go over to the Allies and help them in an offensive that would destroy Turkey or at least divert all naval and military forces to the Dardanelles, and thus leave Constantinople itself vulnerable. From time to time, he had been given reports that attractive young women had been interrogated at small army posts not far from the Dardanelles and Gelibou, but thus far there had been nothing to lead him to their master. That master must be a man, he believed, for those women who had been interrogated had been able to keep silent under even the most hideous tortures and had died without revealing the identity of 'N.' Could it be Nicholas Estofari, the fat grain merchant who had made such lavish gifts to the Sultan so as to ingratiate himself at the palace? It was possible. The fat old fool was notorious for his whoring, but Major Hakim Istefan somehow could not believe that a man like that could have surrounded himself with such faithful and stoic young beauties who would die rather than reveal the name of their master.

No, it must be someone else, someone who knew almost from the War Ministry itself, what was being planned. A traitor in the higher echelons was more dangerous, for he was certain to be on the best of terms with the highest officials, and perhaps even the Sultan himself.

He lifted the riding crop and slashed it down at the offending papers. Then there was a knock at the door, and Sergeant Gruila Bekir entered and smartly saluted.

Sergeant Gruila Bekir was his chief torturer and interrogator. The man was squat, nearly bald, and almost toothless. But, at fifty, he was still as redoubtable a cocksmith as he had been when he was a boy. The man was a rogue and ought to have been hanged a thousand times over, but he was invaluable to his master; in the guerrilla warfare in the Balkans he had twice saved the life of Major Hakim Istefan. More than that, he knew how to procure an attractive female who might give the tortured intelligence head a few hours of diversion, for, although Major Hakim Istefan could no longer fuck, he could amuse himself with his lips and his cruel talon-like fingers, or force the handle of his riding crop into the quaking cunt or the shuddering bottomhole of a haughty beauty.

Or again, he could force her under that same whip to crouch between his legs and to lick at his disfigured, incomplete prick, the insides of his thighs and his bottomhole, and to wallow in the degradation that succeeded in giving him such triumph as he could still enjoy from the treacherous bitches.

"Well, idiot," he growled, but the noncommissioned officer grinned, understanding that his cruel master thus revealed a kind of special fondness for him.

"Excellency Major, a really choice piece this afternoon! Bedrack just brought her in."

"Ah! Tell me about her. It's been a tiring day and I'm in need of a little vacation. So are you, and you would play Zeus to Europa, I'll be bound."

"The major is very clever, but he knows that his sergeant has little schooling and therefore cannot always understand his fine terms," the sergeant grinned to show his nearly toothless gums.

"No matter. But to fully educate you, Bekir, Zeus is

Turkish Delights

the Greek name given to the king of the gods in the olden days. And Europa was a beautiful girl at the riverbank whom the god desired. So he transformed himself into a bull, Bekir, and fucked her. There! Do you understand that?"

"Oh, yes, yes, Excellency Major!" the sergeant cackled, bobbing his bald head repeatedly. "Very good!"

"Now, go on with your story. What about this choice morsel Bedrack has brought to us? What's her name, what's she accused of, and and what do you propose to do to her? You know I value your opinions in these matters."

"She's nice, very nice, and with big breasts and such an ass, Excellency," Sergeant Bekir's pudgy hands described fantastic circles in the air. "Her name is Nicea Korolos, Excellency. She claims to be from Athens, only she doesn't have a passport, and when Bedrack went to the Hotel George to check on her papers, her maid was very impertinent with him and slapped his face for daring to question her mistress."

"And then?"

"He had them both taken in, Excellency."

"Two of them, eh? You will tell Bedrack I'm going to give him corporal's stripes for bringing in such fine merchandise, and for being so thoughtful, and you'll stand him a drink tonight, at least that. Now let's have these two bitches in and we'll see what to do with them. Is your whip hand as eager as ever?"

"Surely, Excellency Major! Good hard whip on bare ass. That'll teach the bitches not to come to Constantinople and fool with us, won't it, Excellency Major?"

A few moments later, two deliciously attractive young

women were led in by the grinning private who had taken it upon himself to arrest them and bring them in because their papers were not in order. He saluted his superior officer, turned on his heel and disappeared, and the fat bald sergeant ambled forward to stand between the two as they stared across Major Hakim Istefan's cluttered desk.

Nicea Korolos was an enchanting beauty of about twenty-seven. Her pale golden hair was coiffed in a loose knot at the back of her head, leaving her ears bare and her forehead displayed in all its high-arching purity. She had a dainty, aquiline nose, a soft, sweet mouth, and large blue eyes.

"I am an actress from Athens, and this is my maid, Euphrosyne Sapiros, who is also from Athens," she said indignantly. "I was to give a performance tonight at Medea, but, because of this silly war, half of my baggage has been lost in transit. Undoubtedly, my passport and other papers are in it. But I assure you that if you make inquiry, at the Nogelu Theater and ask of the manager, Mr. Antonescu, he will tell you exactly who I am! This is an indignity and I protest it! We Greeks have nothing to do with this war, and I have come here to entertain the people of your barbaric country."

"Gently, Nicea, gently," he chuckled, enjoying the look of indignation that sparkled in her eyes and the color that flamed in her cheeks at the use of her first name. "Anyone can walk in here and claim she is the wife of the Sultan, but then she has to prove it. This Antonescu, he is an oily character who ought to have been hanged long ago. However, to relieve your anxiety

Turkish Delights

and to prove to you that we are not quite so barbaric as you think I am going to send one of my men over to the theater to find him. Meanwhile, you will wait in a special little room that we provide for strangers, until, of course, your identity is established. After that, of course, you will have permission to go. Bekir!"

"Sir?"

"Escort these ladies to the waiting chamber."

The fat, bald, toothless sergeant grinned. The two attractive women, exchanging a fearful glance, dubiously followed him. He led them down the stairs to the damp cellar, along whose corridor there were cells and even more ominous-looking heavy metal doors that opened into torture chambers. When he reached the end of the corridor, he took out a key and opened one of the metal doors, shoved them into the cell, slammed the door, and turned the key in the lock behind them with a guffaw of salacious laughter. It would be dark inside, but the bitches would soon discover what delightful little furnishings were there for their benefit!

An hour later, Private Dostri Bedrack knocked at the major's office, was admitted and confided to the cadaverous-looking sadist that the manager of the theater understood that a young Greek woman purportedly Nicea Korolos was to appear tonight at the theater, but he did not recognize her by sight, having had only some correspondence from her agent in Athens.

Moreover, he hastened to agree, that in view of wartime vigilance essential to the safety of the city, it would not be wise to permit an unknown and unidentified female to appear before a Turkish audience. This answer was precisely what Major Hakim Istefan had anticipated, for he had a dossier on Antonescu, who had been engaged in illicit smuggling several years ago and could at any time be brought in for interrogation and sentence. The theater manager was therefore only too eager to sacrifice the welfare of these two women in order to save his own skin.

"Let us pay a little visit to the ladies, who must be quite lonely by now and quite ready to have a visitor, eh?" he said to his sergeant, as he rose from his desk and strode toward the door.

The fat sergeant grinned and winked. "I was thinking that myself, Major! Which one do you want yourself?"

"I'll take the so-called lady, Bekir. You may have the maid. And this time I think I will wield the whip myself. And let us pose them in an interesting way. She says she's from the theater? Well then, she will appreciate a theatrical setting, I'm sure."

A few moments later, Sergeant Bekir unlocked the metal door at the end of the cellar corridor. In his hand was a pine torch, which he at once thrust into the iron bracket just inside the cell. There was a simultaneous cry of terror and surprise, as the two young women beheld their surroundings for the first time.

It was a windowless room with a low ceiling, perhaps the size of a large living room. The walls and the floor themselves were damp, and at certain times of the year, through the crumbling mortar near the corners of the walls, rats were known to enter. Major Hakim Istefan recalled as his brooding eyes swiftly swept over the room, how, six months ago, an aristocratic Turkish woman who

Turkish Delights

had actually been a Greek spy and who had been shot by a firing squad the following morning, had clung to his booted legs, groveling on her knees, babbling that she would fuck him or suck him or anything, just so he took her out of this cell and away from the horrible rats. He accepted her offer, of course, but he had left her there all night and instructed Sergeant Bekir to toss in bits of food certain to attract the hungry rodents.

Several rusted iron rings had been set in the wall here and there, and there was a heavy wooden pillory far to the right, which could be used as a whipping post. In the center of the room, a heavy wooden ladder rose at an angle to meet with an upright round post to which it was fixed. Three sets of buckling straps were attached to the ladder, for it was a flogging ladder. There was also a low pair of stocks with a heavy round footstool in front of them, and this was for the *bastinado*. However, it could also be used for flogging the back or buttocks, depending on how the victim was placed. For the *bastinado*, the victim was placed seated on the stool, with her ankles locked in the clamp-holes of the lower frame, her bare feet thus outthrust and straddled on the other side.

A thin, supple bamboo rod, or sometimes an acacia switch, was then used to flog the soles and the heels. Then again, for a simple flogging, she would be seated on the stool, but with her neck engaged in the upper middle yoke hole and her wrists clamped in two smaller holes at the sides, with her ankles equally pinioned. To further the torment, bits of gravel, thorns, and pebbles and other uncomfortable substances could be placed upon the surface of the stool.

But hardly had the two women comprehended the significance of their surroundings than their eyes lit upon a panoply of whips, thongs, straps, and rods on the wall, exactly to the left of the door.

"How dare you keep us in a place like this!" the pale golden-haired actress indignantly exclaimed, her voice trembling with anger and shame. "I am not used to this sort of treatment! I shall complain to the Greek Ambassador!"

"You have my permission to do this, Nicea, but only after I have released you. It appears that the manager of the theater where you were going to give your performance for us barbaric Turks cannot identify you. And, being a true Turkish patriot at wartime, he feels as I do that your presence might incite some unpleasant incidents. Besides, it is much too convenient to invent a story of lost luggage. We shall try our best, Sergeant Bekir and I, to obtain more specific details on your background. We'll start with your maid, this little Euphrosyne. She is really very pretty and tasty. I wonder, Nicea, if you've tasted her?"

For a moment, the lovely, sensitive-featured blond woman did not quite comprehend the lascivious meaning of her interlocutor; then, her cheeks flaming, she stepped back and said in a low, shaking voice, "You are an abominable beast to dare say such a thing to two helpless women, no matter who they may be!"

"Now that is very theatrical, Nicea. But I much prefer my own brand of theatrics. Bekir, make Euphrosyne comfortable, will you?"

Euphrosyne Sapiros uttered a cry of terror as the fat,

bald sergeant advanced toward her, licking his fleshy lips, an unmistakable lustful glitter in his beady eyes. She was about twenty, tall and slim, but with a stunningly contrasting pair of full, round high-perched titties and a magnificently rounded, upstandingly contoured behind which even her petticoats and thick dress did not conceal.

The sergeant seized her by one wrist and doubled it behind her back, making her bend over with a shriek of pain, and first began to rip off her dress and then petticoats.

"I protest! You've no right! We're not criminals, do you understand?" Nicea cried out to the sadistic officer. "Let her go! She's done nothing!"

"It's amusing how often maids know so much more about their mistresses than their mistresses themselves. Leave her stockings and her knickers on, for the time being. Eh, Bekir, that's good. Now let's see—I think on the ladder and on her back."

"On her back, Excellency Major?" the fat sergeant demanded dumbfoundedly.

"Yes, you idiot, I know what I'm doing, even though you don't," the officer snapped.

The weeping black-haired girl tried vainly to cover the thick bush of her cunt and to hide her magnificently ivory-tinted titties with their wide, pale-coral love circles and pouting buds, but in a few moments the sergeant had forced her towards the ladder, with her back against the rungs, swiftly corded her ankles, lashed another cord around her waist, and finally, standing on a higher footstool nearby, bound her wrists high above her head. Her eyes enormous with terror, tears running down her cheeks, her titties rising and falling rapidly, the helpless girl sobbed out:

"Oh, mistress, what are they going to do to me? I'm a good girl. I've done nothing wrong. Oh, please tell them!"

Major Hakim Istefan made another sign with his hand and the sergeant seized the beautiful golden-haired actress. She cried out angrily, tried to slap him, to knee him and to twist out of his grasp, but Bekir struck her a glancing blow against the cheek with his heavy fist, dazing her.

By the time she had recovered, she found herself standing against the wall opposite the door, her arms above her head and tied to one of the solid metal rings, stripped down to only her corset, stockings, and shoes. Her naked breasts, proud, young, widely-spaced soft pink-tinted pears were exposed to the greedy eyes of her two tormentors.

Sergeant Bekir strode to the panoply of whips and after some hesitation took down a plaited leather whip about two feet long, it's final tip an additional two inches in length, being made of about six tiny narrow strips of tanned goatskin. The short, heavy handle clutched in his right hand, he moved slowly back towards the ladder and Euphrosyne writhed and shrieked trying to free herself.

"Oh, mistress, mistress! He's going to whip me! Oh, don't let him, I'm so afraid. Oh, please, let me go. I've done nothing!"

"Excellency Major?" the sergeant turned to his satanic master for orders.

Turkish Delights

"Amuse yourself, Bekir, but not too hard with that whip. Flick me those nice big titties and that belly. See if you can dart the tip of that whip right into the sweet little belly button, and a few times on the insides of those fine thighs, and a few more into that furry cunt of hers. Perhaps it'll make her hot for your prick, Bekir."

"You vile, shabby, ignoble creature! How dare you treat poor Euphrosyne this way. I demand you send for the Greek Ambassador at once! This is unjust, and you've no right to do this to us!" Nicea screamed.

"Gently, Nicea. Your turn will come soon enough. And if I'm wrong, you will have all my apologies and I'm sure Sergeant Bekir can find some ointment for the little marks left on your pretty maid. Besides, if you haven't already tried her, you'll have your chance. You can console each other, you might say," Major Hakim Istefan drawled, savoring the torment of the two helpless victims.

His eyes feasted on their revealed charms, and he preferred the sensitive, older woman who showed him thus far only her titties. She would show a great deal more before this day was done.

Sergeant Bekir planted himself about two feet away from the ladder, facing the dark-haired weeping young maid and playfully flicked the whip out to touch her collarbone. Her eyes rolled madly. She tugged at her bonds and tried to flatten herself more than ever against the wooden ladder.

"My, how she's afraid of it, Excellency," the sergeant grinned with an obscene cackle. "I'll warm her up, though. Don't you fear."

So saying, he drew back the whip and deftly flicked Euphrosyne's right nipple, and she twisted herself as much as her bonds would allow, babbling entreaties of mercy. But already the whip had risen and then shot out again, and the other nipple this time felt the savage kiss of the thin strips of goatskin.

Her body seemed to jump, but the solid ladder held her tightly to its caresses. Mad with pain and shame, desperately trying to close her thighs, for she could see the sergeant's eyes fixed on her virgin cunt, Euphrosyne uselessly supplicated for mercy. For fully half an hour the sadistic Turkish Intelligence Head allowed this subordinate to ply the whip over the maid's creamy nakedness.

At times, it flicked lightly, with an intimation of more stinging kisses to come, touching the navel, the abdomen, the pubic hair, into the soft pouting pink lips of Euphrosyne's cunt itself. Then, giving her no time to prepare herself or understand where the lash would next fall or with what strength, Sergeant Bekir directed the whip in a diagonal cut over her belly, or across both naked titties, to leave fiery welts that drew harrowing cries of indescribable agony from the shuddering, half-fainting brunette maid.

"Now, perhaps you'll tell us a little more about yourself, my dear girl," Major Hakim Istefan lit a cigar and approached the shuddering, welted body of his victim.

The smell of sweat and of urine—the urine of fear—was intoxicating for him, and he approached as closely as he could, staring at her breasts, her contorted, tear-drenched face, the chattering teeth and the flaring nostrils. Then he extended the hot end of the cigar towards the bush of her cunt.

"Quickly!" he snarled.

Euphrosyne's eyes were hypnotically fixed to the red glow of the tip of the lit cigar. With all her strength, she tried to back herself into the ladder, and then babbled hysterically, "I'm just her maid, it's true! She's an actress. I worked with her for two years and she's a fine, generous woman. I can tell you nothing else."

"Perhaps we've made a mistake, Bekir," the Major turned to his subordinate with a look of deceptive ingenuousness.

"That would be too bad, Major."

"Yes. But on the other hand, we have no great love for Greeks here. If she's a great actress, we would have heard of her long before this, eh, sergeant? But I don't think she is because she hasn't convinced me yet that she is one. So all Greece will lose is two pretty girls, and they will do much better here amusing our soldiers, don't you agree?"

"Oh, surely, Excellency Major," the fat, bald non-commissioned officer sniggered.

"I think it's time for the mistress to console the maid, Bekir. Help her to do that." Major Hakim Istefan leaned to whisper in his sergeant's ear and the sergeant, with a bellow of laughter, at once responded.

"Excellency Major, why, that's a wonderful idea, that is. I wish I'd thought of it myself. At once, Excellency Major."

Casting aside his whip, the fat sergeant approached the wall against which Nicea was tethered. Unfastening her wrists, he brutally ripped off her corset, although she tried to strike at him with her little fists.

Frenzied with shame, beseeching her satanic tormentor to call the Greek Ambassador, to spare her, she was dragged to the ladder and forced upon it. Sergeant Bekir thrust her forward so that her titties and cunt rubbed against Euphrosyne's. Meanwhile, the Major aided him in tethering the two women together in this salacious tableau that was to end in enforced lesbianism under the lash.

"There, now the two of them can console each other, eh, Bekir? And hand me the whip this time," Major Hakim Istefan commanded.

Nicea turned her face back over her shoulder and cried out hoarsely, "It's filthy, it's inhuman! You coward, you cruel, horrid beast to shame us so! You'll pay for this. You wait and see if you don't! The Greek Ambassador will prove who I am."

"But first you must prove who he is, sweetheart," the Turkish officer sarcastically rejoined.

Then, raising his arm, he sent the whip whistling across the young blond woman's slender back. She caught her breath and writhed, gritting her teeth, determined not to make an outcry to give him satisfaction. But even that convulsive movement had ground her titties and cunt against her maid's; and, at the same movement, revolted by this contact, Euphrosyne jerked her body backward.

Waiting for this, the major regaled her with a furious backhanded stroke that leaped the thong over both her jutting round bottom globes and drew an agonized scream from the aristocratic young beauty.

Turkish Delights

"Now you've had a taste of it, my darling Nicea," he chuckled thickly. "I'd advise you to commune with Euphrosyne. You can distract yourself that way, you know, and the whip will be a kind of delight for you. Besides, I'm sure, with a figure like Euphrosyne has, you've probably tried that nasty little game in bed at night, you Greek whore!"

His eyes narrowing to pinpoints of glittering, cruel light, his lips twisted, he began to whip the young actress. Using the full force of the thong, he struck horizontally over her bottom from the tops of her hips to the base, and then varied the torture for a few moments by flicking the thin strands against the small of her back, her shoulder blades, and her neck, and even around to bite at the outer curves of her panting titties.

Her voice became hoarse and slurred with the shrill cries of agony that the lash, so expertly wielded, wrenched from her. Panting, sweating, babbling incoherent entreaties, Nicea could no longer control the movements of her naked body. Each time the whip fell, she lunged forward and ground her cunt against her maid's. She felt Euphrosyne's titties against her as the burning kiss of the whip added a new welt and yet another to her soft pink flesh and produced a new, lascivious, involuntary contortion.

"I'll flay the skin off your ass, Nicea, if you don't start to rub your cunt against Euphrosyne's and make her come," the Major snarled.

Again the lash cracked wickedly as it wrapped around the ripest center of the young Greek actress's bottom. With a wild shriek of agony, she cast aside all prudery and pride and, her mouth fused with her maid's, began lasciviously to rub and squirm herself, while Euphrosyne wept and moaned and finally began to imitate her mistress.

And when at last both women were drawn to orgasm, under the infernal persuasion of the lash, Major Hakim Istefan flung it aside and ordered the sergeant to hand him his ivory-handled riding crop. Then, prying open Nicea's welted bottomcheeks, he thrust the ivory-handle in as far as it would go. Then he made another sign, and the half-fainting, golden-haired young woman was taken down from the ladder and her wrists tied above her to one of the wall rings, but this time with her face to the wall and with the obscene emergence of the riding crop sticking out of her asshole.

Mounting a footstool, the sergeant, unbuttoning his trousers, liberated his enormous, thick prick and began to prod Euphrosyne's furry cunthole. The girl shrieked desperately, even imploring her mistress for help. But there was to be none for her. And as the Head of Turkish Intelligence watched, his face flushed, his eyes sparkling, fat, bald Sergeant Bekir fucked the naked young maid, exclaiming triumphantly, "She's a virgin, Excellency Major! And by the bowels of Shaitan, she's tight as the very devil!"

And when he had finished with the weeping girl, he moved over to the wall. There, haggard and trembling, her body drenched with sweat and with tears, Nicea understood what was in store for her. But the whip had broken her courage, and she did not even rebel as the fat sergeant, a hand on one of her titties, the other used to

Turkish Delights

pry open the lips of her cunt, inserted his greased weapon and crammed home to the very hilt. Here again, he triumphantly announced, "But this one isn't a virgin, Excellency Major, though she's tight as the very devil! I'll loosen you up, you blond bitch!"

His hands pressed against his crotch, his eyes dark and brooding, Major Hakim Istefan watched the brutal rape of the two Greek women. And when Nicea, her head bowed, her titties rising and falling convulsively, sagged in her bonds, he turned to his assistant.

"Let's go get some sleep and then a good dinner, Bekir. Then we can come back and see just how talkative these bitches are going to be."

You've heard of the writers
but didn't know where to find them

Samuel R. Delany • Pat Califia • Carol Queen • Lars Eighner • Felice Picano • Lucy Taylor • Aaron Travis • Michael Lassell • Red Jordan Arobateau • Michael Bronski • Tom Roche • Maxim Jakubowski • Michael Perkins • Camille Paglia • John Preston • Laura Antoniou • Alice Joanou • Cecilia Tan • Michael Perkins • Tuppy Owens • Trish Thomas • Lily Burana

You've seen the sexy images
but didn't know where to find them

Robert Chouraqui • Charles Gatewood • Richard Kern • Eric Kroll • Vivienne Maricevic • Housk Randall • Barbara Nitke • Trevor Watson • Mark Avers • Laura Graff • Michele Serchuk • Laurie Leber

You can find them all in
Masquerade

a publication designed expressly for the connoisseur of the erotic arts.

ORDER TODAY
SAVE 50%
1 year (6 issues) for $15; 2 years (12 issues) for only $25!

Essential. —*Skin Two*

The best newsletter I have ever seen! —*Secret International*

Very informative and enticing. —*Redemption*

A professional, insider's look at the world of erotica. —*Screw*

I recommend a subscription to **MASQUERADE**... It's good stuff. —*Black Sheets*

MASQUERADE presents some of the best articles on erotica, fetishes, sex clubs, the politics of porn and every conceivable issue of sex and sexuality. —*Factsheet Five*

Fabulous. —*Tuppy Owens*

MASQUERADE is absolutely lovely ... marvelous images. —*Le Boudoir Noir*

Highly recommended. —*Eidos*

DIRECT

Masquerade/Direct • DEPT X74L • 801 Second Avenue • New York, NY 10017 • FAX: 212.986.7355
MC/VISA orders can be placed by calling our toll-free number: 800.375.2356

☐ PLEASE SEND ME A 1 YEAR SUBSCRIPTION FOR $30 *NOW* $15 !
☐ PLEASE SEND ME A 2 YEAR SUBSCRIPTION FOR $60 *NOW* $25!

NAME _____
ADDRESS _____
CITY _____ STATE _____ ZIP _____
TEL ( ) _____
PAYMENT: ☐ CHECK ☐ MONEY ORDER ☐ VISA ☐ MC
CARD # _____ EXP. DATE _____

No C.O.D. orders. Please make all checks payable to Masquerade/Direct. Payable in U.S. currency only.

MASQUERADE BOOKS

MASQUERADE

VISCOUNT LADYWOOD
GYNECOCRACY
$7.95/511-5
Julian, whose parents feel he shows just a bit too much spunk, is sent to a very special private school, in hopes that he will learn to discipline his wayward soul. Once there, Julian discovers that his program of study has been devised by the deliciously stern Mademoiselle de Chambonnard. In no time, Julian is learning the many ways of pleasure—under the firm hand of this demanding headmistress.

EDITED BY CHARLOTTE ROSE
50 PLAYGIRL FANTASIES
$6.50/460-7
A steamy selection of women's fantasies straight from the pages of *Playgirl*—the leading magazine of sexy entertainment for women. These tales of seduction—specially selected by no less an authority than Charlotte Rose, author of such bestselling women's erotica as *Women at Work* and *The Doctor is In*—are sure to set your pulse racing.

N. T. MORLEY
THE PARLOR
$6.50/496-8
Lovely Kathryn gives in to the ultimate temptation. The mysterious John and Sarah ask her to be their slave—an idea that turns Kathryn on so much that she can't refuse! But who are these two mysterious strangers? Little by little, Kathryn not only learns to serve, but comes to know the inner secrets of her stunning keepers.

JULIAN ANTHONY GUERRA, EDITOR
COME QUICKLY:
FOR COUPLES ON THE GO
$6.50/461-5
The increasing pace of daily life is no reason to forgo a little carnal pleasure whenever the mood strikes. Here are over sixty of the hottest fantasies around—all designed to get you going in less time than it takes to dial 976. A super-hot volume especially for couples on a modern schedule.

ERICA BRONTE
LUST, INC.
$6.50/467-4
Lust, Inc. explores the extremes of passion that lurk beneath even the coldest, most business-like exteriors. Join in the sexy escapades of a group of high-powered professionals whose idea of office decorum is like nothing you've ever encountered! Business attire not required....

VANESSA DURIES
THE TIES THAT BIND
$6.50/510-7
The incredible confessions of a thrillingly unconventional woman. From the first page, this chronicle of dominance and submission will keep you gasping with its vivid depictions of sensual abandon. At the hand of Masters Georges, Patrick, Pierre and others, this submissive seductress experiences pleasures she never knew existed....

M. S. VALENTINE
THE CAPTIVITY OF CELIA
$6.50/453-4
Colin is mistakenly considered the prime suspect in a murder, forcing him to seek refuge with his cousin, Sir Jason Hardwicke. In exchange for Colin's safety, Jason demands Celia's unquestioning submission—knowing she will do anything to help her lover. Sexual extortion!

AMANDA WARE
BOUND TO THE PAST
$6.50/452-6
Anne accepts a research assignment in a Tudor mansion. Upon arriving, she finds herself aroused by James, a descendant of the mansion's owners. Together they uncover the perverse desires of the mansion's long-dead master—desires that bind Anne inexorably to the past—not to mention the bedpost!

SACHI MIZUNO
SHINJUKU NIGHTS
$6.50/493-3
Another tour through the lives and libidos of the seductive East, from the author of *Passion in Tokyo*. No one is better than Sachi Mizuno at weaving an intricate web of sensual desire, wherein many characters are ensnared and enraptured by the demands of their long-denied carnal natures. One by one, each surrenders social convention for the unashamed pleasures of the flesh.

PASSION IN TOKYO
$6.50/454-2
Tokyo—one of Asia's most historic and seductive cities. Come behind the closed doors of its citizens, and witness the many pleasures that await. Lusty men and women from every stratum of Japanese society free themselves of all inhibitions....

MARTINE GLOWINSKI
POINT OF VIEW
$6.50/433-X
With the assistance of her new, unexpectedly kinky lover, she discovers and explores her exhibitionist tendencies—until there is virtually nothing she won't do before the horny audiences her man arranges! Unabashed acting out for the sophisticated voyeur.

BUY ANY 4 BOOKS & CHOOSE 1 ADDITIONAL BOOK, OF EQUAL OR LESSER VALUE, AS YOUR FREE GIFT

MASQUERADE BOOKS

RICHARD McGOWAN
A HARLOT OF VENUS
$6.50/425-9
A highly fanciful, epic tale of lust on Mars! Cavortia—the most famous and sought-after courtesan in the cosmopolitan city of Venus—finds love and much more during her adventures with some of the most remarkable characters in recent erotic fiction.

M. ORLANDO
THE ARCHITECTURE OF DESIRE
Introduction by Richard Manton.
$6.50/490-9
Two novels in one special volume! In *The Hotel Justine*, an elite clientele is afforded the opportunity to have any and all desires satisfied. *The Villa Sin* is inherited by a beautiful woman who soon realizes that the legacy of the ancestral estate includes bizarre erotic ceremonies. Two pieces of prime real estate.

CHET ROTHWELL
KISS ME, KATHERINE
$5.95/410-0
Beautiful Katherine can hardly believe her luck. Not only is she married to the charming and oh-so-agreeable Nelson, she's free to live out all her erotic fantasies with other men. Katherine has discovered Nelson to be far more devoted than the average spouse—and the duo soon begin exploring a relationship more demanding than marriage!

MARCO VASSI
THE STONED APOCALYPSE
$5.95/401-1/mass market
"Marco Vassi is our champion sexual energist." —VLS
During his lifetime, Marco Vassi praised by writers as diverse as Gore Vidal and Norman Mailer, and his reputation was worldwide. *The Stoned Apocalypse* is Vassi's autobiography; chronicling a cross-country trip on America's erotic byways, it offers a rare glimpse of a generation's sexual imagination.

ROBIN WILDE
TABITHA'S TEASE
$5.95/387-2
When poor Robin arrives at The Valentine Academy, he finds himself subject to the torturous teasing of Tabitha—the Academy's most notoriously domineering co-ed. But Tabitha is pledge-mistress of a secret sorority dedicated to enslaving young men. Robin finds himself the utterly helpless (and wildly excited) captive of Tabitha & Company's weird desires! A marathon of ticklish torture!

ERICA BRONTE
PIRATE'S SLAVE
$5.95/376-7
Lovely young Erica is stranded in a country where lust knows no bounds. Desperate to escape, she finds herself trading her firm, luscious body to any and all men willing and able to help her. Her adventure has its ups and downs, ins and outs—all to the undeniable pleasure of lusty Erica!

CHARLES G. WOOD
HELLFIRE
$5.95/358-9
A vicious murderer is running amok in New York's sexual underground—and Nick O'Shay, a virile detective with the NYPD, plunges deep into the case. He soon becomes embroiled in an elusive world of fleshly extremes, hunting a madman seeking to purge America with fire and blood sacrifices. Set in New York's infamous sexual underground.

OLIVIA M. RAVENSWORTH
THE MISTRESS OF CASTLE ROHMENSTADT
$5.95/372-4
Lovely Katherine inherits a secluded European castle from a mysterious relative. Upon arrival she discovers, much to her delight, that the castle is a haven of sensual pleasure. Katherine learns to shed her inhibitions and enjoy her new home's many delights. Soon, Castle Rohmenstadt is the home of every perversion known to man.

CLAIRE BAEDER, EDITOR
LA DOMME: A DOMINATRIX ANTHOLOGY
$5.95/366-X
A steamy smorgasbord of female domination! Erotic literature has long been filled with heartstopping portraits of domineering women, and now the most memorable have been brought together in one beautifully brutal volume. A must for all fans of true Woman Power.

TINY ALICE
THE GEEK
$5.95/341-4
"An accomplishment of which anybody may be proud." —Philip José Farmer
The Geek is told from the point of view of a chicken, who reports on the various perversities he witnesses as part of a traveling carnival. When a gang of renegade lesbians kidnaps Chicken and his geek, all hell breaks loose.

CHARISSE VAN DER LYN
SEX ON THE NET
$5.95/399-6
Electrifying erotica from one of the Internet's hottest and most widely read authors. Encounters of all kinds—straight, lesbian, dominant/submissive and all sorts of extreme passions—are explored in thrilling detail.

STANLEY CARTEN
NAUGHTY MESSAGE
$5.95/333-3
Wesley Arthur discovers a lascivious message on his answering machine. Aroused beyond his wildest dreams by the acts described, Wesley becomes obsessed with tracking down the woman behind the seductive voice. His search takes him through strip clubs, sex parlors and no-tell motels—and finally to his randy reward....

MASQUERADE BOOKS

AKBAR DEL PIOMBO

SKIRTS
$4.95/115-2
Randy Mr. Edward Champdick enters high society—and a whole lot more—in his quest for ultimate satisfaction. For it seems that once Mr. Champdick rises to the occasion, nothing can bring him down.

DUKE COSIMO
$4.95/3052-0
A kinky romp played out against the boudoirs, bathrooms and ballrooms of the European nobility, who seem to do nothing all day except each other. The lifestyles of the rich and licentious are revealed in all their glory.

A CRUMBLING FAÇADE
$4.95/3043-1
The return of that incorrigible rogue, Henry Pike, who continues his pursuit of sex, fair or otherwise, in the most elegant homes of the most debauched aristocrats.

CAROLE REMY

BEAUTY OF THE BEAST
$5.95/332-5
A shocking tell-all, written from the point-of-view of a prize-winning reporter. And what reporting she does! All the secrets of an uninhibited life are revealed, and each lusty tableau is painted in glowing colors.

DAVID AARON CLARK

THE MARQUIS DE SADE'S JULIETTE
$4.95/240-X
The Marquis de Sade's infamous Juliette returns—and emerges as the most perverse and destructive nightstalker modern New York will ever know.

Praise for David Aaron Clark:

"David Aaron Clark has delved into one of the most sensationalistically taboo aspects of eros, sadomasochism, and produced a novel of unmistakable literary imagination and artistic value."
—Carlo McCormick, Paper

ANONYMOUS

NADIA
$5.95/267-1
Follow the delicious but neglected Nadia as she works to wring every drop of pleasure out of life—despite an unhappy marriage. A classic title providing a peek into the secret sexual lives of another time and place.

NIGEL McPARR

THE STORY OF A VICTORIAN MAID
$5.95/241-8
What were the Victorians really like? Chances are, no one believes they were as stuffy as their Queen, but who would have imagined such unbridled libertines! Follow her from exploit to smutty exploit!

MOLLY WEATHERFIELD

CARRIE'S STORY
$5.95/444-5
"I had been Jonathan's slave for about a year when he told me he wanted to sell me at an auction. I wasn't in any condition to respond when he told me this..." Desire and depravity run rampant in this story of uncompromising mastery and irrevocable submission.

BREN FLEMMING

CHARLY'S GAME
$4.95/221-3
A rich woman's gullible daughter has run off with one of the toughest leather dykes in town—and sexy P.I. Charly is hired to lure the girl back. One by one, wise and wicked women ensnare one another in their lusty nets!

ISADORA ALMAN

ASK ISADORA
$4.95/61-0
Six years' worth of Isadora Alman's syndicated columns on sex and relationships. Today's world is more perplexing than ever—and Alman can help untangle the most personal of knots.

TITIAN BERESFORD

THE WICKED HAND
$5.95/343-0
With an Introduction by *Leg Show*'s Dian Hanson. A collection of fetishistic tales featuring the absolute subjugation of men by lovely, domineering women.

CINDERELLA
$6.50/500-X
Beresford triumphs again with this intoxicating tale, filled with castle dungeons and tightly corseted ladies-in-waiting, naughty viscounts and impossibly cruel masturbatrixes—nearly every conceivable method of erotic torture is explored and described in lush, vivid detail.

JUDITH BOSTON
$4.95/273-6
Young Edward would have been lucky to get the stodgy old companion he thought his parents had hired for him. Instead, an exquisite woman arrives at his door, and Edward finds his lewd behavior never goes unpunished by the unflinchingly severe Judith Boston! Together they take the downward path to perversion!

NINA FOXTON
$5.95/443-7
An aristocrat finds herself bored by run-of-the-mill amusements for "ladies of good breeding." Instead of taking tea with proper gentlemen, naughty Nina "milks" them of their most private essences. No man ever says "No" to the lovely Nina!

BUY ANY 4 BOOKS & CHOOSE 1 ADDITIONAL BOOK, OF EQUAL OR LESSER VALUE, AS YOUR FREE GIFT

MASQUERADE BOOKS

A TITIAN BERESFORD READER
$4.95/114-4
Wild dominatrixes, perverse masochists, and mesmerizing detail are the hallmarks of the Beresford tale—and encountered here in abundance. The very best scenarios from all of Beresford's bestsellers.

P. N. DEDEAUX
THE NOTHING THINGS
$5.95/404-6
Beta Beta Rho—highly exclusive and widely honored—has taken on a new group of pledges. The five women will be put through the most grueling of ordeals, and punished severely for any shortcomings—much to everyone's delight!

TENDER BUNS
$5.95/396-1
In a fashionable Canadian suburb, Marc Merlin indulges his yen for punishment with an assortment of the town's most desirable and willing women. Things come to a rousing climax at a party planned to cater to just those whims Marc is most able to satisfy....

MICHAEL DRAX
OBSESSIONS
$4.95/3012-1
Victoria is determined to become a model by sexually ensnaring the powerful people who control the fashion industry: Paige, who finds herself compelled to watch Victoria's conquests; and Pietro and Alex, who take turns and then join in for a sizzling threesome. The story of one woman's unslakeable ambition—and lust!

LYN DAVENPORT
DOVER ISLAND
$5.95/384-8
Dr. David Kelly has planted the seeds of his dream— a Corporal Punishment Resort. Soon, many people from varied walks of life descend upon this isolated retreat, intent on fulfilling their every desire. Including Marcy Harris, the perfect partner for the lustful Doctor....

TESSA'S HOLIDAYS
$5.95/377-5
Tessa's lusty lover, Grant, makes sure that each of her holidays is filled with the type of sensual adventure most young women only dream about. What will he dream up next? Only he knows—and he keeps his secrets until the lovely Tessa is ready to explode with desire!

THE GUARDIAN
$5.95/371-6
Felicia grew up under the tutelage of the lash—and she learned her lessons well. Sir Rodney Wentworth has long searched for a woman capable of fulfilling his cruel desires, and after learning of Felicia's talents, sends for her. Felicia discovers that the "position" offered her is delightfully different than anything she could have expected!

LIZBETH DUSSEAU
TRINKETS
$4.95/246-9
"Her bottom danced on the air, pert and fully round. It would take punishment well, he thought." A luscious woman submits to an artist's every whim—becoming the sexual trinket he had always desired.

ANTHONY BOBARZYNSKI
STASI SLUT
$4.95/3050-4
Adina lives in East Germany, where she meets a group of ruthless and corrupt STASI agents who use her for their own perverse gratification—until she uses her talents and attractions in a final bid for total freedom!

JOCELYN JOYCE
PRIVATE LIVES
$4.95/309-0
The lecherous habits of the illustrious make for a sizzling tale of French erotic life. A widow has a craving for a young busboy; he's sleeping with a rich businessman's wife; her husband is minding his sex business elsewhere! Scandalous sexual entanglements run through this tale of upper crust lust!

KIM'S PASSION
$4.95/162-4
The life of an insatiable seductress. Kim leaves India for London, where she quickly takes on the task of bedding every woman in sight!

CAROUSEL
$4.95/3051-2
A young American woman leaves her husband when she discovers he is having an affair with their maid. She then becomes the sexual plaything of Parisian voluptuaries.

SARAH JACKSON
SANCTUARY
$5.95/318-X
Sanctuary explores both the unspeakable debauchery of court life and the unimaginable privations of monastic solitude, leading the voracious and the virtuous on a collision course that brings history to throbbing life.

THE WILD HEART
$4.95/3007-5
A luxury hotel is the setting for this artful web of sex, desire, and love. A newlywed sees sex as a duty, while her hungry husband tries to awaken her to its tender joys. A Parisian entertains wealthy guests for the love of money. Each episode provides a new variation in this lusty Grand Hotel!!

LOUISE BELHAVEL
FRAGRANT ABUSES
$4.95/88-2
The saga of Clara and Iris continues as the now-experienced girls enjoy themselves with a new circle of worldly friends whose imaginations match their own. Perversity follows the lusty ladies around the globe!

SARA H. FRENCH
MASTER OF TIMBERLAND
$5.95/327-9
A tale of sexual slavery at the ultimate paradise resort. One of our bestselling titles, this trek to Timberland has ignited passions the world over—and stands poised to become one of modern erotica's legendary tales.

MASQUERADE BOOKS

RETURN TO TIMBERLAND
$5.95/257-4
Prepare for a vacation filled with delicious decadence, as each and every visitor is serviced by unimaginably talented submissives. The raunchiest camp-out ever!

CHINA BLUE
KUNG FU NUNS
$4.95/3031-8
"She lifted me out of the chair and sat me down on top of the table. She then lifted her skirt. The sight of her perfect legs clad in white stockings and a petite garter belt further mesmerized me...." China Blue returns!

ROBERT DESMOND
THE SWEETEST FRUIT
$4.95/95-5
Connie is determined to seduce and destroy the devoted Father Chadcroft. She corrupts the unsuspecting priest into forsaking all that he holds sacred, and drags him into a hell of unbridled lust.

LUSCIDIA WALLACE
KATY'S AWAKENING
$4.95/308-2
Katy thinks she's been rescued after a terrible car wreck. Little does she suspect that she's been ensnared by a ring of swingers, whose tastes run to domination and unimaginably depraved sex parties. With no means of escape, Katy becomes the newest initiate in this sick private club—and soon finds herself becoming more depraved than even her degenerate captors.

MARY LOVE
MASTERING MARY SUE
$5.95/351-1
Mary Sue is a rich nymphomaniac whose husband is determined to declare her mentally incompetent and gain control of her fortune. He brings her to a castle where, to Mary Sue's delight, she is unleashed for a veritable sex-fest!

THE BEST OF MARY LOVE
$4.95/3099-7
Mary Love leaves no coupling untried and no extreme unexplored in these scandalous selections from *Mastering Mary Sue, Ecstasy on Fire, Vice Park Place, Wanda,* and *Naughtier at Night.*

AMARANTHA KNIGHT
THE DARKER PASSIONS: THE PICTURE OF DORIAN GRAY
$6.50/342-2
In this latest installment in the Darker Passions series, Amarantha Knight takes on Oscar Wilde, resulting in a fabulously decadent tale of highly personal changes. One young man finds his most secret desires laid bare by a portrait far more revealing than he could have imagined....

THE DARKER PASSIONS READER
$6.50/432-1
The best moments from Knight's phenomenally popular Darker Passions series. Here are the most eerily erotic passages from her acclaimed sexual reworkings of *Dracula, Frankenstein, Dr. Jekyll & Mr. Hyde* and *The Fall of the House of Usher.* Be prepared for more than a few thrills and chills from this arousing sampler.

THE DARKER PASSIONS: FRANKENSTEIN
$5.95/248-5
What if you could create a living human? What shocking acts could it be taught to perform, to desire? Find out what pleasures await those who play God....

THE DARKER PASSIONS: THE FALL OF THE HOUSE OF USHER
$5.95/313-9
The Master and Mistress of the house of Usher indulge in every form of decadence, and initiate their guests into the many pleasures to be found in utter submission.

THE DARKER PASSIONS: DR. JEKYLL AND MR. HYDE
$4.95/227-2
It is a story of incredible, frightening transformations achieved through mysterious experiments. Now, Amarantha Knight explores the steamy possibilities of a tale where no one is quite who—or what—they seem. Victorian bedrooms explode with hidden demons!

THE DARKER PASSIONS: DRACULA
$5.95/326-0
The infamous erotic retelling of the Vampire legend.
"Well-written and imaginative, Amarantha Knight gives fresh impetus to this myth, taking us through the sexual and sadistic scenes with details that keep us reading.... A classic in itself has been added to the shelves." —*Divinity*

PAUL LITTLE
THE BEST OF PAUL LITTLE
$6.50/469-0
One of Masquerade's all-time best-selling authors. Known throughout the world for his fantastic portrayals of punishment and pleasure, Little never fails to push readers over the edge of sensual excitement.

ALL THE WAY
$6.95/509-3
Two excruciating novels from Paul Little in one hot volume! *Going All the Way* features an unhappy man who tries to purge himself of the memory of his lover with a series of quirky and uninhibited lovers. *Pushover* tells the story of a serial spanker and his celebrated exploits.

THE DISCIPLINE OF ODETTE
$5.95/334-1
Odette's was sure marriage would rescue her from her family's "corrections." To her horror, she discovers that her beloved has also been raised on discipline. A shocking erotic coupling!

BUY ANY 4 BOOKS & CHOOSE 1 ADDITIONAL BOOK, OF EQUAL OR LESSER VALUE, AS YOUR FREE GIFT

MASQUERADE BOOKS

THE PRISONER
$5.95/330-9
Judge Black has built a secret room below a penitentiary, where he sentences the prisoners to hours of exhibition and torment while his friends watch. Judge Black's House of Corrections is equipped with one purpose in mind: to administer his own brand of rough justice!

TEARS OF THE INQUISITION
$4.95/146-2
The incomparable Paul Little delivers a staggering account of pleasure and punishment. "There was a tickling inside her as her nervous system reminded her she was ready for sex. But before her was...the Inquisitor!"

DOUBLE NOVEL
$4.95/86-6
The Metamorphosis of Lisette Joyaux tells the story of a young woman initiated into a new world of lesbian lusts. *The Story of Monique* reveals the sexual rituals that beckon the ripe and willing Monique.

CHINESE JUSTICE AND OTHER STORIES
$4.95/153-5
The story of the excruciating pleasures and delicious punishments inflicted on foreigners under the leaders of the Boxer Rebellion. Each foreign woman is brought before the authorities and grilled. Scandalous deeds!

CAPTIVE MAIDENS
$5.95/440-2
Three beautiful young women find themselves powerless against the debauched landowners of 1824 England. They are banished to a sexual slave colony, and corrupted by every imaginable perversion. Soon, they come to crave the treatment of their unrelenting captors, and find themselves insatiable.

SLAVE ISLAND
$5.95/441-0
A leisure cruise is waylaid, finding itself in the domain of Lord Henry Philbrock, a sadistic genius. The ship's passengers are kidnapped and spirited to his island prison, where the women are trained to accommodate the most bizarre sexual cravings of the rich, the famous, the pampered and the perverted. An incredible bestseller, which cemented Little's reputation as a master of contemporary erotic literature.

ALIZARIN LAKE
SEX ON DOCTOR'S ORDERS
$5.95/402-X
A chronicle of selfless devotion to mankind! Beth, a nubile young nurse, uses her considerable skills to further medical science by offering incomparable and insatiable assistance in the gathering of important specimens. No man leaves naughty Nurse Beth's station without surrendering exactly what she needs!

THE EROTIC ADVENTURES OF HARRY TEMPLE
$4.95/127-6
Harry Temple's memoirs chronicle his amorous adventures from his initiation at the hands of insatiable sirens, through his stay at a house of hot repute, to his encounters with a chastity-belted nympho!

JOHN NORMAN
TARNSMAN OF GOR
$6.95/486-0
This legendary—and controversial—series returns! *Tarnsman* finds Tarl Cabot transported to Counter-Earth, better known as Gor. He must quickly accustom himself to the ways of this world, including the caste system which exalts some as Priest-Kings or Warriors, and debases others as slaves. A spectacular world unfolds in this first volume of John Norman's million-selling Gorean series.

OUTLAW OF GOR
$6.95/487-9
In this second volume, Tarl Cabot returns to Gor, where he might reclaim both his woman and his role of Warrior. But upon arriving, he discovers that his name, his city and the names of those he loves have become unspeakable. In his absence, Cabot has become an outlaw, and must discover his new purpose on this strange planet, where danger stalks the outcast, and even simple answers have their price....

PRIEST-KINGS OF GOR
$6.95/488-7
The third volume of John Norman's million-selling, controversial Gor series. Tarl Cabot, brave Tarnsman of Gor, searches for the truth about his lovely wife Talena. Does she live, or was she destroyed by the mysterious, all-powerful Priest-Kings? Cabot is determined to find out— while knowing that no one who has approached the mountain stronghold of the Priest-Kings has ever returned alive....

RACHEL PEREZ
ODD WOMEN
$4.95/123-3
These women are sexy, smart, tough—some even say odd. But who cares, when their combined ass-ets are so sweet! An assortment of Sapphic sirens proves once and for all that comely ladies come best in pairs.

ALIZARIN LAKE
SEX ON DOCTOR'S ORDERS
$5.95/402-X
Beth, a nubile young nurse, uses her considerable skills to further medical science by offering incomparable and insatiable assistance in the gathering of important specimens. No man leaves naughty Nurse Beth's station without surrendering exactly what she needs!

THE EROTIC ADVENTURES OF HARRY TEMPLE
$4.95/127-6
Harry Temple's memoirs chronicle his amorous adventures from his initiation at the hands of insatiable sirens, through his stay at a house of hot repute, to his encounters with a chastity-belted nympho!

AFFINITIES
$4.95/113-6
"Kelsy had a liking for cool upper-class blondes, the long-legged girls from Lake Forest and Winnetka who came into the city to cruise the lesbian bars on Halsted, looking for breathless ecstasies...." A scorching tale of lesbian libidos unleashed, from a writer more than capable of exploring every nuance of female passion in vivid detail.

MASQUERADE BOOKS

SYDNEY ST. JAMES

RIVE GAUCHE
$5.95/317-1
The Latin Quarter, Paris, circa 1920. Expatriate bohemians couple with abandon—before eventually abandoning their ambitions amidst the intoxicating temptations waiting to be indulged in every bedroom.

THE HIGHWAYWOMAN
$4.95/174-8
A young filmmaker making a documentary about the life of the notorious English highwaywoman, Bess Ambrose, becomes obsessed with her mysterious subject. It seems that Bess touched more than hearts—and plundered the treasures of every man and maiden she met on the way. Incredible extremes of passion are reached by not only the voluptuous filmmaker, but her insatiable subject!

GARDEN OF DELIGHT
$4.95/3058-X
A vivid account of sexual awakening that follows an innocent but insatiably curious young woman's journey from the furtive, forbidden joys of dormitory life to the unabashed carnality of the wild world. A coming of age story unlike any other!

MARCUS VAN HELLER

TERROR
$5.95/247-7
Another shocking exploration of lust by the author of the ever-popular *Adam & Eve*. Set in Paris during the Algerian War, Terror explores the place of sexual passion in a world drunk on violence.

KIDNAP
$4.95/90-4
P. I. Harding is called in to investigate a mysterious kidnapping case involving the rich and powerful. Along the way he has the pleasure of "interrogating" an exotic dancer named Jeanne and a beautiful English reporter, as he finds himself enmeshed in the crime underworld.

ALEXANDER TROCCHI

THONGS
$4.95/217-5
"...In Spain, life is cheap, from that glittering tragedy in the bullring to the quick thrust of the stiletto in a narrow street in a Barcelona slum. No, this death would not have called for further comment had it not been for one striking fact. The naked woman had met her end in a way he had never seen before—a way that had enormous sexual significance. My God, she had been..." Trocchi's acclaimed classic returns.

HELEN AND DESIRE
$4.95/3093-8
Helen Seferis' flight from the oppressive village of her birth became a sexual tour of a harsh world. From brothels in Sydney to harems in Algiers, Helen chronicles her adventures fully in her diary. Each encounter is examined in the scorching and uncensored diary of the sensual Helen!

THE CARNAL DAYS OF HELEN SEFERIS
$4.95/3086-5
P.I. Anthony Harvest is assigned to save Helen Seferis, a beautiful Australian who has been abducted. Following clues in her explicit diary of adventures, he pursues the lovely, doomed Helen—the ultimate sexual prize.

DON WINSLOW

THE INSATIABLE MISTRESS OF ROSEDALE
$6.50/494-1
The story of the perfect couple: Edward and Lady Penelope, who reside in beautiful and mysterious Rosedale manor. While Edward is a true connoisseur of sexual perversion, it is Lady Penelope whose mastery of complete sensual pleasure makes their home infamous. Indulging one another's bizarre whims is a way of life for this wicked couple, and none who encounter the extravagances of Rosedale will forget what they've learned....

SECRETS OF CHEATEM MANOR
$6.50/434-8
Edward returns to his late father's estate, to find it being run by the majestic Lady Amanda. Edward can hardly believe his luck—Lady Amanda is assisted by her two beautiful, lonely daughters, Catherine and Prudence. What the randy young man soon comes to realize is the love of discipline that all three beauties share.

KATERINA IN CHARGE
$5.95/409-7
When invited to a country retreat by a mysterious couple, the two randy young ladies can hardly resist! But do they have any idea what they're in for? Whatever the case, the imperious Katerina will make her desires known very soon—and demand that they be fulfilled...

THE MANY PLEASURES OF IRONWOOD
$5.95/310-4
Seven lovely young women are employed by The Ironwood Sportsmen's Club A small and exclusive club with seven carefully selected sexual connoisseurs, Ironwood is dedicated to the relentless pursuit of sensual pleasure.

CLAIRE'S GIRLS
$5.95/442-9
You knew when she walked by that she was something special. She was one of Claire's girls, a woman carefully dressed and groomed to fill a role, to capture a look, to fit an image crafted by the sophisticated proprietress of an exclusive escort agency. High-class whores blow the roof off!

N. WHALLEN

TAU'TEVU
$6.50/426-7
In a mysterious land, the statuesque and beautiful Vivian learns to subject herself to the hand of a mysterious man. He systematically helps her prove her own strength, and brings to life in her an unimagined sensual fire. But who is this man, who goes only by the name of Orpheo?

BUY ANY 4 BOOKS & CHOOSE 1 ADDITIONAL BOOK, OF EQUAL OR LESSER VALUE, AS YOUR FREE GIFT

MASQUERADE BOOKS

COMPLIANCE
$5.95/356-2
Fourteen stories exploring the pleasures of release. Characters from all walks of life learn to trust in the skills of others, only to experience the thrilling liberation of submission. Here are the joys to be found in some of the most forbidden sexual practices around....

THE MASQUERADE READERS
THE VELVET TONGUE
$4.95/3029-6
An orgy of oral gratification! *The Velvet Tongue* celebrates the most mouth-watering, lip-smacking, tongue-twisting action. A feast of fellatio and *soixante-neuf* awaits readers of excellent taste at this steamy suck-fest.

A MASQUERADE READER
$4.95/84-X
A sizzling sampler. Strict lessons are learned at the hand of *The English Governess*. Scandalous confessions are found in *The Diary of an Angel*, and the story of a woman whose desires drove her to the ultimate sacrifice in *Thongs* completes the collection.

THE CLASSIC COLLECTION
PROTESTS, PLEASURES, RAPTURES
$5.95/400-3
Invited for an allegedly quiet weekend at a country vicarage, a young woman is stunned to find herself surrounded by shocking acts of sexual sadism. Soon, her curiosity is piqued, and she begins to explore her own capacities for cruelty.

THE YELLOW ROOM
$5.95/378-3
The "yellow room" holds the secrets of lust, lechery, and the lash. There, bare-bottomed, spread-eagled, and open to the world, demure Alice Darvell soon learns to love her lickings. In the second tale, hot heiress Rosa Coote and her adventures in punishment and pleasure.

SCHOOL DAYS IN PARIS
$5.95/325-2
The rapturous chronicles of a well-spent youth! Few Universities provide the profound and pleasurable lessons one learns in after-hours study—particularly if one is young and available, and lucky enough to have Paris as a playground. A stimulating look at the pursuits of young adulthood.

MAN WITH A MAID
$4.95/307-4
The adventures of Jack and Alice have delighted readers for eight decades! A classic of its genre, *Man with a Maid* tells an outrageous tale of desire, revenge, and submission. This tale qualifies as one of the world's most popular adult novels—with over 200,000 copies in print!

MAN WITH A MAID II
$4.95/3071-7
Jack's back! With the assistance of the perverse Alice, he embarks again on a trip through every erotic extreme. Jack leaves no one unsatisfied—least of all, himself—and Alice is always certain to outdo herself in her capacity to corrupt and control. An incendiary sequel!

MAN WITH A MAID: THE CONCLUSION
$4.95/3013-X
The conclusion to the epic saga of lust that has thrilled readers for decades. The adulterous woman who is corrected with enthusiasm and the maid who receives grueling guidance are just two who benefit from these lessons!

CONFESSIONS OF A CONCUBINE III: PLEASURE'S PRISONER
$5.95/357-0
Filled with pulse-pounding excitement—including a daring escape from the harem and an encounter with an unspeakable sadist—*Pleasure's Prisoner* adds an unforgettable chapter to this thrilling confessional.

CONFESSIONS OF A CONCUBINE II: HAREM SLAVE
$4.95/226-4
The concubinage continues, as the true pleasures and privileges of the harem are revealed. For the first time, readers are invited behind the veils that hide uninhibited, unimaginable pleasures from the world....

LADY F.
$4.95/102-0
An uncensored tale of Victorian passions. Master Kidrodstock suffers deliciously at the hands of the stunningly cruel and sensuous Lady Flayskin—the only woman capable of taming his wayward impulses. A fevered chronicle of punishing passions.

CLASSIC EROTIC BIOGRAPHIES
JENNIFER III
$5.95/292-2
The further adventures of erotica's most daring heroine. Jennifer, the quintessential beautiful blonde, has a photographer's eye for details—particularly of the masculine variety!

JENNIFER AGAIN
$4.95/220-5
One of modern erotica's most famous heroines. Once again, the insatiable Jennifer seizes the day—and extracts from it every last drop of sensual pleasure! No man is immune to this vixen's charms.

JENNIFER
$4.95/107-1
From the bedroom of a notoriously insatiable dancer to an uninhibited ashram, *Jennifer* traces the exploits of one thoroughly modern woman as she lustfully explores the limits of her own sexuality.

THE ROMANCES OF BLANCHE LA MARE
$4.95/101-2
When Blanche loses her husband, it becomes clear she'll need a job. She sets her sights on the stage—and soon encounters a cast of lecherous characters intent on making her path to suckcess as hot and hard as possible!

PETER JASON
WAYWARD
$4.95/3004-0
A mysterious countess hires a tour bus for an unusual vacation. Traveling through Europe's most notorious cities, she picks up friends, lovers, and acquaintances from every walk of life in pursuit of pleasure.

MASQUERADE BOOKS

ROMY ROSEN
SPUNK
$6.95/492-5
A scintillating tale of unearthly beauty, outrageous decadence, and brutal exploitation. Casey, a lovely model poised upon the verge of super-celebrity, falls hard for a insatiable young rock singer—not suspecting that his sexual appetite has led her to experiment with a dangerous new aphrodisiac. Casey becomes an addict, and her craving plunges her into a strange underworld, where bizarre sexual compulsions are indulged behind the most exclusive doors and the only chance for redemption lies with a shadowy young man with a secret of his own.

CYBERSEX CONSORTIUM
THE PERV'S GUIDE TO THE INTERNET
$6.95/471-2
You've heard the objections: cyberspace is soaked with sex, piled high with prurience, mired in immorality. Okay—so where is it!? Tracking down the good stuff—the real good stuff—can waste an awful lot of expensive time, and frequently leave you high and dry. But now, the Cybersex Consortium presents an easy-to-use guide for those intrepid adults who know what they want. No horny hacker can afford to pass up this map to the kinkiest rest stops on the Info Superhighway.

AMELIA G, EDITOR
BACKSTAGE PASSES
$6.96/438-0
A collection of some of the most raucous writing around. Amelia G, editor of the goth-sex journal *Blue Blood*, has brought together some of today's most irreverant writers, each of whom has outdone themselves with an edgy, antic tale of modern lust. Punks, metalheads, and grunge-trash roam the pages of *Backstage Passes*, and no one knows their ways better...

GERI NETTICK WITH BETH ELLIOT
MIRRORS: PORTRAIT OF A LESBIAN TRANSSEXUAL
$6.95/435-6
The alternately heartbreaking and empowering story of one woman's long road to full selfhood. Born a male, Geri Nettick knew something just didn't fit. And even after coming to terms with her own gender dysphoria—and taking steps to correct it—she still fought to be accepted by the lesbian feminist community to which she felt she belonged. A fascinating, true tale of struggle and discovery.

TRISTAN TAORMINO & DAVID AARON CLARK, EDITORS
RITUAL SEX
$6.95/391-0
While many people believe the body and soul to occupy almost completely independent realms, the many contributors to *Ritual Sex* know—and demonstrate—that the two share more common ground than society feels comfortable acknowledging. From personal memoirs of ecstatic revelation, to fictional quests to reconcile sex and spirit, *Ritual Sex* delves into forbidden areas with gusto, providing an unprecedented look at private life.

DAVID MELTZER
UNDER
$6.95/290-6
The story of a sex professional living at the bottom of the social heap. After surgeries designed to increase his physical allure, corrupt government forces drive the cyber-gigolo underground—where even more bizarre cultures await him.

ORF
$6.95/110-1
He is the ultimate musician-hero—the idol of thousands, the fevered dream of many more. And like many musicians before him, he is misunderstood, misused—and totally out of control. Every last drop of feeling is squeezed from a modern-day troubadour and his lady love.

TAMMY JO ECKHART
PUNISHMENT FOR THE CRIME
$6.95/427-5
Peopled by characters of rare depth, these stories explore the true meaning of dominance and submission, and offer some surprising revelations. From an encounter between two of society's most despised individuals, to the explorations of longtime friends, these tales take you where few others have ever dared....

THOMAS S. ROCHE, EDITOR
NOIROTICA: AN ANTH. OF EROTIC CRIME STORIES
$6.95/390-2
A collection of darkly sexy tales, taking place at the crossroads of the crime and erotic genres. Thomas S. Roche has gathered together some of today's finest writers of sexual fiction, all of whom explore the murky terrain where desire runs irrevocably afoul of the law.

AMARANTHA KNIGHT, EDITOR
SEDUCTIVE SPECTRES
$6.95/464-X
Breathtaking tours through the erotic supernatural via the macabre imaginations of today's best writers. Never before have ghostly encounters been so alluring, thanks to a cast of otherworldly characters well-acquainted with the pleasures of the flesh.

BUY ANY 4 BOOKS & CHOOSE 1 ADDITIONAL BOOK, OF EQUAL OR LESSER VALUE, AS YOUR FREE GIFT

MASQUERADE BOOKS

SEX MACABRE
$6.95/392-9
Horror tales designed for dark and sexy nights. Amarantha Knight—the woman behind the Darker Passions series, as well as the spine-tingling anthologies *Flesh Fantastic* and *Love Bites*—has gathered together erotic stories sure to make your skin crawl, and heart beat faster.

FLESH FANTASTIC
$6.95/352-X
Humans have long toyed with the idea of "playing God": creating life from nothingness, bringing life to the inanimate. Now Amarantha Knight, author of the "Darker Passions" series, collects stories exploring not only the act of Creation, but the lust that follows....

GARY BOWEN
DIARY OF A VAMPIRE
$6.95/331-7
"Gifted with a darkly sensual vision and a fresh voice, [Bowen] is a writer to watch out for."
—Cecilia Tan
The chilling, arousing, and ultimately moving memoirs of an undead—but all too human—soul. Bowen's Rafael, a red-blooded male with an insatiable hunger for the same, is the perfect antidote to the effete malcontents haunting bookstores today. *Diary of a Vampire* marks the emergence of a bold and brilliant vision, firmly rooted in past and present.

LAURA ANTONIOU, EDITOR
NO OTHER TRIBUTE
$6.95/294-9
A collection sure to challenge Political Correctness in a way few have before, with tales of women kept in bondage to their lovers by their deepest passions. Love pushes these women beyond acceptable limits, rendering them helpless to deny anything to the men and women they adore. A volume dedicated to all Slaves of Desire.

SOME WOMEN
$6.95/300-7
Over forty essays written by women actively involved in consensual dominance and submission. Professional mistresses, lifestyle leatherdykes, whipmakers, titleholders—women from every conceivable walk of life lay bare their true feelings about explosive issues.

BY HER SUBDUED
$6.95/281-7
These tales all involve women in control—of their lives, their lovers, their men. So much in control that they can remorselessly break rules to become powerful goddesses of the men who sacrifice all to worship at their feet.

RENÉ MAIZEROY
FLESHLY ATTRACTIONS
$6.95/299-X
Lucien was the son of the wantonly beautiful actress, Marie-Rose Hardanges. When she decides to let a "friend" introduce her son to the pleasures of love, Marie-Rose could not have foretold the excesses that would lead to her own ruin and that of her cherished son.

JEAN STINE
THRILL CITY
$6.95/411-9
Thrill City is the seat of the world's increasing depravity, and Jean Stine's classic novel transports you there with a vivid style you'd be hard pressed to ignore. No writer is better suited to describe the unspeakable extremes of this modern Babylon.

SEASON OF THE WITCH
$6.95/268-X
"A future in which it is technically possible to transfer the total mind...of a rapist killer into the brain dead but physically living body of his female victim. Remarkable for intense psychological technique. There is eroticism but it is necessary to mark the differences between the sexes and the subtle altering of a man into a woman."
—The Science Fiction Critic

JOHN WARREN
THE TORQUEMADA KILLER
$6.95/367-8
Detective Eva Hernandez gets her first "big case": a string of vicious murders taking place within New York's SM community. Eva assembles the evidence, revealing a picture of a world misunderstood and under attack—and gradually comes to understand her own place within it.

THE LOVING DOMINANT
$6.95/218-3
Everything you need to know about an infamous sexual variation—and an unspoken type of love. Mentor—a longtime player in scene—guides readers through this world and reveals the too-often hidden basis of the D/S relationship: care, trust and love.

GRANT ANTREWS
MY DARLING DOMINATRIX
$6.95/447-X
When a man and a woman fall in love, it's supposed to be simple, uncomplicated, easy—unless that woman happens to be a dominatrix. Curiosity gives way to unblushing desire in this story of one man's awakening to the joys of willing slavery.

LAURA ANTONIOU WRITING AS "SARA ADAMSON"
THE TRAINER
$6.95/249-3
The Marketplace—the ultimate underground sexual realm includes not only willing slaves, but the exquisite trainers who take submissives firmly in hand. And now these mentors divulge the desires that led them to become the ultimate figures of authority.

THE SLAVE
$6.95/173-X
This second volume in the "Marketplace" trilogy further elaborates the world of slaves and masters. One talented submissive longs to join the ranks of those who have proven themselves worthy of entry into the Marketplace. But the delicious price is staggeringly high....

MASQUERADE BOOKS

THE MARKETPLACE
$6.95/3096-2
"Merchandise does not come easily to the Marketplace.... They haunt the clubs and the organizations.... Some are so ripe that they intimidate the poseurs, the weekend sadists and the furtive dilettantes who are so endemic to that world. And they never stop asking where we may be found...."

DAVID AARON CLARK
SISTER RADIANCE
$6.95/215-9
Rife with Clark's trademark vivisections of contemporary desires, sacred and profane. The vicissitudes of lust and romance are examined against a backdrop of urban decay in this testament to the allure of the forbidden.

THE WET FOREVER
$6.95/117-9
The story of Janus and Madchen—a small-time hood and a beautiful sex worker on the run from one of the most dangerous men they have ever known—*The Wet Forever* examines themes of loyalty, sacrifice, redemption and obsession amidst Manhattan's sex parlors and underground S/M clubs. Its combination of sex and suspense led Terence Sellers to proclaim it "evocative and poetic."

MICHAEL PERKINS
EVIL COMPANIONS
$6.95/3067-9
Set in New York City during the tumultuous waning years of the Sixties, *Evil Companions* has been hailed as "a frightening classic." A young couple explores the nether reaches of the erotic unconscious in a shocking confrontation with the extremes of passion.

THE SECRET RECORD: MODERN EROTIC LITERATURE
$6.95/3039-3
Michael Perkins surveys the field with authority and unique insight. Updated and revised to include the latest trends, tastes, and developments in this misunderstood and maligned genre.

AN ANTHOLOGY OF CLASSIC ANONYMOUS EROTIC WRITING
$6.95/140-3
Michael Perkins has collected the very best passages from the world's erotic writing. "Anonymous" is one of the most infamous bylines in publishing history—and these steamy excerpts show why! Includes excerpts from some of the most important titles in the history of erotic literature.

LIESEL KULIG
LOVE IN WARTIME
$6.95/3044-X
Madeleine knew that the handsome SS officer was a dangerous man, but he was just a cabaret singer in Nazi-occupied Paris, trying to survive in a perilous time. When Josef fell in love with her, he discovered that a beautiful and amoral woman can sometimes be wildly dangerous.

HELEN HENLEY
ENTER WITH TRUMPETS
$6.95/197-7
Helen Henley was told that women just don't write about sex—much less the taboos she was so interested in exploring. So Henley did it alone, flying in the face of "tradition," by writing this touching tale of arousal and devotion in one couple's kinky relationship.

ALICE JOANOU
BLACK TONGUE
$6.95/258-2
"Joanou has created a series of sumptuous, brooding, dark visions of sexual obsession, and is undoubtedly a name to look out for in the future."
—Redeemer

Exploring lust at its most florid and unsparing, *Black Tongue* is a trove of baroque fantasies—each redolent of forbidden passions. Joanou creates some of erotica's most mesmerizing and unforgettable characters.

TOURNIQUET
$6.95/3060-1
A heady collection of stories and effusions from the pen of one our most dazzling young writers. Strange tales abound, from the story of the mysterious and cruel Cybele, to an encounter with the sadistic entertainment of a bizarre after-hours cafe. A complex and riveting series of meditations on desire.

CANNIBAL FLOWER
$4.95/72-6
The provocative debut volume from this acclaimed writer. "She is waiting in her darkened bedroom, as she has waited throughout history, to seduce the men who are foolish enough to be blinded by her irresistible charms.... She is the goddess of sexuality, and *Cannibal Flower* is her haunting siren song."
—Michael Perkins

TUPPY OWENS
SENSATIONS
$6.95/3081-4
Tuppy Owens tells the unexpurgated story of the making of *Sensations*—the first big-budget sex flick. Originally commissioned to appear in book form after the release of the film in 1975, *Sensations* is finally released under Masquerade's stylish Rhino*ceros* imprint.

SOPHIE GALLEYMORE BIRD
MANEATER
$6.95/103-9
Through a bizarre act of creation, a man attains the "perfect" lover—by all appearances a beautiful, sensuous woman, but in reality something far darker. Once brought to life she will accept no mate, seeking instead the prey that will sate her hunger for vengeance. A biting take on the war of the sexes, this debut goes for the jugular of the "perfect woman" myth.

BUY ANY 4 BOOKS & CHOOSE 1 ADDITIONAL BOOK, OF EQUAL OR LESSER VALUE, AS YOUR FREE GIFT

MASQUERADE BOOKS

PHILIP JOSÉ FARMER
FLESH
$6.95/303-1
Space Commander Stagg explored the galaxies for 800 years. Upon his return, Stagg is made the centerpiece of an incredible public ritual—one that will repeatedly take him to the heights of ecstasy, and inexorably drag him toward the depths of hell.

A FEAST UNKNOWN
$6.95/276-0
"Sprawling, brawling, shocking, suspenseful, hilarious..." —Theodore Sturgeon
Farmer's supreme anti-hero returns. "I was conceived and born in 1888." Slowly, Lord Grandrith—armed with the belief that he is the son of Jack the Ripper—tells the story of his remarkable and unbridled life. His story begins with his discovery of the secret of immortality—and progresses to encompass the furthest extremes of human behavior. A classic of speculative erotica.

THE IMAGE OF THE BEAST
$6.95/166-7
Herald Childe has seen Hell, glimpsed its horror in an act of sexual mutilation. Childe must now find and destroy an inhuman predator through the streets of a polluted and decadent Los Angeles of the future. One clue after another leads Childe to an inescapable realization about the nature of sex and evil....

DANIEL VIAN
ILLUSIONS
$6.95/3074-1
Two tales of danger and desire in Berlin on the eve of WWII. From private homes to lurid cafés, passion is exposed in stark contrast to the brutal violence of the time. Two sexy tales examining a remarkably decadent age.

PERSUASIONS
$6.95/183-7
A double novel, including the classics *Adagio* and *Gabriela and the General*, this volume traces desire around the globe. Two classics of international lust!

SAMUEL R. DELANY
THE MAD MAN
$8.99/408-9
"Reads like a pornographic reflection of Peter Ackroyd's *Chatterton* or A. S. Byatt's *Possession*.... Delany develops an insightful dichotomy between [his protagonist]'s two worlds: the one of cerebral philosophy and dry academia, the other of heedless, 'impersonal' obsessive sexual extremism. When these worlds finally collide...the novel achieves a surprisingly satisfying resolution...." —Publishers Weekly
For his thesis, graduate student John Marr researches the life of Timothy Hasler: a philosopher whose career was cut tragically short over a decade earlier. On another front, Marr finds himself increasingly drawn toward shocking, depraved sexual entanglements with the homeless men of his neighborhood, until it begins to seem that Hasler's death might hold some key to his own life as a gay man in the age of AIDS.

EQUINOX
$6.95/157-8
The Scorpion has sailed the seas in a quest for every possible pleasure. Her crew is a collection of the young, the twisted, the insatiable. A drifter comes into their midst and is taken on a fantastic journey to the darkest, most dangerous sexual extremes—until he is finally a victim to their boundless appetites.

ANDREI CODRESCU
THE REPENTANCE OF LORRAINE
$6.95/329-5
"One of our most prodigiously talented and magical writers." —NYT Book Review
By the acclaimed author of *The Hole in the Flag* and *The Blood Countess*. An aspiring writer, a professor's wife, a secretary, gold anklets, Maoists, Roman harlots—and more—swirl through this spicy tale of a harried quest for a mythic artifact. Written when the author was a young man, this lusty yarn was inspired by the heady days of the Sixties.

LEOPOLD VON SACHER-MASOCH
VENUS IN FURS
$6.95/3089-X
This classic 19th century novel is the first uncompromising exploration of the dominant/submissive relationship in literature. The alliance of Severin and Wanda epitomizes Sacher-Masoch's dark obsession with a cruel, controlling goddess and the urges that drive the man held in her thrall. This special edition includes the letters exchanged between Sacher-Masoch and Emilie Mataja, an aspiring writer he sought to cast as the avatar of the forbidden desires expressed in his most famous work.

BADBOY

JULIAN ANTHONY GUERRA, EDITOR
COME QUICKLY: FOR BOYS ON THE GO
$6.50/413-5
The increasing pace of daily life is no reason a guy has to forgo a little carnal pleasure whenever the mood strikes him. Here are over sixty of the hottest fantasies around—all designed to get you going in less time than it takes to dial 976. Julian Anthony Guerra, the editor behind the phenomenally popular *Men at Work* and *Badboy Fantasies*, has put together this volume especially for you—a man on a modern schedule, who still appreciates a little old-fashioned action.

MATT TOWNSEND
SOLIDLY BUILT
$6.50/416-X
The tale of the tumultuous relationship between Jeff, a young photographer, and Mark, the butch electrician hired to wire Jeff's new home. For Jeff, it's love at first sight; Mark, however, has more than a few hang-ups. Soon, both are forced to reevaluate their outlooks, and are assisted by a variety of hot men....

MASQUERADE BOOKS

JOHN PRESTON

MR. BENSON
$4.95/3041-5
A classic erotic novel from a time when there was no limit to what a man could dream of doing.... Jamie is an aimless young man lucky enough to encounter Mr. Benson. He is soon led down the path of erotic enlightenment, learning to accept this man as his master. Jamie's incredible adventures never fail to excite—especially when the going gets rough!

TALES FROM THE DARK LORD
$5.95/323-6
A new collection of twelve stunning works from the man *Lambda Book Report* called "the Dark Lord of gay erotica." The relentless ritual of lust and surrender is explored in all its manifestations in this heart-stopping triumph of authority and vision from the Dark Lord!

TALES FROM THE DARK LORD II
$4.95/176-4
The second volume of acclaimed eroticist John Preston's masterful short stories. Also includes an interview with the author, and an explicit screenplay written for pornstar Scott O'Hara.

THE ARENA
$4.95/3083-0
There is a place on the edge of fantasy where every desire is indulged with abandon. Men go there to unleash beasts, to let demons roam free, to abolish all limits. At the center of each tale are the men who serve there, who offer themselves for the consummation of any passion, whose own bottomless urges compel their endless subservience.

THE HEIR•THE KING
$4.95/3048-2
The ground-breaking novel *The Heir*, written in the lyric voice of the ancient myths, tells the story of a world where slaves and masters create a new sexual society. This edition also includes a completely original work, *The King*, the story of a soldier who discovers his monarch's most secret desires. Available only from Badboy.

THE MISSION OF ALEX KANE

SWEET DREAMS
$4.95/3062-8
It's the triumphant return of gay action hero Alex Kane! In *Sweet Dreams*, Alex travels to Boston where he takes on a street gang that stalks gay teenagers. Mighty Alex Kane wreaks a fierce and terrible vengeance on those who prey on gay people everywhere!

GOLDEN YEARS
$4.95/3069-5
When evil threatens the plans of a group of older gay men, Kane's got the muscle to take it head on. Along the way, he wins the support—and very specialized attentions—of a cowboy plucked right out of the Old West. But Kane and the Cowboy have a surprise waiting for them....

DEADLY LIES
$4.95/3076-8
Politics is a dirty business and the dirt becomes deadly when a political smear campaign targets gay men. Who better to clean things up than Alex Kane! Alex comes to protect the dreams, and lives, of gay men imperiled by lies.

STOLEN MOMENTS
$4.95/3098-9
Houston's evolving gay community is victimized by a malicious newspaper editor who is more than willing to sacrifice gays on the altar of circulation. He never counted on Alex Kane, fearless defender of gay dreams and desires.

SECRET DANGER
$4.95/111-X
Homophobia: a pernicious social ill not confined by America's borders. Alex Kane and the faithful Danny are called to a small European country, where a group of gay tourists is being held hostage by ruthless terrorists. Luckily, the Mission of Alex Kane stands as firm foreign policy.

LETHAL SILENCE
$4.95/125-X
The Mission of Alex Kane thunders to a conclusion. Chicago becomes the scene of the right-wing's most noxious plan—facilitated by unholy political alliances. Alex and Danny head to the Windy City to take up battle with the mercenaries who would squash gay men underfoot.

JAY SHAFFER

WET DREAMS
$6.50/495-X
Sweaty, sloppy sex runs throughout this collection of super-hot, hypermasculine sex-tales from one of our most accomplished Badboys. Each of these stories takes a hot, hard look at the obsessions that keep men up all night. Provocative and affecting, this is a night full of dreams you won't forget in the morning.

SHOOTERS
$5.95/284-1
No mere catalog of random acts, *Shooters* tells the stories of a variety of stunning men and the ways they connect in sexual and non-sexual ways. A virtuoso storyteller, Shaffer always gets his man.

ANIMAL HANDLERS
$4.95/264-7
In Shaffer's world, each and every man finally succumbs to the animal urges deep inside. And if there's any creature that promises a wild time, it's a beast who's been caged for far too long.

FULL SERVICE
$4.95/150-0
Wild men build up steam until they finally let loose. No-nonsense guys bear down hard on each other as they work their way toward release in this finely detailed assortment of masculine fantasies. One of gay erotica's most insightful chroniclers of male passion.

BUY ANY 4 BOOKS & CHOOSE 1 ADDITIONAL BOOK, OF EQUAL OR LESSER VALUE, AS YOUR FREE GIFT

MASQUERADE BOOKS

D. V. SADERO
REVOLT OF THE NAKED
$4.95/261-2
In a distant galaxy, there are two classes of humans: Freemen and Nakeds. Freemen are full citizens; Nakeds live only to serve their Masters, and obey every sexual order with haste and devotion.

IN THE ALLEY
$4.95/144-6
Hardworking men—from cops to carpenters—bring their own special skills and impressive tools to the most satisfying job of all: capturing and breaking the male human beast. Hot, incisive and way over the top!

SCOTT O'HARA
DO-IT-YOURSELF PISTON POLISHING
$6.50/489-5
Longtime sex-pro Scott O'Hara draws upon his acute powers of seduction to lure you into a world of hard, horny men long overdue for a tune-up. Pretty soon, you'll pop your own hood for the servicing you know you need....

SUTTER POWELL
EXECUTIVE PRIVILEGES
$6.50/383-X
No matter how serious or sexy a predicament his characters find themselves in, Powell conveys the sheer exuberance of their encounters with a warm humor rarely seen in contemporary gay erotica.

GARY BOWEN
MAN HUNGRY
$5.95/374-0
By the author of *Diary of a Vampire*. A riveting collection of stories from one of gay erotica's new stars. Dipping into a variety of genres, Bowen crafts tales of lust unlike anything being published today.

KYLE STONE
FIRE & ICE
$5.95/297-3
A collection of stories from the author of the infamous adventures of PB 500. Randy, powerful, and just plain bad, Stone's characters always promise one thing: enough hot action to burn away your desire for anyone else....

HOT BAUDS
$5.95/285-X
The author of *Fantasy Board* and *The Initiation of PB 500* combed cyberspace for the hottest fantasies of the world's horniest hackers. Stone has assembled the first collection of the raunchy erotica so many gay men cruise the Information Superhighway for.

FANTASY BOARD
$4.95/212-4
The author of the scalding sci-fi adventures of PB 500 explores the more foreseeable future—through the intertwined lives (and private parts) of a collection of randy computer hackers. On the Lambda Gate BBS, every hot and horny male is in search of a little virtual satisfaction.

THE CITADEL
$4.95/198-5
The sequel to *The Initiation of PB 500*. Having proven himself worthy of his stunning master, Micah—now known only as '500'—will face new challenges and hardships after his entry into the forbidding Citadel. Only his master knows what awaits—and whether Micah will again distinguish himself as the perfect instrument of pleasure....

THE INITIATION OF PB 500
$4.95/141-1
An interstellar accident strands a young stud on an alien planet. He is a stranger on their planet, unschooled in their language, and ignorant of their customs. But this man, Micah—now known only by his number—will soon be trained in every last detail of erotic personal service. And, once nurtured and transformed into the perfect physical specimen, he must begin proving himself worthy of the master who has chosen him....

RITUALS
$4.95/168-3
Via a computer bulletin board, a young man finds himself drawn into a series of sexual rites that transform him into the willing slave of a mysterious stranger. Gradually, all vestiges of his former life are thrown off, and he learns to live for his Master's touch....

JOHN ROWBERRY
LEWD CONDUCT
$4.95/3091-1
Flesh-and-blood men vie for power, pleasure and surrender in each of these feverish stories, and no one walks away from his steamy encounter unsated. Rowberry's men are unafraid to push the limits of civilized behavior in search of the elusive and empowering conquest. One of gay erotica's first success stories.

ROBERT BAHR
SEX SHOW
$4.95/225-6
Luscious dancing boys. Brazen, explicit acts. Unending stimulation. Take a seat, and get very comfortable, because the curtain's going up on a show no discriminating appetite can afford to miss.

JASON FURY
THE ROPE ABOVE, THE BED BELOW
$4.95/269-8
The irresistible Jason Fury returns—this time, telling the tale of a vicious murderer preying upon New York's go-go boy population. No one is who or what they seem, and in order to solve this mystery and save lives, each studly suspect must lay bare his soul—and more! Never has a private dick worked so hard!

ERIC'S BODY
$4.95/151-9
Meet Jason Fury—blond, blue-eyed and up for anything. Fury's sexiest tales are collected in book form for the first time. Follow the irresistible Jason through sexual adventures unlike any you have ever read....

MASQUERADE BOOKS

"BIG" BILL JACKSON
EIGHTH WONDER
$4.95/200-0
From the bright lights and back rooms of New York to the open fields and sweaty bods of a small Southern town, "Big" Bill always manages to cause a scene, and the more actors he can involve, the better! Like the man's name says, he's got more than enough for everyone, and turns nobody down....

1 800 906-HUNK
THE connection for hot handfuls of eager guys! No credit card needed—so call now for access to the hottest party line available. Spill it all to bad boys from across the country! (Must be over 18.) Pick one up now.... $3.98 per min.

LARS EIGHNER
WHISPERED IN THE DARK
$5.95/286-8
A volume demonstrating Eighner's unique combination of strengths: poetic descriptive power, an unfailing ear for dialogue, and a finely tuned feeling for the nuances of male passion.
AMERICAN PRELUDE
$4.95/170-5
Eighner is widely recognized as one of our best, most exciting gay writers. He is also one of gay erotica's true masters—and *American Prelude* shows why. Wonderfully written, blisteringly hot tales of all-American lust.
B.M.O.C.
$4.95/3077-6
In a college town known as "the Athens of the Southwest," studs of every stripe are up all night—studying, naturally. In *B.M.O.C.*, Lars Eighner includes the very best of his short stories, sure to appeal to the collegian in every man. Relive university life the way it was supposed to be, with a cast of handsome honor students majoring in Human Homosexuality.

EDITED BY DAVID LAURENTS
SOUTHERN COMFORT
$6.50/466-6
Editor David Laurents now unleashes another collection of today's most provocative gay writing. The tales here focus on the American South—and reflect not only Southern literary tradition, but the many contributions the region has made to the iconography of the American Male.
WANDERLUST:
HOMOEROTIC TALES OF TRAVEL
$5.95/395-3
A volume dedicated to the special pleasures of faraway places. Gay men have always had a special interest in travel—and not only for the scenic vistas. *Wanderlust* celebrates the freedom of the open road, and the allure of men who stray from the beaten path....

THE BADBOY BOOK OF EROTIC POETRY
$5.95/382-1
Over fifty of today's best poets. Erotic poetry has long been the problem child of the literary world—highly creative and provocative, but somehow too frank to be "literature." Both learned and stimulating, *The Badboy Book of Erotic Poetry* restores eros to its rightful place of honor in contemporary gay writing.

AARON TRAVIS
BIG SHOTS
$5.95/448-8
Two fierce tales in one electrifying volume. In *Beirut*, Travis tells the story of ultimate military power and erotic subjugation; *Kip*, Travis' hypersexed and sinister take on film noir, appears in unexpurgated form for the first time—including the final, overwhelming chapter.
EXPOSED
$4.95/126-8
A volume of shorter Travis tales, each providing a unique glimpse of the horny gay male in his natural environment! Cops, college jocks, ancient Romans—even Sherlock Holmes and his loyal Watson—cruise these pages, fresh from the throbbing pen of one of our hottest authors.
BEAST OF BURDEN
$4.95/105-5
Five ferocious tales. Innocents surrender to the brutal sexual mastery of their superiors, as taboos are shattered and replaced with the unwritten rules of masculine conquest. Intense, extreme—and totally Travis.
IN THE BLOOD
$5.95/283-3
Written when Travis had just begun to explore the true power of the erotic imagination, these stories laid the groundwork for later masterpieces. Among the many rewarding rarities included in this volume: "In the Blood" —a heart-pounding descent into sexual vampirism, written with the furious erotic power that has distinguished Travis' work from the beginning.
THE FLESH FABLES
$4.95/243-4
One of Travis' best collections. *The Flesh Fables* includes "Blue Light," his most famous story, as well as other masterpieces that established him as the erotic writer to watch. And watch carefully, because Travis always buries a surprise somewhere beneath his scorching detail....
SLAVES OF THE EMPIRE
$4.95/3054-7
"*Slaves of the Empire* is a wonderful mythic tale. Set against the backdrop of the exotic and powerful Roman Empire, this wonderfully written novel explores the timeless questions of light and dark in male sexuality. Travis has shown himself expert in manipulating the most primal themes and images. The locale may be the ancient world, but these are the slaves and masters of our time...."   —John Preston

BUY ANY 4 BOOKS & CHOOSE 1 ADDITIONAL BOOK, OF EQUAL OR LESSER VALUE, AS YOUR FREE GIFT

MASQUERADE BOOKS

BOB VICKERY
SKIN DEEP
$4.95/265-5
So many varied beauties no one will go away unsatisfied. No tantalizing morsel of manflesh is overlooked—or left unexplored! Beauty may be only skin deep, but a handful of beautiful skin is a tempting proposition.

JR
FRENCH QUARTER NIGHTS
$5.95/337-6
A randy roundup of this author's most popular tales. *French Quarter Nights* is filled with sensual snapshots of the many places where men get down and dirty—from the steamy French Quarter to the steam room at the old Everard baths. In the best tradition of gay erotica, these are nights you'll wish would go on forever....

TOM BACCHUS
RAHM
$5.95/315-5
The imagination of Tom Bacchus brings to life an extraordinary assortment of characters, from the Father of Us All to the cowpoke next door, the early gay literati to rude, queercore mosh rats. No one is better than Bacchus at staking out sexual territory with a swagger and a sly grin.

BONE
$4.95/177-2
Queer musings from the pen of one of today's hottest young talents. A fresh outlook on fleshly indulgence yields more than a few pleasant surprises. Horny Tom Bacchus maps out the tricking ground of a new generation.

KEY LINCOLN
SUBMISSION HOLDS
$4.95/266-3
A bright young talent unleashes his first collection of gay erotica. From tough to tender, the men between these covers stop at nothing to get what they want. These sweat-soaked tales show just how bad boys can really get—especially when given a little help by an equally lustful stud.

HODDY ALLEN
AL
$5.95/302-3
Al is a remarkable young man. With his long brown hair, bright green eyes and eagerness to please, many would consider him the perfect submissive. Many would like to mark him as their own—but it is at that point that Al stops. One day Al relates the entire astounding tale of his life....

CALDWELL/EIGHNER
QSFX2
$5.95/278-7
The wickedest, wildest, other-worldliest yarns from two master storytellers—Clay Caldwell and Lars Eighner. Both eroticists take a trip to the furthest reaches of the sexual imagination, sending back ten stories proving that as much as things change, one thing will always remain the same....

CLAY CALDWELL
ASK OL' BUDDY
$5.95/346-5
Set in the underground SM world, Caldwell takes you on a journey of discovery—where men initiate one another into the secrets of the rawest sexual realm of all. And when each stud's initiation is complete, he takes his places among the masters—eager to take part in the training of another hungry soul...

STUD SHORTS
$5.95/320-1
"If anything, Caldwell's charm is more powerful, his nostalgia more poignant, the horniness he captures more sweetly, achingly acute than ever."
—Aaron Travis
A new collection of this legend's latest sex-fiction. With his customary candor, Caldwell tells all about cops, cadets, truckers, farmboys (and many more) in these dirty jewels.

TAILPIPE TRUCKER
$5.95/296-5
Trucker porn! In prose as free and unvarnished as a cross-country highway, Caldwell tells the truth about Trag and Curly—two men hot for the feeling of sweaty manflesh. Together, they pick up—and turn out—a couple of thrill-seeking punks.

SERVICE, STUD
$5.95/336-8
Another look at the gay future. The setting is the Los Angeles of a distant future. Here the all-male populace is divided between the served and the servants—guaranteeing the erotic satisfaction of all involved.

QUEERS LIKE US
$4.95/262-0
"This is Caldwell at his most charming."
—Aaron Travis
For years the name Clay Caldwell has been synonymous with the hottest, most finely crafted gay tales available. *Queers Like Us* is one of his best: the story of a randy mailman's trek through a landscape of willing, available studs.

ALL-STUD
$4.95/104-7
This classic, sex-soaked tale takes place under the watchful eye of Number Ten: an omniscient figure who has decreed unabashed promiscuity as the law of his all-male land. One stud, however, takes it upon himself to challenge the social order, daring to fall in love. Finally, he is forced to fight for not only himself, but the man to whom he has committed himself.

CLAY CALDWELL AND AARON TRAVIS
TAG TEAM STUDS
$6.50/465-8
Thrilling tales from these two legendary eroticists. The wrestling world will never seem the same, once you've made your way through this assortment of sweaty, virile studs. But you'd better be wary—should one catch you off guard, you just might spend the rest of the night pinned to the mat.... A double dose of roughstuff, available only from Badboy.

MASQUERADE BOOKS

LARRY TOWNSEND

LEATHER AD: S
$5.95/407-0
The second half of Townsend's acclaimed tale of lust through the personals—this time told from a Top's perspective. A simple ad generates many responses, and one man finds himself in the enviable position of putting these studly applicants through their paces.....

LEATHER AD: M
$5.95/380-5
The first of this two-part classic. John's curious about what goes on between the leatherclad men he's fantasized about. He takes out a personal ad, and starts a journey of self-discovery that will leave no part of his life unchanged.

1 900 745-HUNG

Hardcore phone action for real men. A scorching assembly of studs is waiting for your call—and eager to give you the headtrip of your life! Totally live, guaranteed one-on-one encounters. (Must be over 18.) No credit card needed. $3.98 per minute.

BEWARE THE GOD WHO SMILES
$5.95/321-X
Two lusty young Americans are transported to ancient Egypt—where they are embroiled in regional warfare and taken as slaves by marauding barbarians. The key to escape from this brutal bondage lies in their own rampant libidos, and urges as old as time itself.

THE CONSTRUCTION WORKER
$5.95/298-1
A young, hung construction worker is sent to a building project in Central America, where he finds that man-to-man sex is the accepted norm. The young stud quickly fits in—until he senses that beneath the constant sexual shenanigans there moves an almost supernatural force.

2069 TRILOGY
(This one-volume collection only $6.95)244-2
For the first time, Larry Townsend's early science-fiction trilogy appears in one massive volume! Set in a future world, the 2069 Trilogy includes the tight plotting and shameless male sexual pleasure that established him as one of gay erotica's first masters.

MIND MASTER
$4.95/209-4
Who better to explore the territory of erotic dominance than an author who helped define the genre—and knows that ultimate mastery always transcends the physical.

THE LONG LEATHER CORD
$4.95/201-9
Chuck's stepfather never lacks money or clandestine male visitors with whom he enacts intense sexual rituals. As Chuck comes to terms with his own desires, he begins to unravel the mystery behind his stepfather's secret life.

MAN SWORD
$4.95/188-8
France's King Henri III, unimaginably spoiled by his mother—the infamous Catherine de Medici—was groomed from a young age to assume the throne of France. Along the way, he encounters enough sexual schemers and politicos to alter one's picture of history forever!

THE FAUSTUS CONTRACT
$4.95/167-5
Two attractive young men desperately need $1000. Will do anything. Travel OK. Danger OK. Call anytime... Two cocky young hustlers get more than they bargained for in this story of lust and its discontents.

THE GAY ADVENTURES OF CAPTAIN GOOSE
$4.95/169-1
The hot and tender young Jerome Gander is sentenced to serve aboard the H.M.S. Faerigold—a ship manned by the most hardened, unrepentant criminals. In no time, Gander becomes well-versed in the ways of horny men at sea.

CHAINS
$4.95/158-6
Picking up street punks has always been risky, but in Larry Townsend's classic Chains, it sets off a string of events that must be read to be believed.

KISS OF LEATHER
$4.95/161-6
A look at the acts and attitudes of an earlier generation of gay leathermen, Kiss of Leather is full to bursting with the gritty, raw action that has distinguished Townsend's work for years. Pain and pleasure mix in this tightly plotted tale.

RUN, LITTLE LEATHER BOY
$4.95/143-8
One young man's sexual awakening. A chronic underachiever, Wayne seems to be going nowhere fast. He finds himself bored with the everyday—and drawn to the masculine intensity of a dark and mysterious sexual underground....

RUN NO MORE
$4.95/152-7
The continuation of Larry Townsend's legendary Run, Little Leather Boy. This volume follows the further adventures of Townsend's leatherclad narrator as he travels every sexual byway available to the S/M male.

THE SCORPIUS EQUATION
$4.95/119-5
The story of a man caught between the demands of two galactic empires. Our randy hero must match wits—and more—with the incredible forces that rule his world.

THE SEXUAL ADVENTURES OF SHERLOCK HOLMES
$4.95/3097-0
"A Study in Scarlet" is transformed to expose Mrs. Hudson as a man in drag, the Diogenes Club as an S/M arena, and clues only the redoubtable—and very horny—Sherlock Holmes could piece together. A baffling tale of sex and mystery.

BUY ANY 4 BOOKS & CHOOSE 1 ADDITIONAL BOOK, OF EQUAL OR LESSER VALUE, AS YOUR FREE GIFT

MASQUERADE BOOKS

DONALD VINING
CABIN FEVER AND OTHER STORIES
$5.95/338-4
Eighteen blistering stories in celebration of the most intimate of male bonding. Time after time, Donald Vining's men succumb to nature, and reaffirm both love and lust in modern gay life.

"Demonstrates the wisdom experience combined with insight and optimism can create."
—Bay Area Reporter

DEREK ADAMS
PRISONER OF DESIRE
$6.50/439-9
Scalding fiction from one of Badboy's most popular authors. The creator of horny P.I. Miles Diamond returns with this volume bursting with red-blooded, sweat-soaked excursions through the modern gay libido.

THE MARK OF THE WOLF
$5.95/361-9
I turned to look at the man who stared back at me from the mirror. The familiar outlines of my face seemed coarser, more sinister. An animal? The past comes back to haunt one well-off stud, whose unslakeable thirsts lead him into the arms of many men—and the midst of a perilous mystery.

MY DOUBLE LIFE
$5.95/314-7
Every man leads a double life, dividing his hours between the mundanities of the day and the outrageous pursuits of the night. The creator of sexy P.I. Miles Diamond shines a little light on the wicked things men do when no one's looking.

BOY TOY
$4.95/260-4
Poor Brendan Callan finds himself the guinea pig of a crazed geneticist. The result: Brendan becomes irresistibly alluring—a talent designed for endless pleasure, but coveted by others for the most unsavory means....

HEAT WAVE
$4.95/159-4
"His body was draped in baggy clothes, but there was hardly any doubt that they covered anything less than perfection.... His slacks were cinched tight around a narrow waist, and the rise of flesh pushing against the thin fabric promised a firm, melon-shaped ass...."

MILES DIAMOND AND THE DEMON OF DEATH
$4.95/251-5
Derek Adams' gay gumshoe returns for further adventures. Miles always find himself in the stickiest situations—with any stud whose path he crosses! His adventures with "The Demon of Death" promise another carnal carnival.

THE ADVENTURES OF MILES DIAMOND
$4.95/118-7
The debut of Miles Diamond—Derek Adams' take on the classic American archetype of the hardboiled private eye. "The Case of the Missing Twin" promises to be a most rewarding case, packed as it is with randy studs. Miles sets about uncovering all as he tracks down the randy and delectable Daniel Travis. As Miles soon discovers, every man has a secret desire....

KELVIN BELIELE
IF THE SHOE FITS
$4.95/223-X
An essential and winning volume of tales exploring a world where randy boys can't help but do what comes naturally—as often as possible! Sweaty male bodies grapple in pleasure, proving the old adage: if the shoe fits, one might as well slip right in....

VINCE GILMAN
THE SLAVE PRINCE
$4.95/199-3
A runaway royal learns the true meaning of power when he comes under the hand of Korat—a man well-versed in the many ways of subjugating a young man to his relentless sexual appetite.

JAMES MEDLEY
THE REVOLUTIONARY & OTHER STORIES
$6.50/417-8
Billy, the son of the station chief of the American Embassy in Guatemala, is kidnapped and held for ransom. Frightened at first, Billy gradually develops an unimaginably close relationship with Juan, the revolutionary assigned to guard him. Things soon heat up—thanks to Medley's unforgettable mixture of high adventure and unquenchable lust!

HUCK AND BILLY
$4.95/245-0
Young love is always the sweetest, always the most sorrowful. Young lust, on the other hand, knows no bounds—and is often the hottest of one's life! Huck and Billy explore the desires that course through their young male bodies, determined to plumb the lusty depths of passion.

FLEDERMAUS
FLEDERFICTION: STORIES OF MEN AND TORTURE
$5.95/355-4
Fifteen blistering paeans to men and their suffering. Fledermaus unleashes his most thrilling tales of punishment in this special volume designed with Badboy readers in mind.

VICTOR TERRY
MASTERS
$6.50/418-6
A powerhouse volume of boot-wearing, whip-wielding, bone-crunching bruisers who've got what it takes to make a grown man grovel. From a chance encounter on the Christopher Street pier to an impromptu session with a mysterious and unrelenting visitor, this collection focuses on the most demanding of men—the imperious few to whom so many humbly offer themselves....

SM/SD
$6.50/406-2
Set around a South Dakota town called Prairie, these tales offer compelling evidence that the real rough stuff can still be found where men roam free of the restraints of "polite" society—and take what they want despite all rules.

MASQUERADE BOOKS

WHiPs
$4.95/254-X
Connoisseurs of gay writing have known Victor Terry's work for some time. Cruising for a hot man? You'd better be, because one way or another, these WHiPs—officers of the Wyoming Highway Patrol—are gonna pull you over for a little impromptu interrogation....

MAX EXANDER
DEEDS OF THE NIGHT: TALES OF EROS AND PASSION
$5.95/348-1
MAXimum porn! Exander's a writer who's seen it all—and is more than happy to describe every inch of it in pulsating detail. A whirlwind tour of the hypermasculine libido.

LEATHERSEX
$4.95/210-8
Hard-hitting tales from merciless Max Exander. This time he focuses on the leatherclad lust that draws together only the most willing and talented of tops and bottoms—for an all-out orgy of limitless surrender and control....

MANSEX
$4.95/160-8
"Mark was the classic leatherman: a huge, dark stud in chaps, with a big black moustache, hairy chest and enormous muscles. Exactly the kind of men Todd liked—strong, hunky, masculine, ready to take control...."

TOM CAFFREY
TALES FROM THE MEN'S ROOM
$5.95/364-3
Another collection of keenly observed, passionate tales. From shameless cops on the beat to shy studs on stage, Caffrey explores male lust at its most elemental and arousing. And if there's a lesson to be learned, it's that the Men's Room is less a place than a state of mind—one that every man finds himself in, day after day....

HITTING HOME
$4.95/222-1
One of our newest Badboys weighs in with a scorching collection of stories. Titillating and compelling, the stories in *Hitting Home* make a strong case for there being only one thing on a man's mind.

TORSTEN BARRING
PRISONERS OF TORQUEMADA
$5.95/252-3
Another volume sure to push you over the edge. How cruel is the "therapy" practiced at Casa Torquemada? Barring is just the writer to evoke such steamy sexual malevolence.

SHADOWMAN
$4.95/178-0
From spoiled Southern aristocrats to randy youths sowing wild oats at the local picture show, Barring's imagination works overtime in these vignettes of homolust—past, present and future.

PETER THORNWELL
$4.95/149-7
Follow the exploits of Peter Thornwell as he goes from misspent youth to scandalous stardom, all thanks to an insatiable libido and love for the lash. Peter and his sex-crazed sidekicks find themselves pursued by merciless men from all walks of life in this torrid take on Horatio Alger.

THE SWITCH
$4.95/3061-X
Sometimes a man needs a good whipping, and *The Switch* certainly makes a case! Packed with hot studs and unrelenting passions.

BERT McKENZIE
FRINGE BENEFITS
$5.95/354-6
From the pen of a widely published short story writer comes a volume of highly immodest tales. Not afraid of getting down and dirty, McKenzie produces some of today's most visceral sextales.

SONNY FORD
REUNION IN FLORENCE
$4.95/3070-9
Captured by Turks, Adrian and Tristan will do anything to save their heads. When Tristan is threatened by a Sultan's jealousy, Adrian begins his quest for the only man alive who can replace Tristan as the object of the Sultan's lust.

ROGER HARMAN
FIRST PERSON
$4.95/179-9
A highly personal collection. Each story takes the form of a confessional—told by men who've got plenty to confess! From the "first time ever" to firsts of different kinds, *First Person* tells truths too hot to be purely fiction.

J.A. GUERRA
BADBOY FANTASIES
$4.95/3049-0
When love eludes them—lust will do! Thrill-seeking men caught up in vivid dreams, dark mysteries and brief encounters will keep you gasping throughout these tales.

SLOW BURN
$4.95/3042-3
Welcome to the Body Shoppe, where men's lives cross in the pursuit of muscle. Torsos get lean and hard, pecs widen, and stomachs ripple in these sexy stories of the power and perils of physical perfection.

SEAN MARTIN
SCRAPBOOK
$4.95/224-8
Imagine a book filled with only the best, most vivid remembrances...a book brimming with every hot, sexy encounter its pages can hold... Now you need only open up *Scrapbook* to know that such a volume really exists....

BUY ANY 4 BOOKS & CHOOSE 1 ADDITIONAL BOOK, OF EQUAL OR LESSER VALUE, AS YOUR FREE GIFT

MASQUERADE BOOKS

CARO SOLES & STAN TAL, EDITORS
BIZARRE DREAMS
$4.95/187-X
An anthology of stirring voices dedicated to exploring the dark side of human fantasy. *Bizarre Dreams* brings together the most talented practitioners of "dark fantasy," the most forbidden sexual realm of all.

CHRISTOPHER MORGAN
STEAM GAUGE
$6.50/473-9
The first collection of short stories from the author of the bestselling *Muscle Bound*. This volume abounds in manly men doing what they do best—to, with, or for any hot stud who crosses their paths. Frequently published to acclaim in the gay press, Christopher Morgan puts a fresh, contemporary spin on the very oldest of urges.

THE SPORTSMEN
$5.95/385-6
A collection of super-hot stories dedicated to that most popular of boys next door—the all-American athlete. Here are enough tales of carnal grand slams, sexy interceptions and highly personal bests to satisfy the hungers of the most ardent sports fan. Editor Christopher Morgan has gathered those writers who know just the type of guys that make up every red-blooded male's starting line-up....

MUSCLE BOUND
$4.95/3028-8
In the New York City bodybuilding scene, country boy Tommy joins forces with sexy Will Rodriguez in a battle of wits and biceps at the hottest gym in town, where the weak are bound and crushed by iron-pumping gods.

DAVE KINNICK
SORRY I ASKED
$4.95/3090-3
Unexpurgated interviews with gay porn's rank and file. Get personal with the men behind (and under) the "stars," and discover the hot truth about the porn business.

MICHAEL LOWENTHAL, ED.
THE BADBOY EROTIC LIBRARY VOLUME I
$4.95/190-X
Excerpts from *A Secret Life*, *Imre*, *Sins of the Cities of the Plain*, *Teleny* and others demonstrate the uncanny gift for portraying sex between men that led to many of these titles being banned upon publication.

THE BADBOY EROTIC LIBRARY VOLUME II
$4.95/211-6
This time, selections are taken from *Mike and Me* and *Muscle Bound*, *Men at Work*, *Badboy Fantasies*, and *Slowburn*.

ERIC BOYD
MIKE AND ME
$5.95/419-4
Mike joined the gym squad to bulk up on muscle. Little did he know he'd be turning on every sexy muscle jock in Minnesota! Hard bodies collide in a series of workouts designed to generate a whole lot more than rips and cuts.

MIKE AND THE MARINES
$6.50/497-6
Mike takes on America's most elite corps of studs—running into more than a few good men! Join in on the never-ending sexual escapades of this singularly lustful platoon!

ANONYMOUS
A SECRET LIFE
$4.95/3017-2
Meet Master Charles: only eighteen, and quite innocent, until his arrival at the Sir Percival's Royal Academy, where the daily lessons are supplemented with a crash course in pure, sweet sexual heat!

SINS OF THE CITIES OF THE PLAIN
$5.95/322-8
ndulge yourself in the scorching memoirs of young man-about-town Jack Saul. With his shocking dalliances with the lords and "ladies" of British high society, Jack's positively sinful escapades grow wilder with every chapter!

IMRE
$4.95/3019-9
What dark secrets, what fiery passions lay hidden behind strikingly beautiful Lieutenant Imre's emerald eyes? An extraordinary lost classic of fantasy, obsession, gay erotic desire, and romance in a small European town on the eve of WWI.

TELENY
$4.95/3020-2
Often attributed to Oscar Wilde, *Teleny* tells the story of one young man of independent means. He dedicates himself to a succession of forbidden pleasures, but instead finds love and tragedy when he becomes embroiled in a cult devoted to fulfilling only the very darkest of fantasies.

PAT CALIFIA
THE SEXPERT
$4.95/3034-2
You can turn to one authority for answers to virtually any question on the subjects of intimacy and sexual performance—The Sexpert, who responds to real-life sexual concerns with uncanny wisdom and a razor wit.

HARD CANDY

PATRICK MOORE
IOWA
$6.95/423-2
"Moore is the Tennessee Williams of the nineties—profound intimacy freed in a compelling narrative."
—Karen Finley
"Fresh and shiny and relevant to our time. *Iowa* is full of terrific characters etched in acid-sharp prose, soaked through with just enough ambivalence to make it thoroughly romantic."
—Felice Picano
A stunning novel about one gay man's journey into adulthood, and the roads that bring him home again. From the author of the highly praised *This Every Night*.

MASQUERADE BOOKS

STAN LEVENTHAL
BARBIE IN BONDAGE
$6.95/415-1
Widely regarded as one of the most refreshing, clear-eyed interpreters of big city gay male life, Leventhal here provides a series of explorations of love and desire between men. Uncompromising, but gentle and generous, *Barbie in Bondage* is a fitting tribute to the late author's unique talents.

SKYDIVING ON CHRISTOPHER STREET
$6.95/287-6
"Positively addictive." —Dennis Cooper
Aside from a hateful job, a hateful apartment, a hateful world and an increasingly hateful lover, life seems, well, all right for the protagonist of Stan Leventhal's latest novel. Having already lost most of his friends to AIDS, how could things get any worse? But things soon do, and he's forced to endure much more....

PAUL T. ROGERS
SAUL'S BOOK
$7.95/462-3
Winner of the First Annual Editors' Book Award
"Exudes an almost narcotic power.... A masterpiece."
—*Village Voice Literary Supplement*
"A first novel of considerable power... Sinbad the Sailor, thanks to the sympathetic imagination of Paul T. Rogers, speaks to us all." —*New York Times Book Review*
The story of a Times Square hustler called Sinbad the Sailor and Saul, a brilliant, self-destructive, alcoholic, thoroughly dominating character who may be the only love Sindab will ever know.

WALTER HOLLAND
THE MARCH
$6.95/429-1
A moving testament to the power of friendship during even the worst of times. Beginning on a hot summer night in 1980, *The March* revolves around a circle of young gay men, and the many others their lives touch. Over time, each character changes in unexpected ways; lives and loves come together and fall apart, as society itself is horribly altered by the onslaught of AIDS. A kaleidoscopic portrait of friendship, love, loss, and the myriad triumphs and devestations of contemporary life. From the acclaimed author of *A Journal of the Plague Years*.

RED JORDAN AROBATEAU
LUCY AND MICKEY
$6.95/311-2
The story of Mickey—an uncompromising butch—and her long affair with Lucy, the femme she loves. A raw tale of pre-Stonewall lesbian life.
"A necessary reminder to all who blissfully—some may say ignorantly—ride the wave of lesbian chic into the mainstream." —Heather Findlay

DIRTY PICTURES
$5.95/345-7
"Red Jordan Arobateau is the Thomas Wolfe of lesbian literature... Arobateau's work overflows with vitality and pulsing life. She's a natural—raw talent that is seething, passionate, hard, remarkable."
—Lillian Faderman, editor of *Chloe Plus Olivia*
Dirty Pictures is the story of a lonely butch tending bar—and the femme she finally calls her own.

DONALD VINING
A GAY DIARY
$8.95/451-8
Donald Vining's *Diary* portrays a long-vanished age and the lifestyle of a gay generation all too frequently forgotten. A touching and revealing volume documenting the surprisingly vibrant culture that existed decades before Stonewal.
"*A Gay Diary* is, unquestionably, the richest historical document of gay male life in the United States that I have ever encountered.... It illuminates a critical period in gay male American history."
—*Body Politic*

LARS EIGHNER
GAY COSMOS
$6.95/236-1
A title sure to appeal not only to Eighner's gay fans, but the many converts who first encountered his moving nonfiction work. Praised by the press, *Gay Cosmos* is an important contribution to the burgeoning area of Gay and Lesbian Studies—and sure to provoke many readers.

FELICE PICANO
THE LURE
$6.95/398-8
"The subject matter, plus the authenticity of Picano's research are, combined, explosive. Felice Picano is one hell of a writer." —Stephen King
After witnessing a brutal murder, Noel is recruited by the police, to assist as a lure for the killer. Undercover, he moves deep into the freneticism of Manhattan's gay highlife—where he gradually becomes aware of the darker forces at work in his life. In addition to the mystery behind his mission, he begins to recognize changes: in his relationships with the men around him, in himself...

AMBIDEXTROUS
$6.95/275-2
"Deftly evokes those placid Eisenhower years of bicycles, boners, and book reports. Makes us remember what it feels like to be a child..."
—*The Advocate*
Picano's first "memoir in the form of a novel" tells all: home life, school face-offs, the ingenuous sophistications of his first sexual steps. In three years' time, he's had his first gay fling—and is on his way to becoming the widely praised writer he is today.

BUY ANY 4 BOOKS & CHOOSE 1 ADDITIONAL BOOK, OF EQUAL OR LESSER VALUE, AS YOUR FREE GIFT

MASQUERADE BOOKS

MEN WHO LOVED ME
$6.95/274-4

"Zesty...spiked with adventure and romance...a distinguished and humorous portrait of a vanished age."
—Publishers Weekly

In 1966, Picano abandoned New York, determined to find true love in Europe. When the older and wiser Picano returns to New York at last, he plunges into the city's thriving gay community—experiencing the frenzy and heartbreak that came to define Greenwich Village society in the 1970s.

WILLIAM TALSMAN
THE GAUDY IMAGE
$6.95/263-9

"To read The Gaudy Image now...it is to see first-hand the very issues of identity and positionality with which gay men were struggling in the decades before Stonewall. For what Talsman is dealing with...is the very question of how we conceive ourselves gay."
—from the introduction by Michael Bronski

ROSEBUD

THE ROSEBUD READER
$5.95/319-8

Rosebud has contributed greatly to the burgeoning genre of lesbian erotica—to the point that authors like Lindsay Welsh, Aarona Griffin and Valentina Cilescau are among the hottest and most closely watched names in lesbian and gay publishing. Here are the finest moments from Rosebud's contemporary classics.

RANDY TUROFF
LUST NEVER SLEEPS
$6.50/475-5

A powerful volume of highly erotic, touchingly real fiction from the editor of Lesbian Words. Turoff accurately and insightfully depicts a circle of modern women, telling the stories of their lives and loves through a series of interconnected stories. Like the stories in Lust Never Sleeps, each of Turoff's women very capably stands on her own two feet—even while gaining resonance and deeper meaning from the relationships she has built to the others in her world. A stirring evocation of contemporary lesbian community.

RED JORDAN AROBATEAU
ROUGH TRADE
$6.50/470-4

Famous for her unflinching portrayal of lower-class dyke life and love, Arobateau outdoes herself with these tales of butch/femme affairs and unrelenting passions. Unapologetic and distinctly non-homogenized, Rough Trade is a must for all fans of challenging lesbian literature.

BOYS NIGHT OUT
$6.50/463-1

A Red hot volume of short fiction from this lesbian literary sensation. As always, Arobateau takes a good hard look at the lives of everyday women, noting well the struggles and triumphs each woman experiences. Never one to shrink from the less-than-chic truth, Red Jordan Arobateau has carved herself a niche as the foremost chronicler of working class dyke life.

ALISON TYLER
DARK ROOM: AN ONLINE ADVENTURE
$6.50/455-0

Dani, a successful photographer, can't bring herself to face the death of her lover, Kate. An ambitious journalist, Kate was found mysteriously murdered, leaving her lover with only fond memories of a too-brief relationship. Determined to keep the memory of her lover alive, Dani goes online under Kate's screen alias—and begins to uncover the truth behind the crime that has torn her world apart.

BLUE SKY SIDEWAYS & OTHER STORIES
$6.50/394-5

A variety of women, and their many breathtaking experiences with lovers, friends—and even the occasional sexy stranger. From blossoming young beauties to fearless vixens, Tyler finds the sexy pleasures of everyday life.

DIAL "L" FOR LOVELESS
$5.95/386-4

Meet Katrina Loveless—a private eye talented enough to give Sam Spade a run for his money. In her first case, Katrina investigates a murder implicating a host of society's darlings—including wealthy Tessa and Baxter Saint Claire, and the lovely, tantalizing, infamous Geneva twins. Loveless untangles the mess— while working herself into a variety of highly compromising knots with the many lovelies who cross her path!

THE VIRGIN
$5.95/379-1

Veronica answers a personal ad in the "Women Seeking Women" category—and discovers a whole sensual world she never knew existed! And she never dreamed she'd be prized as a virgin all over again, by someone who would deflower her with a passion no man could ever show....

THE BLUE ROSE
$5.95/335-X

The tale of a modern sorority—fashioned after a Victorian girls' school. Ignited to the heights of passion by erotic tales of the Victorian age, a group of lusty young women are encouraged to act out their forbidden fantasies—all under the tutelage of Mistresses Emily and Justine, two avid practitioners of hard-core discipline!

K. T. BUTLER
TOOLS OF THE TRADE
$5.95/420-8

A sparkling mix of lesbian erotica and humor. An encounter with ice cream, cappuccino and chocolate cake; an affair with a complete stranger; a pair of faulty handcuffs; and love on a drafting table. Seventeen tales.

MASQUERADE BOOKS

LOVECHILD
GAG
$5.95/369-4
From New York's poetry scene comes this explosive volume of work from one of the bravest, most cutting young writers you'll ever encounter. The poems in *Gag* take on American hypocrisy with uncommon energy, and announce Lovechild as a writer of unforgettable rage.

ELIZABETH OLIVER
THE SM MURDER: MURDER AT ROMAN HILL
$5.95/353-8
Intrepid lesbian P.I.s Leslie Patrick and Robin Penny take on a really hot case: the murder of the notorious Felicia Roman. The circumstances of the crime lead the pair on an excursion through the leatherdyke underground, where motives—and desires—run deep.

PAGAN DREAMS
$5.95/295-7
Cassidy and Samantha plan a vacation at a secluded bed-and-breakfast, hoping for a little personal time alone. Their hostess, however, has different plans. The lovers are plunged into a world of dungeons and pagan rites, as Anastasia steals Samantha for her own.

SUSAN ANDERS
CITY OF WOMEN
$5.95/375-9
Stories dedicated to women and the passions that draw them together. Designed strictly for the sensual pleasure of women, these tales are set to ignite flames of passion from coast to coast.

PINK CHAMPAGNE
$5.95/282-5
Tasty, torrid tales of butch/femme couplings. Tough as nails or soft as silk, these women seek out their antitheses, intent on working out the details of their own personal theory of difference.

ANONYMOUS
LAVENDER ROSE
$4.95/208-6
From the writings of Sappho, Queen of the island Lesbos, to the turn-of-the-century *Black Book of Lesbianism*; from *Tips to Maidens* to *Crimson Hairs*, a recent lesbian saga—here are the great but little-known lesbian writings and revelations. A one volume survey of hot and historic lesbian writing.

LAURA ANTONIOU, EDITOR
LEATHERWOMEN
$4.95/3095-4
These fantasies, from the pens of new or emerging authors, break every rule imposed on women's fantasies. The hottest stories from some of today's newest and most outrageous writers make this an unforgettable exploration of the female libido.

LEATHERWOMEN II
$4.95/229-9
Writings of women on the edge—resulting in a collection sure to ignite libidinal flames. Leave taboos behind, because these Leatherwomen know no limits....

AARONA GRIFFIN
PASSAGE AND OTHER STORIES
$4.95/3057-1
An S/M romance. Lovely Nina is frightened by her lesbian passions, until she finds herself infatuated with a woman she spots at a local café. One night Nina follows her, and finds herself enmeshed in an endless maze leading to a world where women test the edges of sexuality and power.

VALENTINA CILESCU
MY LADY'S PLEASURE: WOMAN WITH A MAID VOLUME I
$5.95/412-7
Dr. Claudia Dungarrow, a lovely, powerful, but mysterious figure at St. Matilda's College, attempts to seduce virginal Elizabeth Stanbridge, she sets off a chain of events that eventually ruins her career. Claudia vows revenge—and makes her foes pay deliciously....

DARK VENUS: MISTRESS WITH A MAID, VOLUME 2
$6.50/481-X
This thrilling saga of cruel lust continues! *Mistress with a Maid* breathes new life into the conventions of dominance and submission. What emerges is a picture of unremitting desire—whether it be for supreme erotic power or ultimate sexual surrender.

THE ROSEBUD SUTRA
$4.95/242-6
"Women are hardly ever known in their true light, though they may love others, or become indifferent towards them, may give them delight, or abandon them, or may extract from them all the wealth that they possess." So says *The Rosebud Sutra*—a volume promising women's inner secrets. One woman learns to use these secrets in a quest for pleasure with a succession of lady loves....

THE HAVEN
$4.95/165-9
J craves domination, and her perverse appetites lead her to the Haven: the isolated sanctuary Ros and Annie call home. Soon J forces her way into the couple's world, bringing unspeakable lust and cruelty into their lives.

MISTRESS MINE
$5.95/445-3
Sophia Cranleigh sits in prison, accused of authoring the "obscene" *Mistress Mine*. What she has done, however, is merely chronicle the events of her life—to the outrage of many. For Sophia has led no ordinary life, but has slaved and suffered—deliciously—under the hand of the notorious Mistress Malin. How long had she languished under the dominance of this incredible beauty?

BUY ANY 4 BOOKS & CHOOSE 1 ADDITIONAL BOOK, OF EQUAL OR LESSER VALUE, AS YOUR FREE GIFT

MASQUERADE BOOKS

LINDSAY WELSH

SECOND SIGHT
$6.50/507-7
The debut of Dana Steele—lesbian superhero!
During an attack by a gang of homophobic youths, Dana is thrown onto subway tracks—touching the deadly third rail. Miraculously, she survives, and finds herself endowed with superhuman powers. Not wishing to waste her extraordinary new lease on life, Dana decides to devote her powers to the protection of her lesbian sisters, no matter how daunting the danger they face. With the help of her lover Astrid, Dana stands poised to become a legend in her own time.

NASTY PERSUASIONS
$6.50/436-4
A hot peek into the behind-the-scenes operations of Rough Trade—one of the world's most famous lesbian clubs. Join Slash, Ramone, Cherry and many others as they bring one another to the height of torturous ecstasy—all in the name of keeping Rough Trade the premier name in sexy entertainment for women.

MILITARY SECRETS
$5.95/397-X
Colonel Candice Sproule heads a highly specialized boot camp. Assisted by three dominatrix sergeants, Col. Sproule takes on the talented submissives sent to her by secret military contacts. Then comes Jesse—whose pleasure in being served matches the Colonel's own. This new recruit sets off fireworks in the barracks—and beyond....

ROMANTIC ENCOUNTERS
$5.95/359-7
Beautiful Julie, the most powerful editor of romance novels in the industry, spends her days igniting women's passions through books—and her nights fulfilling those needs with a variety of lovers. Finally, through a sizzling series of coincidences, Julie's two worlds come together explosively!

THE BEST OF LINDSAY WELSH
$5.95/368-6
A collection of this popular writer's best work. This author was one of Rosebud's early bestsellers, and remains highly popular. A sampler set to introduce some of the hottest lesbian erotica to a wider audience.

NECESSARY EVIL
$5.95/277-9
What's a girl to do? When her Mistress proves too systematic, too by-the-book, one lovely submissive takes the ultimate chance—choosing and creating a Mistress who'll fulfill her heart's desire. Little did she know how difficult it would be—and, in the end, rewarding....

A VICTORIAN ROMANCE
$5.95/365-1
Lust-letters from the road. A young Englishwoman realizes her dream—a trip abroad under the guidance of her eccentric maiden aunt. Soon, the young but blossoming Elaine comes to discover her own sexual talents, as a hot-blooded Parisian named Madelaine takes her Sapphic education in hand.

A CIRCLE OF FRIENDS
$4.95/250-7
The story of a remarkable group of women. The women pair off to explore all the possibilities of lesbian passion, until finally it seems that there is nothing—and no one—they have not dabbled in.

BAD HABITS
$5.95/446-1
What does one do with a poorly trained slave? Break her of her bad habits, of course! The story of the ultimate finishing school, *Bad Habits* was an immediate favorite with women nationwide.
"Talk about passing the wet test!... If you like hot, lesbian erotica, run—don't walk—and pick up a copy of Bad Habits." —Lambda Book Repor

ANNABELLE BARKER

MOROCCO
$4.95/148-9
A luscious young woman stands to inherit a fortune—if she can only withstand the ministrations of her cruel guardian until her twentieth birthday. With two months left, Lila makes a bold bid for freedom, only to find that liberty has its own excruciating and delicious price....

A.L. REINE

DISTANT LOVE & OTHER STORIES
$4.95/3056-3
In the title story, Leah Michaels and her lover, Ranelle, have had four years of blissful, smoldering passion together. When Ranelle is out of town, Leah records an audio "Valentine:" a cassette filled with erotic reminiscences....

A RICHARD KASAK BOOK

EDITED BY SHAR REDNOUR

VIRGIN TERRITORY 2
$12.95/506-9
The follow-up volume to the groundbreaking *Virgin Territory*. This volume includes the work of many women inspired by the success of VT, and their stories should prove just as liberating. Focusing on the many "firsts" of a woman's erotic life, *Virgin Territory 2* provides one of the sole outlets for serious discussion of the myriad possibilities available to and chosen by many contemporary lesbians. A necessary addition to the library of any reader interested in the state of contemporary sexuality.

VIRGIN TERRITORY
$12.95/457-7
An anthology of writing by women about their first-time erotic experiences with other women. From the longings and ecstasies of awakening dykes to the sometimes awkward pleasures of sexual experimentation on the edge, each of these true stories reveals a different, radical perspective on one of the most traditional subjects around: virginity.

MASQUERADE BOOKS

MICHAEL FORD, EDITOR
ONCE UPON A TIME:
EROTIC FAIRY TALES FOR WOMEN
$12.95/449-6
How relevant to contemporary lesbians are the lessons of these age-old tales? The contributors to *Once Upon a Time*—some of the biggest names in contemporary lesbian literature—retell their favorite fairy tales, adding their own surprising—and sexy—twists. *Once Upon a Time* is sure to be one of contemporary lesbian literature's classic collections.

HAPPILY EVER AFTER:
EROTIC FAIRY TALES FOR MEN
$12.95/450-X
A hefty volume of bedtime stories Mother Goose never thought to write down. Adapting some of childhood's most beloved tales for the adult gay reader, the contributors to *Happily Ever After* dig up the subtext of these hitherto "innocent" diversions—adding some surprises of their own along the way.

MICHAEL BRONSKI, EDITOR
TAKING LIBERTIES: GAY MEN'S ESSAYS ON POLITICS, CULTURE AND SEX
$12.95/456-9
"Offers undeniable proof of a heady, sophisticated, diverse new culture of gay intellectual debate. I cannot recommend it too highly." —Christopher Bram
A collection of some of the most divergent views on the state of contemporary gay male culture published in recent years. Michael Bronski here presents some of the community's foremost essayists weighing in on such slippery topics as outing, masculine identity, pornography, the pedophile movement, political strategy—and much more. Includes essays by Pulitzer Prize-winning playwright Tony Kushner, conservative firebrands Bruce Bawer and Andrew Sullivan, literary sensation John Preston, and many others.

FLASHPOINT: GAY MALE SEXUAL WRITING
$12.95/424-0
A collection of some of the most provocative testaments to gay eros. Michael Bronski presents over twenty of the genre's best writers, exploring areas such as Enlightenment, True Life Adventures and more. Sure to be one of the most talked about and influential volumes ever dedicated to the exploration of gay sexuality.

HEATHER FINDLAY, EDITOR
A MOVEMENT OF EROS:
25 YEARS OF LESBIAN EROTICA
$12.95/421-6
One of the most scintillating overviews of lesbian erotic writing ever published. Heather Findlay has assembled a roster of stellar talents, each represented by their best work. Tracing the course of the genre from its pre-Stonewall roots to its current renaissance, Findlay examines each piece, placing it within the context of lesbian community and politics.

CHARLES HENRI FORD & PARKER TYLER
THE YOUNG AND EVIL
$12.95/431-3
"*The Young and Evil* creates [its] generation as *This Side of Paradise* by Fitzgerald created his generation." —Gertrude Stein
Originally published in 1933, *The Young and Evil* was an immediate sensation due to its unprecedented portrayal of young gay artists living in New York's notorious Greenwich Village. From flamboyant drag balls to squalid bohemian flats, these characters followed love and art wherever it led them—with a frankness that had the novel banned for many years.

MICHAEL ROWE
WRITING BELOW THE BELT:
CONVERSATIONS WITH EROTIC AUTHORS
$19.95/363-5
"An in-depth and enlightening tour of society's love/hate relationship with sex, morality, and censorship." —James White Review
Journalist Michael Rowe interviewed the best erotic writers and presents the collected wisdom in *Writing Below the Belt*. Rowe speaks frankly with cult favorites such as Pat Califia, crossover success stories like John Preston, and up-and-comers Michael Lowenthal and Will Leber. A volume dedicated to chronicling the insights of some of this overlooked genre's most renowned pratitioners. An acclaimed look at this vital literature.

LARRY TOWNSEND
ASK LARRY
$12.95/289-2
One of the leather community's most respected scribes here presents the best of his advice to leathermen worldwide. Starting just before the onslaught of AIDS, Townsend wrote the "Leather Notebook" column for *Drummer* magazine. Now, readers can avail themselves of Townsend's collected wisdom, as well as the author's contemporary commentary—a careful consideration of the way life has changed in the AIDS era. From Daddies to dog collars, and belts to bruises, *Ask Larry* is an essential volume for any man worth his leathers.

MICHAEL LASSELL
THE HARD WAY
$12.95/231-0
"Lassell is a master of the necessary word. In an age of tepid and whining verse, his bawdy and bittersweet songs are like a plunge in cold champagne." —Paul Monette

The first collection of renowned gay writer Michael Lassell's poetry, fiction and essays. As much a chronicle of post-Stonewall gay life as a compendium of a remarkable writer's work.

BUY ANY 4 BOOKS & CHOOSE 1 ADDITIONAL BOOK, OF EQUAL OR LESSER VALUE, AS YOUR FREE GIFT

MASQUERADE BOOKS

AMARANTHA KNIGHT, EDITOR
LOVE BITES
$12.95/234-5
A volume of tales dedicated to legend's sexiest demon—the Vampire. Not only the finest collection of erotic horror available—but a virtual who's who of promising new talent. A must for fans of both the horror and erotic genres.

RANDY TUROFF, EDITOR
LESBIAN WORDS: STATE OF THE ART
$10.95/340-6
"This is a terrific book that should be on every thinking lesbian's bookshelf." —Nisa Donnelly
One of the widest assortments of lesbian nonfiction writing in one revealing volume. Dorothy Allison, Jewelle Gomez, Judy Grahn, Eileen Myles, Robin Podolsky and many others are represented by some of their best work, looking at not only the current fashionability the media has brought to the lesbian "image," but important considerations of the lesbian past via historical inquiry and personal recollections.

ASSOTTO SAINT
SPELLS OF A VOODOO DOLL
$12.95/393-7
"Angelic and brazen." —Jewelle Gomez
A fierce, spellbinding collection of the poetry, lyrics, essays and performance texts of Assotto Saint—one of the most important voices in the renaissance of black gay writing. Saint, aka Yves François Lubin, was the editor of two seminal anthologies: 1991 Lambda Literary Book Award winner, *The Road Before Us: 100 Gay Black Poets* and *Here to Dare: 10 Gay Black Poets*. He was also the author of two books of poetry, *Stations* and *Wishing for Wings*.

WILLIAM CARNEY
THE REAL THING
$10.95/280-9
"Carney gives us a good look at the mores and lifestyle of the first generation of gay leathermen. A chilling mystery/romance novel as well." —Pat Califia
With a new introduction by Michael Bronski. *The Real Thing* has long served as a touchstone in any consideration of gay "edge fiction." First published in 1968, this uncompromising story of American leathermen received instant acclaim. *The Real Thing* finally returns from exile, ready to thrill a new generation.

EURYDICE
F/32
$10.95/350-3
"It's wonderful to see a woman...celebrating her body and her sexuality by creating a fabulous and funny tale." —Kathy Acker
With the story of Ela, Eurydice won the National Fiction competition sponsored by Fiction Collective Two and Illinois State University. A funny, disturbing quest for unity, *f/32* prompted Frederic Tuten to proclaim "almost any page... redeems us from the anemic writing and banalities we have endured in the past decade..."

SAMUEL R. DELANY
THE MOTION OF LIGHT IN WATER
$12.95/133-0
"A very moving, intensely fascinating literary biography from an extraordinary writer. Thoroughly admirable candor and luminous stylistic precision; the artist as a young man and a memorable picture of an age." —William Gibson
Award-winning author Samuel R. Delany's autobiography covers the early years of one of science fiction's most important voices. *The Motion of Light in Water* follows Delany from his early marriage to the poet Marilyn Hacker, through the publication of his first, groundbreaking work. Delany paints a vivid and compelling picture of New York's East Village in the early '60s.

THE MAD MAN
$23.95/193-4/hardcover
Delany's fascinating examination of human desire. For his thesis, graduate student John Marr researches the life and work of the brilliant Timothy Hasler: a philosopher whose career was cut tragically short over a decade earlier. Marr soon begins to believe that Hasler's death might hold some key to his own life as a gay man in the age of AIDS.
"What Delany has done here is take the ideas of the Marquis de Sade one step further, by filtering extreme and obsessive sexual behavior through the sieve of post-modern experience...." —*Lambda Book Report*
"Delany develops an insightful dichotomy between [his protagonist]'s two worlds: the one of cerebral philosophy and dry academia, the other of heedless, 'impersonal' obsessive sexual extremism. When these worlds finally collide ... the novel achieves a surprisingly satisfying resolution...." —*Publishers Weekly*

BARRY HOFFMAN, EDITOR
THE BEST OF GAUNTLET
$12.95/202-7
Gauntlet has, with its semi-annual issues, always publishing the widest possible range of opinions. The most provocative articles have been gathered by editor-in-chief Barry Hoffman, to make *The Best of Gauntlet* a riveting exploration of American society's limits.

FELICE PICANO
DRYLAND'S END
$12.95/279-5
The science fiction debut of the highly acclaimed author of *Men Who Loved Me* and *Like People in History*. Set five thousand years in the future, *Dryland's End* takes place in a fabulous techno-empire ruled by intelligent, powerful women. While the Matriarchy has ruled for over two thousand years and altered human language, thought and society, it is now unraveling. Military rivalries, religious fanaticism and economic competition threaten to destroy the mighty empire. A Lambda Literary Award nominee in the Science Fiction category, Picano's first foray into the genre has met with a wildly enthusiastic response.

MASQUERADE BOOKS

ROBERT PATRICK
TEMPLE SLAVE
$12.95/191-8
"You must read this book." —Quentin Crisp
"This is nothing less than the secret history of the most theatrical of theaters, the most bohemian of Americans and the most knowing of queens. Patrick writes with a lush and witty abandon, as if this departure from the crafting of plays has energized him. *Temple Slave* is also one of the best ways to learn what it was like to be fabulous, gay, theatrical and loved in a time at once more and less dangerous to gay life than our own." —Genre
The fascinating, fictionalized tale of the birth of gay theater, from this award-winning playwright.

CHEA VILLANUEVA
JESSIE'S SONG
$9.95/235-3
"It conjures up the strobe-light confusion and excitement of urban dyke life.... Read about these dykes and you'll love them." —Rebecca Ripley
Based largely upon her own experience, Villanueva's work is remarkable for its frankness, and delightful in its iconoclasm. Unconcerned with political correctness, this writer has helped expand the boundaries of "serious" lesbian writing.

GUILLERMO BOSCH
RAIN
$12.95/232-9
"Rain is a trip..." —Timothy Leary
An adult fairy tale, *Rain* takes place in a time when the mysteries of Eros are played out against a background of uncommon deprivation. The tale begins on the 1,537th day of drought—when one man comes to know the true depths of thirst. In a quest to sate his hunger for some knowledge of the wide world, he is taken through a series of extraordinary, unearthly encounters that promise to change not only his life, but the course of civilization around him. A haunting and provocative debut, and a moving fable for our time.

LAURA ANTONIOU, EDITOR
LOOKING FOR MR. PRESTON
$23.95/288-4
Edited by Laura Antoniou, *Looking for Mr. Preston* includes work by Lars Eighner, Pat Califia, Michael Bronski, Joan Nestle, and others who contributed interviews, essays and personal reminiscences of John Preston—a man whose career spanned the industry. Preston was the author of over twenty books, and edited many more. Ten percent of the proceeds from sale of the book will go to the AIDS Project of Southern Maine, for which Preston served as President of the Board.

CECILIA TAN, EDITOR
SM VISIONS: THE BEST OF CIRCLET PRESS
$10.95/339-2
"Fabulous books! There's nothing else like them."
—Susie Bright, *Best American Erotica and Herotica 3*
Circlet Press, devoted exclusively to the erotic science fiction and fantasy genre, is now represented by the best of its very best: *SM Visions*—sure to be one of the most thrilling and eye-opening rides through the erotic imagination ever published.

KATHLEEN K.
SWEET TALKERS
$12.95/192-6
Kathleen K., a highly successful businesswoman, opens up her diary for a rare peek at her day-to-day life. What makes Kathleen's story unusual is the nature of her business—she is a popular phone sex operator, and she now reveals a number of secrets and surprises.

RUSS KICK
**OUTPOSTS:
A CATALOG OF RARE AND DISTURBING ALTERNATIVE INFORMATION**
$18.95/0202-8
A huge, authoritative guide to some of the most bizarre publications available today! Rather than simply summarize the plethora of opinions crowding the American scene, Kick has tracked down and compiled reviews of work penned by political extremists, conspiracy theorists, hallucinogenic pathfinders, sexual explorers, and others. Each review is followed by ordering information for the many readers sure to want these publications for themselves.

MICHAEL LOWENTHAL, EDITOR
THE BEST OF THE BADBOYS
$12.95/233-7
The very best of the leading Badboys is collected here, in this testament to the artistry that has catapulted these "outlaw" authors to bestselling status. John Preston, Aaron Travis, Larry Townsend, and others are here represented by their most provocative writing.

LUCY TAYLOR
UNNATURAL ACTS
$12.95/181-0
"A topnotch collection..." —*Science Fiction Chronicle*
Unnatural Acts plunges deep into the dark side of the psyche and brings to life a disturbing vision of erotic horror. Unrelenting angels and hungry gods play with souls and bodies in Taylor's murky cosmos: where heaven and hell are merely differences of perspective; where redemption and damnation lie behind the same shocking acts. A frightening look at the disturbing, dark side of human desire, and the uncharted territory between life and death.

BUY ANY 4 BOOKS & CHOOSE 1 ADDITIONAL BOOK, OF EQUAL OR LESSER VALUE, AS YOUR FREE GIFT

MASQUERADE BOOKS

TIM WOODWARD, EDITOR
THE BEST OF SKIN TWO
$12.95/130-6

A groundbreaking journal from the crossroads of sexuality, fashion, and art, *Skin Two* specializes in provocative essays by the finest writers working in the "radical sex" scene. Collected here are the articles and interviews that established the magazine's reputation. Including interviews with cult figures Tim Burton, Clive Barker and Jean Paul Gaultier.

MICHAEL PERKINS
THE GOOD PARTS: AN UNCENSORED GUIDE TO LITERARY SEXUALITY
$12.95/186-1

Michael Perkins, one of America's only critics to regularly scrutinize sexual literature, presents sex as seen in the pages of over 100 major fiction and nonfiction volumes from the past twenty years. A one-of-a-kind compendium of "mainstream" sex-writing.

COMING UP:
THE WORLD'S BEST EROTIC WRITING
$12.95/370-8

Author and critic Michael Perkins has scoured the field of erotic writing to produce this anthology sure to challenge the limits of even the most seasoned reader. Using the same sharp eye and transgressive instinct that have established him as America's leading commentator on sexually explicit fiction, Perkins here presents the cream of the current crop.

DAVID MELTZER
THE AGENCY TRILOGY
$12.95/216-7

"...'The Agency' is clearly Meltzer's paradigm of society; a mindless machine of which we are all 'agents,' including those whom the machine supposedly serves...."
—Norman Spinrad

When first published, *The Agency* explored issues of erotic dominance and submission with an immediacy and frankness previously unheard of in American literature, as well as presented a vision of an America consumed and dehumanized by a lust for power.

JOHN PRESTON
MY LIFE AS A PORNOGRAPHER AND OTHER INDECENT ACTS
$12.95/135-7

"...essential and enlightening... [*My Life as a Pornographer*] is a bridge from the sexually liberated 1970s to the more cautious 1990s, and Preston has walked much of that way as a standard-bearer to the cause for equal rights...." —*Library Journal*
"*My Life as a Pornographer*...is not pornography, but rather reflections upon the writing and production of it. In a deeply sex-phobic world, Preston has never shied away from a vision of the redemptive potential of the erotic drive. Better than perhaps anyone in our community, Preston knows how physical joy can bridge differences and make us well."
—*Lambda Book Report*

HUSTLING: A GENTLEMAN'S GUIDE TO THE FINE ART OF HOMOSEXUAL PROSTITUTION
$12.95/137-3

A must-read for any man who's ever considered selling IT, either to make ends meet, or just for fun. John Preston solicited the advice of "working boys" from across the country in his effort to produce the ultimate guide to the hustler's world.
"...fun and highly literary. What more could you expect from such an accomplished activist, author and editor?" —*Drummer*

PAT CALIFIA
SENSUOUS MAGIC
$12.95/458-5

A new classic, destined to grace the shelves of anyone interested in contemporary sexuality.
"*Sensuous Magic* is clear, succinct and engaging even for the reader for whom S/M isn't the sexual behavior of choice.... When she is writing about the dynamics of sex and the technical aspects of it, Califia is the Dr. Ruth of the alternative sexuality set...." —*Lambda Book Report*
"Finally, a 'how to' sex manual that doesn't involve new age mumbo jumbo or 'tricks' that require the agility of a Flying Wallenda.... Califia's strength as a writer lies in her ability to relay information without sounding condescending. If you don't understand a word or concept... chances are it's defined in the handy dictionary in the back...." —*Futuresex*
"For either the uninitiated or the 'old-hand,' Califia is always a sexy delight to read." —*Icon*
"One of the very best sex-manuals ever produced, and certainly the starting point for anyone at all interested in a complete overview of the scene and who wants to explore further or even just work their way back to base." —*Divinity*
"Pat Califia's *Sensuous Magic* is a friendly, non-threatening, helpful guide and resource for 'adventurous couples' who are interested in expanding the erotic boundaries of their sexual relationships.... She captures the power of what it means to enter forbidden terrain, and to do so safely with someone else, and to explore the healing potential, spiritual aspects and the depth of S/M."
—*Bay Area Reporter*
"Don't take a dangerous trip into the unknown—buy this book and know where you're going!"
—*SKIN TWO*

MASQUERADE BOOKS

CARO SOLES, EDITOR
MELTDOWN! AN ANTHOLOGY OF EROTIC SCIENCE FICTION AND DARK FANTASY FOR GAY MEN
$12.95/203-5
Editor Caro Soles has put together one of the most explosive collections of gay erotic writing ever published. *Meltdown!* contains the very best examples of the increasingly popular sub-genre of erotic sci-fi/dark fantasy: stories meant to shock and delight, to send a shiver down the spine and start a fire down below.

LARS EIGHNER
ELEMENTS OF AROUSAL
$12.95/230-2
A guideline for success with one of publishing's best kept secrets: the novice-friendly field of gay erotic writing. Eighner details his craft, providing the reader with sure advice. Because that's what *Elements of Arousal* is all about: the application and honing of the writer's craft, which brought Eighner fame with not only the steamy *Bayou Boy*, but the illuminating *Travels with Lizbeth*.

STAN TAL, EDITOR
**BIZARRE SEX
AND OTHER CRIMES OF PASSION**
$12.95/213-2
From the pages of *Bizarre Sex*. Over twenty small masterpieces of erotic shock make this one of the year's most unexpectedly alluring anthologies. This incredible volume, edited by Stan Tal, includes such masters of erotic horror and fantasy as Edward Lee, Lucy Taylor and Nancy Kilpatrick.

MARCO VASSI
A DRIVING PASSION
$12.95/134-9
Marco Vassi was famous not only for his groundbreaking writing, but for the many lectures he gave regarding sexuality and the complex erotic philosophy he had spent much of his life working out. *A Driving Passion* collects the wit and insight Vassi brought to these lectures, and distills the philosophy that made him an underground sensation.

"The most striking figure in present-day American erotic literature. Alone among modern erotic writers, Vassi is working out a philosophy of sexuality."
—Michael Perkins, *The Secret Record*

"Vintage Vassi." —*Future Sex*

"An intriguing artifact... His eclectic quest for eroticism is somewhat poignant, and his fervor rarely lapses into silliness." —*Publishers Weekly*

THE EROTIC COMEDIES
$12.95/136-5
The Erotic Comedies marked a high point in Vassi's literary career. Short stories designed to shock and transform attitudes about sex and sexuality, *The Erotic Comedies* is both entertaining and challenging—and garnered Vassi some of the most lavish praise of his career. Also includes his groundbreaking writings on the Erotic Experience, including the concept of Metasex—the premise of which was derived from the author's own unbelievable experiences.

"To describe Vassi's writing as pornography would be to deny his very serious underlying purposes.... The stories are good, the essays original and enlightening, and the language and subject-matter intended to shock the prudish."—*Sunday Times* (UK)

"The comparison to [Henry] Miller is high praise indeed.... But reading Vassi's work, the analogy holds—for he shares with Miller an unabashed joy in sensuality, and a questing after experience that is the root of all great literature, erotic or otherwise.... Vassi was, by all accounts, a fearless explorer, someone who jumped headfirst into the world of sex, and wrote about what he found. And as he himself was known to say on more than one occasion, 'The most erotic organ is the mind.'"
—David L. Ulin, *The Los Angeles Reader*

THE SALINE SOLUTION
$12.95/180-2
"I've always read Marco's work with interest and I have the highest opinion not only of his talent but his intellectual boldness." —Norman Mailer
The story of one couple's spiritual crises during an age of extraordianry freedom. While renowned for his sexual philosophy, Vassi also experienced success in with fiction; *The Saline Solution* was one of the high points of his career, while still addressing the issue of sexuality.

THE STONED APOCALYPSE
$12.95/132-2
"...Marco Vassi is our champion sexual energist."
—*VLS*
During his lifetime, Marco Vassi was hailed as America's premier erotic writer. His reputation was worldwide. *The Stoned Apocalypse* is Vassi's autobiography, financed by his other groundbreaking erotic writing. Chronicling a cross-country roadtrip, *The Stoned Apocalypse* is rife with Vassi's insight into the American character and libido. One of the most vital portraits of "the 60s," this volume is a fitting testament to the writer's talents, and the sexual imagination of his generation.

BUY ANY 4 BOOKS & CHOOSE 1 ADDITIONAL BOOK, OF EQUAL OR LESSER VALUE, AS YOUR FREE GIFT

ORDERING IS EASY

MC/VISA orders can be placed by calling our toll-free number
PHONE 800-375-2356/FAX 212-986-7355/E-MAIL masqbks@aol.com
or mail this coupon to:
MASQUERADE DIRECT
DEPT. BMMQA6 801 2ND AVE., NY, NY 10017

BUY ANY FOUR BOOKS AND CHOOSE ONE ADDITIONAL BOOK, OF EQUAL OR LESSER VALUE, AS YOUR FREE GIFT.

QTY.	TITLE	NO.	PRICE
			FREE
			FREE

We Never Sell, Give or Trade Any Customer's Name.

SUBTOTAL

POSTAGE and HANDLING

TOTAL

In the U.S., please add $1.50 for the first book and 75¢ for each additional book; in Canada, add $2.00 for the first book and $1.25 for each additional book. Foreign countries: add $4.00 for the first book and $2.00 for each additional book. No C.O.D. orders. Please make all checks payable to Masquerade Books. Payable in U.S. currency only. New York state residents add 8.25% sales tax. Please allow 4-6 weeks for delivery.

NAME

ADDRESS

CITY _____ STATE _____ ZIP _____

TEL( ) _____

E-MAIL _____

PAYMENT: ☐ CHECK ☐ MONEY ORDER ☐ VISA ☐ MC

CARD NO _____ EXP. DATE _____

THE REVOLUTIONARY

& OTHER STORIES

JAMES MEDLEY

BIG SHOTS

"Travis is an extraordinary writer...immediate and intimidating, fevered and anxious."
—Michael Bronski, *The Guide*

AARON TRAVIS

THE SLAVE

SARA ADAMSON

"...perverse SM Erotica, mixing hetero and homosexuality in the tradition of Anne Rice's **Beauty** series."
—*Lambda Book Report*

DOVER ISLAND

LYN DAVENPORT

PROTESTS, PLEASURES, RAPTURES

ANONYMOUS

MASQUERADE

SLAVE ISLAND

He created a secret civilization where females served as love slaves

ANONYMOUS

MASQUERADE

RIVE GAUCHE
SYDNEY ST. JAMES

TEARS OF THE INQUISITION

PAUL LITTLE

$4.95 • MASQUERADE BOOKS.

Chinese Justice
and Other Stories

$4.95 • MASQUERADE BOOKS

PAUL LITTLE

POINT OF VIEW

MARTINE GŁOWINSKI

MASQUERADE

Tender Buns

P. N. DEDEAUX

MASQUERADE

TABITHA'S TEASE

ROBIN WILDE

MASQUERADE

KATERINA IN CHARGE

DON WINSLOW

SECRETS OF CHEATEM MANOR

DON WINSLOW

MASQUERADE

MASQUERADE

The Many Pleasures of
IRONWOOD

DON WINSLOW